KEY OF
GOLD

BY LAWRENCE SCHOONOVER

THE BURNISHED BLADE

THE GENTLE INFIDEL

THE GOLDEN EXILE

THE QUICK BROWN FOX

THE SPIDER KING

THE QUEEN'S CROSS

THE REVOLUTIONARY

THE PRISONER OF TORDESILLAS

THE CHANCELLOR

KEY OF GOLD

KEY OF GOLD

a novel by

LAWRENCE SCHOONOVER

LITTLE, BROWN AND COMPANY · BOSTON · TORONTO

LIBRARY OF CONGRESS CATALOG CARD NO. 68-11533

SECOND PRINTING

Published simultaneously in Canada
by Little, Brown & Company (Canada) Limited

PRINTED IN THE UNITED STATES OF AMERICA

for
RUTH MORGENTHAU KNIGHT
with affection that
grows through the years

BOOK I

BENEDICT of Seville returned to his home, tired in body but in a satisfied frame of mind. His day had been rewarding. From dawn to dusk he had visited the sick, some in the hovels of the poor, many more in fine mansions of the rich.

Of the two classes he preferred to treat his nobler patients, for their ailments were easier to cure, consisting largely of imaginary aches and pains. There were the elderly dowagers, fretting about the dowries of their unmarried daughters, eating themselves into unhealthy corpulence to quiet their nervous stomachs. There were also the men, the aging thin old dons, well past the fourth decade and hence in those days, on the downgrade of life, whose strength had failed and whose pride was hurt because they no longer received summonses to fight for God, Queen and King against the Moor. Nothing so wounded such men as to discover that they were no longer fit to fight. There were also the profitable, perennially recurring young lechers, who, in the pride of their youth, falsely assumed that they could spend all night in a brothel and wake up as fresh and alert as if they had behaved themselves. Imperiously they would summon Dr. Benedict and demand a restorative to wipe out their midnight follies and put themselves on their feet again, as if a doctor were a confessor who could absolve soul and body of sin with a word, and start the patient afresh as if nothing had happened. In medicine, mused Dr. Benedict, as he reached to his sleeve for the key to his front door, there are no magic words to help you. There is only the physic, the herbs and the wonderful concoctions of the Jews, Moors, Byzantines, Romans, Greeks and, long before them, the lore of the Egyptian priest-physicans passed down in unbroken line through countless generations of doctors. Some of this lore was fraudulent but most of it was empirical, effective and sincerely devoted to the alleviation of the suffering of their fellowmen.

For those of his patients whose ailments were imaginary or due to the unusual stress of the times, he had marvelous remedies in his pharmacopoeia. An apprentice physician, chosen for his youth, good looks and engaging manners, would present to him a lacquered chest full of small glass vials each containing a different colored liquid. Dr. Benedict would gravely choose a color, having first glanced at the decor of the sickroom, that pleasantly matched or violently contrasted. He would measure out a few drops and administer it by mouth to the patient, who next day would be soothed, calm, hopeful and in a friendly mood. "Send for me if the trouble returns," he would say, with just the right mixture of deference and professional dignity. They always did. No one knew that the liquid in all the vials was identical, namely, a strong extract of poppy; or that the rainbow hues were harmless vegetable coloring. To render the hypochondriac tranquil, he knew, was the only treatment when

worry, and worry alone, makes one sick. He often smiled at the
veneration they showed for his box of vials. But he did not hold
it in contempt. It had done much good; it could do no harm; it
increased his reputation and it constituted an unfailing source of
income.

His was a lowly profession, though he had grown rich in it,
richer than anyone knew. He dressed simply and rode a mule,
not a horse, and he hid his wealth. Physicians, barbers and
surgeons, tooth-pullers, bonesetters and veterinarians, all were
landless men, classed with peasant farmers, and all were easy to
rob. The tax collectors considered them fair game, and the tax
collectors were increasingly more exacting as the war against
Granada became more costly each year. King Ferdinand and
Queen Isabella cared little that the treasury was empty, now
that victory was in sight.

His ample income also enabled him to spend much time
among the humble, whose genuine sicknesses and deplorable
poverty pained him, both professionally and aesthetically. His
poor patients were apt to pay him in chickens, sausages, vegetables, eggs and, when they could, a country smoked ham. These
he took, out of respect for the fierce pride of the poor, especially
the Spanish poor, which he knew by instinct, as only a man
could whose ancestors have lived in Spain for so long that no
one remembered when they first had migrated hither. But Dr.
Benedict, unlike most Spaniards, knew that one ancestor had
come quite recently, as recently as two hundred years before.
Where that first ancestor had lived was not certain, but family
tradition and the name Benedict traced it to England in the
reign of Edward I, who, having procured other means of wealth,
deported his Jewish subjects.

Dr. Benedict was at great pains to conceal this dangerous

[5]

secret, particularly dangerous in Spain since the year 1478, when the Papal Inquisition, a relatively moderate organization, came under the control of the Spanish state and became the Spanish Inquisition, the most efficient fund raising arm of government ever devised. Rome was irked at its secular character, protested against its high-handed exactions, and secretly fumed that all the money from fines, confiscations, attainders and escheats went into the coffers of the Spanish treasury and never a penny to Rome. But Rome concealed its irritation, for the king and queen of Spain had accomplished what no Spanish rulers for seven hundred years had been able to do: they were driving the Moor into smaller and smaller territory, confining the infidel, like a frog in a drying puddle, to a shrinking area in the south. Outpost after outpost, castle after castle, city after city had fallen before the armies of Ferdinand and Isabella. Now only the citadel of Granada remained. All Christendom took pride in the Reconquest. Many predicted the final expulsion of the Moor in a matter of months, or a year at the most.

In the prosecution of such a war it was only to be expected that extraordinary fiscal measures would have to be taken. Someone had to pay; and there was no richer source of wealth than the Jews and the crypto-Jews. Spain was full of them. Many had lived there since the year 1290, when England expelled them en masse, two hundred years before. In 1306 France also had expelled them, a hundred and eighty-five years before. Spain, needing their talent and wealth, had received them; and in Spain they had prospered for eight generations. Was not, went the Spanish argument, a heavy tax, especially in wartime when hate rose high against the infidel Moors, better than deportations like those of England and France? Most Christian princes, preoccupied with their own problems — in Germany

[6]

there was a massive witch hunt in progress, and ten thousand men, women and children with odd mannerisms had recently been burned at the stake — considered the Jewish problem in Spain a purely internal affair. Only the worldly, lighthearted Italians chuckled cynically at the mounting religious intolerance among the Spaniards.

After so many generations in Spain, knowing no other home-land, intensely patriotic, speaking a more polished Spanish than their contemporaries because they were more literate, the Span-ish Jews, indistinguishable from other Spaniards by reason of centuries of residence and much intermingling of blood, con-sidered themselves temporarily embarrassed but not actually endangered by the new Spanish Inquisition's enormous exac-tions, and they looked askance at some of their stubborn breth-ren who flaunted their Jewishness, who made a show of their wealth and occasionally got themselves burned like the witches in Germany. The trouble would pass. It always did. And no one thought it would happen to him personally if he exercised reasonable precaution, least of all Dr. Benedict of Seville, now pausing to open the door of his house and reaching for his key.

An ill-dressed youth with a vaguely military look about him, wearing a dagger at his belt, suddenly appeared out of the shadows and ran up to him and plucked him by the sleeve of his long academic gown. The doctor was accompanied by two apprentices, one of whom carried a fat purse containing the day's fees that had been paid in coin, the other carrying, in a couple of saddlebags slung over the mule, a collection of fees that had been paid in kind. Some of the fees were still cackling.

Both apprentices rushed forward to protect their master, menacing the intruder with their staffs. But it was not an

assassin they confronted. This was not the face of violence. It was simply a frightened face, and very young.

"What is it, lad?" the doctor said.

"You are Dr. Benedict, the most famous physician of Seville?" said the youth. He spoke like a peasant, but there was a noble cast to his countenance, curiously incongruous with his rough speech.

Benedict smiled. "I am certainly Dr. Benedict," he replied. "And who may you be, young man, and what ails you? Nothing, I'd say, from the looks of you."

"It isn't me," the young man said. "It's my patron. He's sick. He begs you to come at once to attend him."

"And who is your patron?" It was well to know whom one treated, if only to fix a sensible fee in one's mind.

"I — I am not permitted to say."

Benedict frowned.

"Is your own identity likewise to remain a mystery, young man?"

"Oh no, sir. I am Francisco Pizarro."

Benedict thought a moment, searching in his memory; then he chuckled and the lad saw recognition in his face.

"The son of Don Gonzalo Pizarro?"

"One of them," Pizarro said, blushing scarlet. "One of a legion, they say." His putative father, Gonzalo Pizarro, was a notorious old rascal who had squandered a noble estate, wenched widely, and scattered his illegitimate progeny over all Andalusia.

Dr. Benedict bowed tactfully. "I am honored that your patron has sent you to fetch me, Don Francisco," he said gravely. The title "don" was outrageously flattering and undeserved. Pizarro eyed him sharply, but detected no trace of ridicule in his tone, and Pizarro's ears were tuned to sly taunts at his illegitimacy.

The doctor saw gratitude in his face, and pursued his advantage.

"Now we shall see your patron, Don Francisco. I dare say he is a military man, such as I judge you to be, perhaps even a captain. Is his trouble a wound? I must know what equipment to take. Does he live far? I am somewhat fatigued. As you see, this is the end of my day. I have made many calls. Is he young, old? Is his countenance florid, pale? I will want to take the best medicines for him. It makes a difference."

"My patron is a very old priest," Pizarro blurted out. "His name is — he is called Father Thomas."

"And where does good Father Thomas dwell?" Dr. Benedict asked. The summons had taken on serious overtones. He greatly disliked treating the clergy, who paid him in blessings, and whom, in these troubled times, a crypto-Jew did well to avoid.

"He is in the cloister behind the cathedral," Pizarro said, biting his lip. "I have talked too much. You tricked it out of me."

Dr. Benedict crossed himself and looked toward the sky and replied, "May all the saints forbid that I should trick a brave young man like you! Nor could I succeed, Don Francisco, for you are too clever by far, sharp-witted, keen to observe. No, a physician, like a father confessor, asks questions that the laity may not; and all that is told a physician is equally under the seal. You have told me nothing."

"Then let us go at once. I have two horses."

"Where? I see no horses."

"I tied them in your stables," Pizarro said, grinning.

"It was locked," Benedict said.

"It still is."

"You will go far," Dr. Benedict said, smiling.

The apprentice physicians stabled the doctor's mules; Fran-

cisco Pizarro followed them to the rear to get the two horses his
patron had dispatched, to bring the doctor. Benedict entered his
house.

But first, having glanced over his shoulder, the doctor touched
his fingers hurriedly to his lips, then touched with his fingers a
certain unmarked stone, heart high, beside the door, transferring
the kiss, blessing his house, and calling to mind the little scroll
concealed beneath the stone. On it was written in Hebrew the
central core of the faith of the Jews, as it always had been and
never had changed: it was simple and it was beautiful. It stated
that there was one God, not a multitude of gods; it enunciated
two major commandments: love that God, it commanded, and
love your neighbor. That was all. That was the mystery that
Christians sought to ferret out. It was enough to build a good
life upon.

Glancing again over his shoulder, Benedict smiled. He had
not been observed in his heretical action. The Christians would
not burn him.

The world was not, he thought, very logical, since every
Sunday when he went to church he heard the priest vehemently
adjure the faithful to observe the selfsame commandments, and
the Christian creed affirmed the same unity of God.

He closed the door carefully behind him, locking it with a
golden key. Benedict, like most Spanish urban dwellers of means
and prominence, possessed a gold key with which he opened the
front door of his house. Lately its design had worried him, and
he no longer wore it exposed like a jewel at the belt of his robe,
but hid it, sometimes in his purse, sometimes in his breast,
sometimes in the depths of his long sleeves. Sometimes he even
considered having the lock changed and throwing the key away.
No, it was gold, he thought; better to melt it down and save the

metal. But no again — it was a family heirloom, and family tradition said that the first Dr. Benedict had brought it from England when first he went to Spain and prospered. Therefore keep it, thought Benedict, but do not flaunt it, and wait for better times.

It was certainly not an object that ought to be carelessly exposed, particularly the "web," the operative end, the end that was actually inserted into the lock to throw the bolt and open the door.

The "loop," or handle, the end he held in his fingers while inserting the web — only locksmiths and the man who loved the key knew the technical terms — was fortunately above suspicion. It was shaped something like the Christian cross. If pressed, Dr. Benedict would have sworn on the relics of any saint you might mention (and every church had a pound or two of such venerable bones) that the Christian cross it assuredly was. True, there was an eyelet in the vertical beam, but that, he was prepared to state, was merely to make it easier to hang to his belt. And yet Dr. Benedict knew it was not the Christian cross but the *crux ansata*, the ankh, the immemorial symbol of life of the ancient Egyptians, found in the obscure papyri of their ancient physicians; and hence he revered it as he revered all life, and took some sly comfort in its not being the cross of his Spanish countrymen, which he regarded as an instrument of a hideous old Roman torture. It was in his nature to abhor such a cross, as he abhorred the rack, the thumbscrew and the burning stake. "No wonder they worship our Jesus," he mused. "There have been many, but he was the best. The Shekina upheld him. I would have sworn to anything; I would have recanted all I ever taught just to get them to unnail me and let me down from the cross, that hideous agony. He was three hours a-dying, poor,

[11]

poor young man!" When the bells rang and Dr. Benedict and Maria, his wife, went to the cathedral on Sundays, it was not difficult for him to straddle his conscience and pray that the holiness of such a good man of his race might serve as an example for his own life.

Though not to such stubborn lengths.

Dr. Benedict was far more practical than Jesus.

Around the *crux ansata* of his golden key were two intertwined serpents, beautifully wrought, another symbol of the physician, the caduceus. Hermes, a Greek god, had had such serpents on his staff. No one ever seemed to object to the pagan art of the Greeks and Romans, though occasionally they put fig leaves and concealing draperies on some of the antique statues that the Italians were digging up nowadays out of their gardens and placing in their palaces. A few artistic pieces had found their way to Spain. It was an era of interest in the classic, especially in liberal Italy, where there was a rebirth of pride in the Roman heritage, both Christian and non-Christian. No, no one would question the caduceus, not even in Spain, though Spain was admittedly more conservative.

The stem of the golden key was without significance. It was simply a finely wrought shaft connecting the loop with the web.

It was the web, the operative end of the key, that worried Dr. Benedict.

The web was shaped in the form of Solomon's seal. This venerable design, a six-pointed star composed of two interlaced equilateral triangles, was the ancient stamp of the Jews. True, Dr. Benedict mused, I have seen it in many church windows in beautifully stained glass, where it represents their Old Testament. But he supposed it must have been placed in the windows in more liberal times. In these latter days it had acquired odious

overtones, almost as hateful as the star and crescent of the
Moors, as religious hatred heightened and the Reconquest swept
south toward Granada and ultimate victory, a victory for which
Benedict prayed like every other good Spaniard. But it was not
prudent nowadays to make a display of Solomon's seal even if it
appeared on so innocuous an object as a front-door key. He
thrust it into his sleeve, and emptied his purse into a jar by the
door, keeping only a few coins of little value.

In the simply furnished but quietly luxurious front hall his
wife advanced to greet him. He kissed her on the brow.

"You look tired, Baruch," she said. "Supper's been waiting.
Come and eat."

He quickly raised his forefinger to his lips and whispered,
"Hush, Maria."

She raised her eyebrows. Usually in the privacy of their home
they called each other Baruch and Miriam, which were the
Hebrew versions of the Christian names by which they were
known and served as terms of endearment.

"I'm afraid we may have to give up our pet names, my dear,
lest by chance we let them slip when we are overheard. At least
on a night like this when I am called to treat one of the clergy.
He may be a high-placed one. He has summoned me by a
nobleman, illegitimate, I grant, but still noble. And he has sent
me a horse to ride."

"Will you ride a horse?" she asked.

The lower classes, by custom, rode mules, lest they aspire to
the status of the dons and caballeros. Jews were prohibited by
law from riding anything else. Thus Dr. Benedict felt doubly
safe on a mule.

"Yes, indeed I will. I mustn't keep this Father Thomas waiting, whoever he is."

"Not even while you take a bite of supper?"

Benedict wrinkled his fine aristocratic nose and sniffed at the good smell of cooking meat that filled the hall from the kitchen below. "What is for supper?"

Maria smiled. "Roast pork, like always on Thursday."

"Good!" he said. "I must reek of it. Cut me a small piece and wrap it in paper. No, not in paper; paper would be suspect; the poor have no paper. Wrap it in an old rag. I will carry it on me and say it is a fee."

"Oh, you silly worried old man! Have we ever once been suspected?" But she ordered a servant to hurry and prepare the little package and dropped it into the doctor's sleeve. "Well, off you go, wrapped in the odor of sanctity."

Benedict chuckled. "Hardly the sweet odor of Aaron's incense; but what can I do?"

Pizarro was waiting impatiently in the street with the horses. Benedict did not close the door behind him and strode down the steps, not once glancing at the heart-high stone, salving his conscience that he could not have kissed it even if he had dared because his right arm was encumbered with his medicine chest, to say nothing of the pork.

"My patron may be displeased," Pizarro warned. "He is not used to being kept waiting."

The doctor swung himself into the saddle. He was an excellent rider but only on rare occasions could he experience the exhilaration of a good strong horse under him. Much walking on his rounds to the sick, much climbing of stairs, much time spent in the open had kept him healthy, and occasionally he wished he could ride with a falcon on his wrist with some of his noble patients when they went hunting. He did not look his forty years, his close-clipped pointed little beard showed not a strand of gray, and he fancied he had a better seat than most caballeros. But of course they never asked him and he knew better than to invite himself.

"Since we must not keep him waiting, let us gallop!" he suggested.

Pizarro paused and frowned.

"Where are your assistant physicians, Dr. Benedict?"

Benedict was ready. He had an excellent excuse for their not accompanying him. They were tight-mouthed and loyal but they were very young and sometimes were nervous in the presence of the clergy. For they had as much to hide as he.

"I neither need nor desire their help," he said smoothly. "Your reverend patron is someone I wish to treat personally. No mere apprentice will touch the person of the patron of Don Francisco Pizarro."

"Thank you, Doctor," the young man said. "But I hope he doesn't blame me for this informality."

"Would not your reverend patron have sent horses for my apprentices also if he had wished a more formal visit?" Dr. Benedict said, smiling.

Pizarro grinned. "Yes, he would have. He thinks of everything. But I hope he isn't angry. His anger is terrible."

"Now, my young friend, let us gallop," Benedict said.

The streets had grown dark, the way scarcely visible in the feeble light that filtered through the wooden grillwork of upper-story windows. From time to time a startled watchman raised his lantern to witness the pair of horsemen flash by in the gloom, the hooves of the horses striking sparks from the cobbles. They were an incongruous couple, the youth riding proud and erect like a caballero, the black-garbed figure that followed looking like some tall aristocratic grandee or a high-placed member of the judiciary. They were obviously persons of importance; there was authority in their appearance and their speed bespoke the urgency of their mission. Instinctively the watchmen saluted and waved them on.

In the vicinity of the cathedral the number of the watchmen increased. Behind the cathedral the whole area was alive with foot soldiers and mounted guardsmen, and bright with torches. At the entrance of the cloisters Pizarro drew rein, blocked by two crossed halberds. A mounted officer standing watch by the sentries questioned him sharply. Pizarro whispered something to him and the burnished pikestaffs immediately parted and the sentries fell back to let them pass. The officer led them through the quiet cloister gardens, not keeping to the paths where the monks were wont to walk and contemplate, telling their beads and saying their offices, but directly across the flowerbeds. Dr. Benedict felt a catch in his throat. No one ever rode horses within these sacred precincts, let alone trample roughshod over the carefully tended flowers. But these horsemen did, and Benedict heartily wished he were not one of them.

At the door of the principal structure within the enclosure, squat and somber like a mausoleum but brilliantly lighted by torchmen and guarded by soldiers, stood a young friar. His face was pale and ascetic, his sunken sleepless eyes reflected the fire of the lights. He looked, to Dr. Benedict, like a man on the verge of losing his self-control, a not infrequent phenomenon in the houses of the very sick. Rich or poor, noble or lowly, they all looked alike when the head of the house was in trouble, and some of the doctor's professional courage returned.

The three dismounted. Grooms appeared and led away the horses. The officer disappeared, tiptoeing away in his jackboots, his mission done.

Pizarro said to the friar, "Reverend sir, this is Dr. Benedict."

"You will enter at once, Doctor," the friar said, and the door opened behind him.

Pizarro whispered, "I must go now. I must not come in." And he added, grinning, "Doctor, for a doctor, you ride like the very devil!"

"At once!" the friar ordered.

Benedict could well have done without the reference to the devil within earshot of the friar, but he liked young Pizarro and he had greatly enjoyed the exhilarating gallop. He smiled and bade the youth adieu, then put on his gravest professional face and followed the friar down a long torch-lighted corridor to a door which was guarded by two sentries. The unusual illumination and the great number of guards was both ominous and revealing. Patently he was called upon to treat an enormously powerful, very frightened, supremely suspicious patient. There was only one such man in Spain.

The guards at the door stood aside. The friar rapped rapidly thrice, then thrice again, and thrice again on the iron-studded oak, and the massive barrier swung open on new-oiled hinges without a sound. A distinguished ecclesiastic with a pectoral cross on his breast said, "You will come in, Dr. Benedict."

I do not believe, Benedict thought wildly, that a bishop ever opened a door for a Jew before! But he entered, his manner poised and respectful.

He saw beside a roaring fire, which rendered the room oppressively hot, a spare old man sitting and sweating in a cushioned armchair. Despite the heat his hands shook as if he were cold, and there was a blanket around his shoulders. Benedict had suspected the identity of his patient, but nevertheless the reality came as a shock. It was Thomas of Torquemada, the

Grand Inquisitor of Castile and Aragon, Confessor to Their Majesties, and next to the King and Queen the most powerful person in Spain. The doctor felt his mouth go dry with fright, and in his mind's eye he saw his own face grow pale as the blood drained from it. His patient was scrutinizing him with eyes that seemed accustomed to the terror his presence inspired and took it as his due.

"Do not be afraid, Dr. Benedict," he said.

"I had no idea —" Benedict began, dropping to his knees. "I beg your blessing, Your Reverend Lord, to the end that my poor ministrations prove efficacious."

Torquemada blessed him languidly and said with a smile, that was not at all formidable, "I never joined more heartily in a suppliant's prayer."

Benedict had knelt somewhat awkwardly, still holding the medicine chest. The bishop advanced and placed it on a table beside Torquemada's chair.

"You will need no assistants, I trust," Torquemada said. It was more a command than a question.

"No, Reverend Lord."

"Then Your Grace will probably wish to return when Dr. Benedict has spoken to me," Torquemada said to the bishop, dismissing him.

The prelate frowned fleetingly, then nodded, smiled and left the room with what dignity he could muster; and doctor and patient were alone.

Clearly Torquemada wished his ailment kept secret, whatever it was, even from his most intimate associates; and Benedict had as yet no notion what it might be. But he raised his voice to a tone intended to carry to anyone listening behind the door and said, "Your Reverend Lord, I observe at once that your indisposition is slight, and Your Lordship will be restored to a state of perfect health within a space of three days."

Torquemada said, "You idiot. Do you suppose for one moment anybody could hear you through that?" indicating with his finger the massive door. Benedict noted that the long lean forefinger was white, presumably owing to a deficiency of blood, and that there was a slight tremor, which might be caused by fatigue or fever or age or fear.

"I hope you are a better doctor than a courtier. Nevertheless, Dr. Benedict, come close and do not shout. My hearing is quite good."

Indeed it is, thought Benedict. You hear everything that is said in Spain! But he took the hint and lowered his voice almost to a whisper; for he knew now that the great man *was* afraid of being overheard. In his closer position as he bent over Torquemada he could smell the fasting breath.

"Your Reverend Lordship should eat more," he said.

"I have not eaten since last Friday," Torquemada said.

Benedict was in a difficult position. "I am only a doctor of the body, sir, and the body is all I can cure. But surely a man of your saintliness need not fast so rigorously — six whole days! I say it as a doctor, Reverend sir; forgive me."

Torquemada looked to the right and looked to the left apprehensively, without moving his head. Benedict noted that the whites of his eyes were healthy, a little bloodshot from insomnia, but not yellow with excess of bile.

"I have not fasted for holiness's sake," Torquemada said. "Someone is poisoning me."

"Incredible!" Benedict said.

"Is it, Doctor? Is it incredible?"

The Grand Inquisitor of Spain was the best protected personage in Christendom. He never traveled without two hundred mounted guards in attendance. Benedict had seen the extraordinary precautions he took to protect his person even in the sacred precincts of the cathedral cloisters.

"Have I not many enemies, God forgive them?"

"The tree that is set on an eminence is exposed to gales, and the house that is set on a hill cannot be hid," Benedict said. "So it is with your Lordship. But so likewise has Your Lordship hosts of friends to look up to Your Eminence."

By a shrewd choice of words the doctor elevated him to the cardinalate.

"Perhaps you possess a courtier's talent after all," Torquemada said, eyeing him.

"Does not someone taste your food?"

"Yes, tastes it, but he does not eat it all. Maybe he takes antidotes first. There are poisons which in small quantities do not kill, in large do; are there not, Dr. Benedict?"

"There are, Reverend Lord."

"You do not, of course, know any of them." His tone was sarcastic.

"Sir, I know a score of them."

"Nor do you, of course, possess any."

"I possess nearly all. I keep them locked in a secret place." It was true. He knew he should not have avowed it, for some were illegal. But many poisons were precious life-saving medicaments.

"I have heard of a grayish powder that tastes like garlic but that causes death if taken over a protracted period," Torquemada said.

Benedict did not know whither this series of questions was

leading. He was irked at the smooth inquisition, but he controlled his irritation.

"It is called arsenic, Reverend Lord. I know it well."

"Do you indeed?"

"In criminal hands it kills. In healing hands, with God's help, it relieves the pain of rheumatism, restores the appetite and revives the failing heart. In the hands of glassmakers dark glass becomes beautifully transparent when arsenic is added to the mix. Like water, wind, and fire it is capable of great good and great evil." Benedict could have added, "especially like fire," but he did not.

"You are candid to indiscretion," Torquemada said, smiling, not unpleasantly. Benedict thought the interview was going very well.

"Is it arsenic poisoning you suspect, Reverend Lord? Do you like the taste of garlic?"

"Who doesn't?" Torquemada said; and indeed garlic, with saffron and pepper, was one of the most popular of Spanish seasonings. But owing to some quirk in his nature, or perhaps his ancient English ancestry, Benedict detested the odor and taste of garlic.

"I don't," he said, "though garlic is beneficial to one's health and keeps one from getting colds, from which it would appear your Lordship now unhappily suffers."

"I suspect arsenic poisoning, Doctor. If someone were poisoning me with arsenic what would be the cure?"

"There wouldn't be any."

"No, you are no courtier," Torquemada said. "I heard you were not. That is why I sent for you."

A dangerous thought occurred to the doctor. Some people heard voices that were not there. Some people saw things that were not there. Some people smelled odors that did not exist. Such people usually went mad and were chained in dungeons to howl out their lives in oblivion and misery, lest they harm themselves or other persons.

"Do you taste garlic in the Host or smell garlic in the wine of Communion?"

The Grand Inquisitor half rose from his chair and directed at Benedict such a glare of concentrated fury as he had never seen before.

"NO!" he shouted. The doctor heard the clank of armor outside the door. Torquemada's shout had penetrated four inches of oak.

"No," Torquemada said more calmly. "But it is a new thought. I shall remember it and be warned. There have been cases where the unspeakable Jews and Moors have defiled the precious body and blood of God with poison. There have been cases. It has been known."

Benedict instantly led the conversation into safe channels.

"What was the last meal Your Reverend Lordship ate?"

"A fish, last Friday. I vomited it up. There was blood in the vomit."

"Black or red?"

"Red, of course. Blood is red."

It was not always, Benedict knew. But he did not press the technical point. Already he had ruled out a host of serious diseases.

"Was it copious, like a flood? Clotted, like a curd?"

"There was very little of it, but I am always on my guard. It was stringy; oh, there is no question that it was there. Naturally I have told no one. I have many enemies; I do not always know who they are; someone has got through to me and poisoned me. I am feared; I am plotted against."

Torquemada had sneezed several times during the interview. The significance of the nasal irritation was not lost on the doctor, who was now forming a solid diagnosis.

"Has Your Lordship suffered a loss of Your Lordship's sense of smell?"

"You demon! How did you know?"

"Your Reverence, I did not know. I must ask questions in order to cure the body, as you must ask questions in order to discharge the duties of your great office in the cure of the souls that God in His wisdom has entrusted to you. Mine is a lowlier office, but I too have my duties."

"Yes, doctors have their duties too. Every Christian has. I lost my sense of smell the day after tasting the poisoned fish. It has now returned, through God's grace, and my fasting. I have dedicated my hunger, which mounts every day. I smell, for example, the odor of meat in this room."

It was obvious to Benedict that his exalted patient had nothing more than a severe stomach upset, with the common nausea that accompanies it. There had been some slight internal nasal bleeding. The highly seasoned fish had further inflamed his already queasy stomach, aggravated by nerves and apprehension, and he had vomited. Had Torquemada been one of his poor patients he would have laughed off the incident and bade him go back to his work. But the ominous symptom in Torquemada was that he thought he was being poisoned. Poor old man, thought Benedict. He thinks the whole world is against him, and he's fasted six whole days. Benedict felt compassion for him, as he did for all his patients whose ills were imaginary. But in a

[23]

person of Torquemada's power such a delusion could lead to harm, much harm, and for many.

"*You* smell of meat," Torquemada said. "Come here."

"I am sorry," Benedict said. "There is meat in my sleeve."

Torquemada plunged in his hand and drew it out, the dirty little rag-wrapped packet.

"A bit of roast pork from a poor widow who gave it me as a fee," Benedict said apologetically. "I am often paid in kind."

"No garlic," said the Grand Inquisitor of Spain, sniffing it.

"She is very poor. She did not season a doctor's fee."

Torquemada said, "Eat some."

Benedict did. "It's rather flat," he said, "but usually she doesn't pay me at all. It was kind of her to give me what she could."

Torquemada watched him narrowly for perhaps three minutes. "You are fortunate, Dr. Benedict, that no one is poisoning you."

Benedict wondered if Torquemada had expected him to drop dead at the first bite. Shortly he was to be glad he had eaten pork in the presence of such a patient.

"I will taste it myself," Torquemada said amiably, and took several large mouthfuls. Benedict sighed. The man who could have fed an army had been starving himself and dared eat only the fee of a doctor. "I find it excellent," he said.

"I will bring you more," Benedict said.

But a veil of distrust dropped over Torquemada's eyes, and he said, "No."

Benedict opened the glittering array of his medicine chest and measured out a little dosage in a small cup. He chose red, of which he thought the Grand Inquisitor would approve.

"This will help Your Lordship," he said.

"Drink it yourself," Torquemada ordered.

"Very well, Reverend Lord."

Benedict downed it.

Again Torquemada scrutinized him.

"You understand," he said.

"Perfectly," the doctor answered.

Minutes passed.

"Now you may physic me," Torquemada said, satisfied. "Mind it's from the same vial."

Benedict had purposely held it in full sight in his hand.

"It is the same."

Torquemada drank it.

Benedict said, "No food at all, complete abstinence, can kill as finally as poisoned food, Your Lordship. I prescribe a bland diet, much milk, preferably the milk of goats."

"It shall be milked in my presence."

"Many vegetables, fresh from the garden, eaten raw; and the soup of oysters, fowl and fish."

"No, no soups."

He would think them too easy to poison, Benedict supposed.

"Soups can be dispensed with, but as a substitute there must be eggs, cooked within the shells, and fruits with the skins on."

Such a diet would be difficult to tamper with and would quiet the patient's mind as well as provide him with nourishment.

"And raw onions," said Benedict emphatically.

"Onions?" Torquemada asked, evidently relishing the thought but speaking rather dreamily. His fasting stomach had reacted quickly to the opiate. The doctor too felt the effects of the draught he had been forced to swallow, but less severely than the patient. Benedict had not fasted for six days. Nevertheless he was apprehensive: it would look bad if his head began to nod.

"There are onions in the cloister gardens," Torquemada said. "I will dig them myself in bare feet and dedicate my humility to God for the benefit of my enemies. So many hate me. And eat them, eat them, eat them!"

Benedict smiled. Torquemada's half-starved, fever-ridden body, weakened by a cold that was verging on pneumonia, instinctively craved the curative power that lay in the common onion, as every peasant knew.

"Yes," said the doctor, wishing that his patient would dismiss him.

"I shall not keep your excellent fee," Torquemada said. His speech was becoming slurred. "Here, take it back."

He drew the doctor to him and fumbled the meat into his sleeve. His fingers felt the key.

"What's this?" he said. He drew it out and poked at it groggily.

"It is my front-door key, Reverend Lord."

"A foul design!"

"I never noticed," Benedict said.

"It's gold, isn't it?"

"Brass, Reverend Lord."

"It looks like gold and it's a foul design."

Benedict took it from the limp fingers, his heart sinking, hoping Torquemada would not remember. But people said Torquemada remembered everything and forgave nothing. Perhaps in his present drugged state he would forget. But if he did remember, the doctor realized he would have to produce it and explain it away somehow. Ferdinand and Isabella were scouring the realm for gold.

[26]

"Ring for my bishop," Torquemada said. "Strike hard or he won't hear you."

With an ivory clapper Benedict struck a large bell which stood on the table. He summons servants with it, Benedict thought. How exalted one must be to have a bishop for a servant. How exalted, how safe, how supremely safe! And how enviable.

"Leave the vial," Torquemada said, rousing. "It eases me."

"But Your Lordship! There is enough in the vial to kill a dozen men! What would become of me if someone were to give you too much?"

"I dare say you'd burn. But I watched the dosage. Don't fret yourself, Dr. Benedict." His head drooped again. "Not gold?"

"Brass, Reverend Lord."

"Brass. Very good. I watched the dosage."

The bishop escorted the doctor to the door.

"The Grand Inquisitor has asked me to leave him the vial of physic," Benedict hastened to explain. "It is a powerful medicine, beneficial in small quantities but capable of noxious, even lethal, effects if taken inadvisedly. I entreat Your Grace not to let it be administered by unqualified persons."

"I see," said the bishop.

"Three drops," muttered Torquemada without raising his head. "Counted 'em." He reached for the vial and clenched it in his hand. "Doctor's full of the same. He is all right, so I am too. Good honest medicine. Good honest doctor. Gold key, though. Foul design."

"It was a powerful sedative," Benedict said. "It has rendered him dreamy, like a little child before he goes to sleep."

"Good night," said Torquemada.

Outside the door the bishop asked, "Did you really drink your own medicine?" His kindly face bore an expression of genuine concern.

"Yes," Benedict said. "He seemed to want me to."

"Are you all right?"

"Quite all right, Your Grace, but very sleepy because of a tiring day and my own sedative. I am quite all right."

"Oh dear, oh dear," the bishop sighed. "The Grand Inquisitor is so uneasy in his mind and drives himself so hard and fasts lik an anchorite and puts all the rest of us to shame. I will send you home in a litter. Do not spread abroad that you are treating the Inquisitor General. But you have calmed him and composed his mind to a degree that I have not seen in a week. You have done him much good. I was so very worried about him."

Benedict of Seville went home in the bishop's own litter, slung between two fat mules, caparisoned in episcopal purple and tinkling with silver bells, dozing and chuckling all the way as watchmen bared their heads and saluted respectfully as he passed. He looked to see if young Pizarro were among his guard, but his eyes could not focus and he could not tell.

Next day Dr. Benedict felt less like chuckling.

HE awoke next day after ten hours of refreshing sleep with a clear mind, but he did not experience the pleasant lassitude that he had come to expect from patients who had taken a similar dosage of his medicine. He was intensely apprehensive. Torquemada's last words, when he was taking his departure, had been about the golden key and its foul design.

Benedict knew that he could explain away the "foul design" of the web as a mechanical coincidence. And the design of the handle, the only elaborately decorated part, was perfectly Christian and orthodox: so went the arguments, already preparing in his agile mind. That which was not a Christian cross was merely a reputable symbol of the physician's art.

But the fact that the key was gold was unfortunate. Possession of so costly an object rendered him suspect in Torquemada's eyes. Loyal Spaniards were expected to have donated all their gold objects long since to the King and Queen to aid in the long, holy and immensely expensive war against the Moors of Granada.

[29]

If I see him again, and I hope I don't, Benedict mused, I could say I donated it to the tax collector as a patriotic gesture and I could show him a receipt. But no, that would not do. I said it was brass.

Perhaps I could get a new one made of brass, he thought. But no, again. He knew there wasn't time. If the Grand Inquisitor summoned him again the call would come before so complex an object could be duplicated, especially by a brass founder, who would not only do cruder work but who unquestionably would be swamped nowadays by royal orders for handguns and cannon, the new fire weapons that were proving so effective and which naturally would take precedence over a luxury item like a front-door key. If, on the other hand, the Grand Inquisitor waited that long to summon him he would probably not summon him at all. But he remembered the look in Torquemada's eyes when he saw the key, and he knew he must place himself swiftly beyond all suspicion. Patently, the key must become brass, the same key, and all in one day.

He sent his apprentices to make his rounds and rode his mule alone into a part of town that was seldom frequented by Christians, except of course the tax collectors. Here lived a substantial community of Jews. It occurred to him that, ironically, they were safer than he was. Jews who lived openly and quietly as Jews were seldom interfered with in the practice of their religion and never in their businesses, arts or professions, which had always been essential to the wealth of the realm and were now doubly so in wartime. Since they had never been baptized, they were tolerated, though subjected to countless discriminatory taxes and disabilities and socially scorned; and they were preached to interminably by tedious mendicant friars who hoped to convert them. They listened patiently. A few were converted.

But woe betide the crypto-Jew, the man who had been baptized or whose ancestors had, and who still secretly remained a Jew, like Dr. Benedict. Such a man was in a special class and a special hatred was reserved for him; he was a lapsed heretic and for him there was no mercy. It did not matter at all if, like Benedict, he was not especially religious. Of all men I am the least fanatic, he muttered to himself; but I may find myself in a class of zealots whom I dislike for their extreme impracticality. I just want to get along and cause no trouble and do what little good one man can do in this queer contradictory world.

In this part of the city some of the Jewish houses were ostentatious, but the majority were quietly prosperous with a studied attempt to appear poor. There were numerous shops and the countinghouses of the money changers. And there was a small establishment owned by an eccentric old scholar named Tubal.

Tubal was an alchemist. Benedict had occasionally bought medicines from him when he could not get them from Christian apothecaries, medicines easy to adulterate or so poisonous that most people would not sell them for fear of the authorities. Tubal made and sold the purest calomel, the whitest lunar caustic, the strongest alcohol to be found anywhere in Seville.

There was much gossip about him. He was said to have emigrated from Granada many years before when, having cast the horoscope of the sultan, the stars revealed that he would be the last and that Granada would fall. He was known to speak Arabic, Hebrew, Spanish and Greek. Some said he possessed the Philosophers' Stone and could change base metals to gold. Some said he knew the vowels of the Tetragrammaton and could work miracles with The Name. Some said he kept a reconstructed corpse in his cellar and, on occasion, would send it on private errands, though others said it was only a poor feeble-minded giant he had taken in, given shelter to and kept as a servant. He was said to have great secret wealth and to know high statesmen. It was whispered that King Ferdinand, notoriously superstitious, had once visited his shop in disguise and there taken a drug that would assure a prince instead of a princess to Queen Isabella. Benedict scoffed at such fancies and discounted gossip. But he was forced to concede that Tubal, the alchemist, engaged in a highly suspect profession with a degree of immunity granted only to lunatics and persons with powerful friends, or to those against whom not a shred of incriminating evidence could be found.

He hitched his mule to the post in front of Tubal's shop and entered.

Tubal's face was arresting. His beard was white and untrimmed and gave him something of a Biblical patriarchal appearance. On his head he wore a peaked fur cap; escaping from the edges was a white aureole of unkempt hair. But there was a strictly modern touch, modern as the year 1491. He wore a pair of thick spectacles of Venetian glass, costly, unusual things and difficult to procure. Benedict, whose eyesight was excellent, supposed it was the penalty of poring too long over alchemistical manuscripts and peering into the white hot fires of alembics. His hands were gnarled and stained with old acid burns. Doctor and alchemist greeted each other with Spanish politeness and professional reserve.

"From time to time I have bought medicines here," Benedict said.

"I was honored by your patronage," Tubal said.

"They were sometimes of special kinds," Benedict said.

Tubal said, "Were they? I do not remember."

"Kinds I could not get elsewhere, or could get only in impure form. Yours were pure, and I used them only for healing purposes."

"That is always commendable," Tubal said. "Now that I bethink me I remember them well. You wish to buy more? Powdered mummy that preserves? Reflect how long the Egyptian mummies have remained in a state of preservation. Costly, but how else can your patients assure immortality, or at least a protracted life span? A catapasm of unicorn horn specially compounded with Baltic amber? I have just received a small shipment from the north and I will share it with you. No? Something more special still? I may not have it, though I shall try to procure it for you. Well?"

"I have heard it said that certain alchemists of great skill can convert baser metals to gold," Dr. Benedict said.

Tubal smiled, noncommittal, and said nothing. Nearly every day some impoverished grandee came to him with the same request.

"Is it true?"

"A man of your learning ought to know that great strides are being made in that direction, but I do not take such commissions myself; nor shall I, till my own experiments prove more conclusive. Yet in time to come, yes, baser metals shall be transubstantiated into the nobler ones. I cannot help you, yet, Doctor."

"I came to ask if you could do the opposite. It is important to me."

"I do not understand."

"Can you convert gold into, say, brass?"

"Ah, that is quite different. Yes. It is hard to rise. It is easy to step down. To brass, yes, or at least into the semblance of brass. No one can tell the difference."

"I realize it's an unusual request."

"Indeed it is, Señor Doctor."

But it was not, not really. Many people were hiring alchemists to disguise their gold objects, most often as silver, sometimes as copper or brass. Most often they were Jews or crypto-Jews or crypto-Moors, but a surprisingly large number were irreproachable Christians who could attest the *limpieza* of their blood for generations. For Tubal it was becoming a profitable business. Since someone else would do it if he did not, he always obliged.

"It is a difficult procedure, requiring great knowledge," he said mysteriously. "Unskilled artisans simply dip them in a molten bath of the baser metal. The fraud is instantly detectable."

"That is why I have come to you."

"It is an object of great value?"

"Not great, but of some sentiment."

"Perhaps that is the greatest," Tubal said, nodding.

"It is my front-door key."

"A front-door key. I understand," Tubal said. "I would do the same in your place, Señor Doctor. May I see it?"

Benedict showed it to him.

The alchemist started, stared at it closely, bringing it so close to his glasses that his breath condensed on the metal, and muttered something in Hebrew that Benedict did not catch, though it sounded like "desecration."

"It is a curious mixture of designs," Tubal said, calmer but in a distinct manner. "The holy is mixed with the profane."

Benedict noted that the alchemist did not specify which he considered holy, which profane; but he knew in his heart what

[34]

Tubal meant and he honored him for the faith he did not share, not to such stubborn lengths, at least.

"It is only a key," Benedict said, shrugging. "Only a front-door key. But it is very old and I do not wish to donate it to Their Catholic Majesties in the crusade against the infidel, holy as such a crusade may be. Can you disguise it?"

The alchemist said with a sigh, "Yes, I can disguise it, as we all must disguise, scheme, contrive, juggle, sidestep, shunt and put on false faces to survive. I should do the same were I your age. But I did not know this about you, my brother."

"Know what?" Benedict said, alarmed. He was ready to leave the shop.

"Did I say I *knew* something?" the alchemist asked. "I know nothing. You have told me nothing. Indeed, my eyesight is so poor that I do not remember ever seeing you before, nor would I recognize you on the street. Would you care to give me the key?"

In the jaws of an iron pincers the alchemist took the key and immersed it in an amber fluid for perhaps thirty seconds. When tiny bubbles appeared on the surface he drew it out and held it in the fire, turning it over and over. The key turned a rusty red, but whether from action of the heat or some chemical action the doctor did not know. Then with a chamois skin the alchemist rubbed it, and the key turned silver. Dr. Benedict realized that the chamois skin was impregnated with mercury, or perhaps lunar caustic, which the doctor used to burn off warts. The alchemist chattered about inconsequentialities, the weather, the war, the state of the health of the city and his hope that the doctor was not overtiring himself in his treatment of the sick. Deftly and swiftly the alchemist continued to work and his chatter was obviously intended to distract the doctor's attention and obscure whatever he was doing with the key. Benedict smiled. How often had he obscured his own secrets in exactly the same manner when dealing with patients. Yet it must have been mercury, for the key now shone like liquid silver, moonlight on water.

The alchemist held the golden key once again in the fire and the silver lost its sheen and turned chalky white, on which having cooled it in water, he burnished it with a bit of the horn of some beast, which he said was a unicorn's horn, but which Benedict supposed was nothing more than a piece of deer's antler. Shortly, again the key shone silver, but less brilliantly.

"I do not follow the process," Benedict said. "I do not understand what you are doing."

"I am false-facing that which is gold," Tubal said.

The alchemist now dipped the key into an emerald green solution, and it was darker when he drew it out, like a sunset compared with a white high-riding moon. Benedict was now utterly bewildered.

"Not too dark," he cautioned.

Again the alchemist burnished the key with a little bunch of chamois skin. Something was unquestionably in the burnisher, probably some other amalgam of liquified metals, for the key again took on a lustrous sheen, only darker. Forthwith Tubal held it once more in the fire, and it became a cheap rusty green.

Benedict was angry.

"You have gone too far," he said.

"Kindly keep silent," the alchemist said. His forehead was sweating from emotion and the heat of his protracted labor.

Benedict accepted the reproach.

The alchemist gently burnished the key again with the beast's horn, and very shortly a metallic sheen reappeared, more subdued, cheaper still, but still something like gold of poor quality.

"It still looks like gold," Benedict said.

"Shouldn't it? Enough to confuse the ignorant and confound the suspicious?" Tubal asked. He called for his assistant, who shuffled his great bulk into the room.

"Fetch me an egg," he ordered.

The blank-faced giant obediently brought an egg, broken in a bowl.

Tubal dipped the key into the egg, frothing it around and around like a cook preparing an omelette, and withdrew it and wiped it dry with a cloth. It was tarnished. He held it up for the doctor's inspection. "Gold does not tarnish," he said.

The doctor answered, "No, it does not."

Tubal took a clean chamois skin and rubbed off most, but not all, of the discoloration, leaving the key again with a brassy-gold distinctly inferior sheen.

"Now, Señor Doctor, it is brass; and any test will prove it so, and with ordinary care it will remain brass for three hundred years."

"I am most grateful," Benedict said, reaching for his purse.

But the alchemist turned his back and walked away, saying, "There is no fee, my brother. We all seek the path to holiness, each in our own way." From the depths of the shop, as Benedict placed the brass key in his purse preparing to depart, while Tubal set himself to compounding a prescription, decidedly unorthodox Benedict heard him pronounce the Ancient Hebrew benediction, uttered in an Arabic accent, "The Lord bless thee and keep thee; the Lord make his face to shine upon thee and be gracious unto thee; the Lord lift up his countenance upon thee and give thee peace." Tubal pronounced "peace" not as *shalom* but as *salaam*, in the way of the Jews of Granada.

Benedict sighed; but he was safe, and he was thankful.

A PERIOD of peace and prosperity now dawned in the life of Benedict of Seville. Never had he been so busy; never had he treated so many wounds. The war against the Moor was rising to its final climactic victory.

Never had the doctor felt so secure, so safe, so above suspicion. In his mind's eye he envisioned the happy future: after victory there would be a lessening of the religious preoccupation that now gripped the country. There would be a relaxation of tensions, a growth of tolerance and the surge of prosperity that always follows the waste of war. Good times were coming, and Benedict saw himself growing old, rich and respected, living out his years in the practice of his art. And when he should become too feeble to make his rounds he would take pleasure in the professional career of his son, and when Juan came home at night he would say, "Well, Juan? How many cases today? What were they like? Did you cure some of them? How much were your fees?" For the Benedicts had always been physicians. And he would teach Juan to distinguish between the fraudulently sick and the truly sick, those sick in the mind and those sick in the body; he would teach him all he knew of the healing art; but above all, he would teach him how to take care of himself. There was always the danger that those who devoted themselves to the care of others forgot to take care of themselves. He mused, "Ideals should be high, but not visionary." Of course, all this was a little premature, since Juan was only nine years old. But Benedict was forehanded. Thus stretched out in the doctor's mind the peaceful happy years to come.

The year 1491 was wearing on to its close. The drought and heat of the Andalusian summer had given way to gentle autumn rains. The waters rose in the Guadalquivir, and the intricate reservoirs and canals, constructed over seven centuries by the Moors, filled with a promise of a new year of plenty and likely of peace at last. The Moors were the best gardeners in the world, as was natural to a people whose origins lay in the desert, the wastes of Arabia, to whom water was a miracle and vegetation a delight. All of those complex irrigation works were now owned and operated by the Spanish Reconquerors, who marveled at the engineering of their infidel predecessors.

Only Granada still stubbornly held out, and Granada was closely invested by the armies of King Ferdinand and Queen Isabella. There was bitter fighting, but everyone knew it was only a matter of time till Granada should fall. It was from these battles that so many of the wounded came to Dr. Benedict for treatment. He rejoiced, like everyone else in Spain, at the coming of certain victory.

But Benedict's happiness about the end of the war was somewhat different from that of most Spaniards. He did not feel the mystical elation that Christians did at the thought of the final solution of the Moorish problem, even though he knew it would lessen the hatred against the Jews. Benedict hated blood. I spend my life staunching it! It belongs to the body, where God put it. How blood could cleanse or wash out guilt or sanctify he simply could not imagine, though Christian and Jew both claimed it did. I am not even a good Jew, he thought, shrugging. He derived much pleasure from reading Isaiah, where he noted with satisfaction that the Lord had said, "I am full of the burnt offerings of rams, and the fat of fat beasts; and I delight not in the blood of bullocks, or of lambs, or of he goats." How much less, Benedict thought, in the blood of man! But he did not pretend to be a theologian; no doubt the experts on both sides had very persuasive arguments in a totally different sense; he read what pleased and comforted him. At least I know something about doctoring, he thought, smiling, contented.

Much of the peace he enjoyed at this time, the last he was ever to know, came from the fact that Torquemada had not summoned him again. I surmise, thought the doctor, that the poor old fellow got over his cold. Well, this is a blessing! He preferred not to think what would have happened to him if Torquemada had died. He hoped, and he now began to believe, he would never be called again to treat this formidable clergyman.

Then one night there was a knock at the door, and Francisco Pizarro stood in the hall. He was very pale and there was a spot on his cloak and his hand clutched at his chest beneath.

"What is it, lad? It is late. My house is closed. Why do you seek me at this hour of the night? I trust nothing is amiss with your patron?"

Pizarro shook his head. "No, Doctor; it's me."

Benedict eyed him clinically and said to the servant, who had locked the door, "Draw up a chair to the fire for Don Francisco. It is cold outside tonight."

[40]

Pizarro slumped into the chair. Benedict gently drew back his cloak and saw the young man's hand smeared with blood, clutching at a rent in his doublet. It was on the left side, shoulder high, just under the collarbone. Someone had aimed at the heart.

"It wasn't my fault," Pizarro said, weakly.

"Of course not," Benedict agreed, his voice low and comforting. "Now just sit quietly, if you please, Don Francisco. You're going to be all right. Just do not talk. Just let me take a look. That's a good lad."

The well-trained servant had called one of the apprentices. Benedict whispered to him; the apprentice nodded and hurried off, returning at once with a small chest, different from the chest of glass vials, and a large transparent glass decanter of amber fluid.

"I told her I was willing to pay," Pizarro said.

"Hush, Don Francisco. Do not weaken yourself by talking."

There was a good deal of blood. It had stained Pizarro's doublet down to the belt. The doctor took a pair of scissors from the chest, which contained his surgical instruments, and prepared to cut away the cloth in the area of the wound, but Pizarro said, "Do not cut my doublet. It's the only one I have."

Benedict hesitated. It was often necessary to cut away clothing and remove scraps of fabric from wounds, and only the very poor ever protested.

"I cannot help it, Don Francisco. I'll not damage it more than somebody else already has. First we must mend *you*, then we shall see to the mending of your garment."

He laid bare an area as large as the palm of his hand, and saw in the skin of Pizarro's chest a knife wound about three inches long. It was bleeding profusely, but not, he noted, with spurts.

When blood spurted from a wound there was danger of death. It occurred to the doctor that it would be distinctly dangerous for a protégé of Torquemada's to die in his house.

"You will be all right, Don Francisco," he said, with more than professional relief. "Drink this. I am going to close the wound." He handed him a copious draught of the amber fluid.

Pizarro smelled it, grinned and drank it down like water. Benedict watched him with a smile. It was remarkable what a young stomach could take.

"I am used to wine, and not of the best," Pizarro said. "I tasted brandy only once before in my life. You must be very rich."

"Do not talk so much," Benedict said. "It weakens you. Brandy is a medicine. In your state it will strengthen you, and you won't hurt so much when I close the wound."

"I am not afraid of pain," Pizarro said. He was watching the doctor carefully, and did not wince in anticipation at what the doctor was doing.

Benedict took a slender iron rod and held it in the fire until it began to glow.

"I am not afraid of the cautery," Pizarro said, and indeed, as Benedict eyed him sharply, he did not appear to be. "All wounds must be closed with the cautery, must they not?"

Benedict laughed. "No, lad, not by all doctors, and very seldom by me. I am only burning off the foreign matter so the probe will be clean."

He plunged it into the brandy; it hissed, and grew cold.

"Now we shall see if the point of the knife broke off and is still in your flesh. If so I must take it out."

"It isn't," Pizarro said. "I saw the knife in her hand afterwards."

"But I must see," Benedict said.

[42]

The apprentice placed powerful hands on Pizarro's shoulders to restrain him. Benedict probed the wound swiftly; the wound was empty and clean; his sensitive fingers felt no obstruction.

"I am sorry to have hurt you," Benedict said. Pizarro had clenched his teeth during the short and painful examination.

"It didn't hurt," he said.

Benedict knew it had. He said approvingly, "You will go far in this world, Don Francisco. You are a brave man."

The pain that Pizarro denied, the weakness from loss of blood and the powerful brandy were loosening his tongue. Also, with the vanity of a very young man, he was itching to relate how he had received the wound, which interested Benedict only mildly. He had already guessed.

"There is a woman in a house by the river," Pizarro said, "A Morisca of great beauty, and very poor, like all those converts. Two friars did me the honor to ask me to accompany them as a guard, though holy men need none, while they searched her house and looked for evidence. Her husband is a laborer of some sort. Naturally we made our visitation while he was away at his work."

"Very wise," Benedict said, nodding to the apprentice, who was melting pitch and preparing a concoction of brandy and beaten egg. Pizarro wondered if he was going to be given another drink.

"She is fair-skinned, for a Morisca, and her eyes grew large and limpid whenever she looked at me. It was obviously an invitation."

It could have been fear, Benedict knew. Fear can make the eyes limpid and large no less than love, but it was not his place to teach anatomy to the vain young man who was interested in learning about it from a more personal approach.

[43]

"The good friars found nothing, no Korans, no horoscopes, no Arabic charms; but later I returned on my own to see what I could find." Pizarro chuckled.

Benedict took a spoon and wet a cotton compress with the egg and brandy mixture, held the edges of the wound together and pressed the compress firmly upon it. Pizarro's chest muscles tightened as the strong alcohol in the brandy bit into his flesh. But Benedict knew it would cleanse it, and the egg would soothe the pain and promote healing. For some reason which no one could explain, wounds treated in this manner healed more rapidly than wounds treated with boiling oil or red-hot cauteries, and the patients seldom developed the severe fever that followed the more orthodox treatment.

"I dare say you went back while her husband was still at work," the doctor suggested.

"Naturally," Pizarro said.

"It would appear that she welcomed you with a knife."

"Not at all," Pizarro said. "Oh, she pushed me away a little at first and began to cry; but I told her I would go get the friars if she made any fuss, and then her eyes got big and inviting just like before. I could see that she wanted me."

The young man had obviously terrorized the poor thing, Benedict realized.

"And without further ado, she gave me such a welcome as I'll never forget to my dying day. There is nothing like the hot Morisco blood for good company in a bed, Señor Doctor."

Adopting his mood, the doctor said, smiling, "But it very nearly turned out to be your dying day, didn't it? A little lower, a little deeper and the knife would have hit the heart, and then not even I could have saved you."

"Oh, she didn't plan to knife me. You can tell when they love

[44]

you. She wanted me to stay. I could tell by the reception she'd given me. Couldn't do enough for me. God, she wiggled like a fish on a hook!"

"I can well believe that," Benedict said, for indeed that was what she was: very much like a fish on a hook. But Benedict said it as if he approved. Meanwhile he was busily dressing the wound. He took a patch of oilcloth, lest Pizarro's blood seep through the compress, and placed it over the compress; and over the whole dressing, which now would not leak, he placed a larger patch of cloth that the apprentice had smeared with pitch. It was still hot enough to be sticky, but not so hot as to blister seriously. It adhered like flexible glue.

"But just then her husband came home. I didn't know it was so late. Just when I was getting my clothes on, just when I was saying, 'I'll pay you, señora, as soon as I can.' You should have seen her face! She went absolutely wild. She screamed at me, 'Get out!' and she called me filthy names. She rushed at me with a knife and slashed at me. It was all for her husband's benefit, of course. I'd have dodged the blow, but the husband lunged at me too and I had to defend myself against both of them. That's how I got the cut."

"Does the husband still live?" Benedict asked.

Pizzaro shrugged. "I don't know. I should think so. I think I only nicked him. He just grunted and slumped over holding his belly. The woman bent over him, screaming that she was innocent and that nothing had happened. She said I was starting to take *off* my clothes instead of just finishing putting them on. Women certainly are clever when they've done something wrong. But I think what really infuriated her was that I didn't happen to have any money to give her as a present for her hospitality. You know these Conversos; money is everything.

God, it was certainly hospitality. Then I told him I was from the Holy Office, and the stupid yokel nearly fainted. He must have a mighty guilty conscience. Now I know he's concealing something."

He might have been concealing a mortal wound, the doctor thought somberly. He was fleetingly tempted to ask the location of the house and the names of the Moriscos and go to offer help; but no. He would be suspect. Perhaps he would send one of the apprentices; but no again. The apprentice would be suspect. If the belly wound were slight some other doctor would treat it. If it were deep no doctor on earth could help, not a belly wound; there was absolutely no cure.

The apprentice was sponging the blood from Pizarro's doublet. Benedict did not like the look on the apprentice's sensitive face. It was red with fury and shame, red as Pizarro's blood, at Pizarro's recital. I think he would like to rip my poultice off and let the Christian bleed to death, Benedict thought. It was obvious to Benedict that the apprentice had a great deal to learn about diplomacy before he qualified as a master physician. If he did not he would never live to be a master, or would always live in poverty. Sensibility should never be carried too far.

"No doubt the victim of your little peccadillo has been treated by some of his own people," Benedict said, looking sternly at his apprentice. "They do not like us to treat them, and they have some quite adequate doctors among themselves. It is idle for us to seek patients among them. That is one of the first things a Christian doctor must learn. Do you feel strong enough to ride back to the cloister, Don Francisco?"

Pizarro looked at his doublet, hesitating. "I cannot show up like this. If my patron saw me I would have to say I had been in a street brawl. But sooner or later he'd find out the truth. No matter how clever the lie, Father Thomas has means of detecting it. Even I do not know how. But I cannot stay out all night either. He would dismiss me."

It was late. One of the women servants in Benedict's household could easily be roused and mend the garment in a matter of minutes, but the blood would have to be washed out and then it would have to dry. There wasn't time.

"You are about the size of José here," Benedict said, nodding to the apprentice. "He will give you his and take yours in exchange."

"His is better than mine," Pizarro said. "Father Thomas would notice and think I stole it."

Benedict hastened to explain, "We were called today to the house of a fashionable patient. Naturally we had to look our best. But my apprentice's usual garb is very much like your own, good, serviceable, not elaborate."

"That is kind of you, Dr. Benedict."

The doctor directed the apprentice to fetch it. "I remember you hung it in the clothes press in your room on the third floor," he said significantly. Actually, the apprentice lived on the second floor, the servants lived on the third. The apprentice nodded, understanding the stratagem, and shortly returned with a servant's doublet. Perhaps, thought the doctor, he will learn diplomacy after all.

Dressed, strengthened by the brandy, and vastly pleased with himself, Pizarro rose to depart.

"Do not disturb the poultice for a week," the doctor said. "Then gently pull it off, and if my prayers and my small skill have aught availed you will find you are healed, and no one will ever be the wiser about your little affair. There will always be a scar, I'm afraid."

Pizarro grinned. "I got it fighting the Moor, didn't I?" But he looked uncomfortable. "About your fee, Doctor, as I said, I do not happen to have —"

Benedict brushed the suggestion away. "The honor of treating your illustrious patron compensates me far beyond your power to repay, and I am happy to have had the honor of treating a trusted member of his household also."

"Nevertheless, I will give you a fee as soon as I can," Pizarro said, bowing handsomely. "Meanwhile I shall find occasion to mention you often to him, praising your skill."

"Oh, please do not do that. I pray that your reverend patron will never need me again as long as he lives," Benedict said in alarm.

"If you should see him again, I trust you will say nothing about this," Pizarro said, touching his wound. "You won't, will you?"

"Of course not, Don Francisco. A doctor's confidences are as sacred as the confessional. Moreover," he added, with a sly wink that was wondrously convincing, "I was young myself once."

"When I think of a doctor's chances!" Pizarro said rather tipsily. "Such chances! It makes me envious."

They heard him gallop away.

"The swine!" the apprentice said.

Benedict lectured him severely. "There are worse, far worse than this young Pizarro," and the apprentice went off to bed hoping one day he too would be as strong, as skillful and as diplomatic as his master.

PIZZARO did not return for further treatment, so Benedict judged that the wound had properly healed.

The doctor's days were filled with toil. He did not neglect his fashionable clientele, who paid so well, but he spent many additional hours, for which he received no pay, in the new hospital that the King and Queen had erected in Seville. Here were wounded soldiers, laid out row upon row on vermin-infested pallets of straw. The terrible wounds inflicted by the new firearms were the most difficult to heal. Benedict prayed that no weapon of war would ever be discovered more cruel than gunpowder. Indeed, it seemed almost unthinkable. Surely, war had now reached the ultimate in destructiveness. When all nations possessed unlimited supplies of cannon and handguns, mankind would come to its senses; a stalemate would ensue and war would fall out of fashion; for in a full-fledged Armageddon with such weapons on both sides, the armies would mutually destroy each other, down to the last man. War would become suicidal, and suicide is unnatural. So perhaps the hideous new weapon would prove a blessing after all.

With the doctor so busy, his apprentices made more and more calls unattended, and at supper, which they ate at the foot of the family table, he would instruct them, teaching them all he knew of the baffling cases they encountered. This professional talk, some of it gory, was good training for Juan who would never be squeamish if exposed to it from childhood. Nor did it bother his wife, who was used to it, though occasionally she would perfume his beard when he reeked from the smoke of the cautery. Once she whispered in his ear, "Baruch, you smell like a Dominican!" He gave her such a look of alarm that she never joked about the matter again.

One night at supper Juan said to his father, "José has not returned."

"Then we shall eat without him, and he shall get a cold supper in his room," Benedict said.

Maria said, "Don't be too hard on him, Benedict. You know how he loses track of time in his work."

"He is entirely too devoted," Benedict said, and lectured Juan and the other apprentice: "I have repeatedly warned José that a doctor must save some time for himself, in the interest of his family, his purse and his health. One doctor cannot cure all the sickness of this world, and if he tries he destroys himself in the process, and the world is deprived of the good he might have accomplished. Never forget that when you are doctors. Therefore José is to be blamed, not praised, for missing supper tonight."

But José, the apprentice, did not come home at all that night, nor the next, nor for a week. Both Benedict and Maria made discreet enquiries among their friends. José had been like a son to them ever since the time when, orphaned and son of a crypto-Jew, they had taken him into their home and raised him as their own to be a doctor when Benedict should grow old. Their enquiries were futile. José had disappeared.

"He may have joined the armies for the assault on Granada," Maria suggested dubiously. "Everyone else has."

"I hope that is all he did," Benedict answered.

The house was gloomy without the intelligent lad.

Then Francisco Pizarro appeared at the doctor's door. His manner was changed and oddly distant. "My patron requires you again," he said.

Benedict said, "I hope your reverend patron keeps well."

"Better than before, Dr. Benedict, but he says he would like to see you."

"And you, Don Francisco? Your wound?"

"Oh that," Pizarro laughed, and struck his chest. "The wound is healed, thanks to you. I am your most grateful patient."

Pizarro paused, as if fighting back a secret he wished to reveal. "You were good to me, Doctor; I cannot yet give you a fee, but I can give you a bit of advice. I could be burned for this, Doctor, but I must warn you to throw away your key."

"My key, Don Francisco?"

"The golden key to your house."

"It isn't gold."

"Father Thomas thinks it is, and he has a keen eye for gold. I should hate to see you fined, or worse, for concealing gold which *los reyes católicos* need so sorely for Spain."

"If your patron is sick again I shall physic him," Benedict said.
"Oh, he is."

"But if, in your kindness for my small part in healing your wound, which not I but God healed and his Holy Saints, my

[51]

meager skill having been only the earthly means to channel His heavenly grace, you come to warn me that the Grand Inquisitor suspects me of disloyalty, I can only protest my innocence, namely, that I am a loyal Christian Spaniard, and my poor front-door key is brass."

"If it's brass you have nothing to fear."

"I will go to your patron now, if he needs me."

"He unquestionably wants to see you," Pizarro said, and added, "I hope for your sake it is brass."

Thomas of Torquemada looked vastly better. He sat by the fire as before but there was no blanket around his shoulders and his color was good. His eyes were not bloodshot, and they were more piercing than ever. The man was perfectly healthy.

"I regret that Your Eminence still suffers from some indisposition of the body, and I present myself to do whatever my poor art can avail," Benedict said.

"My Eminence is better since your last visit," Torquemada said, and sniffed. "No pig in your sleeve, Dr. Benedict? Have you taken an aversion to pork?"

"I have spent the whole day in the hospital of *los reyes católi-cos*," Benedict said, "and the poor soldiers there have no fees for a doctor, but I physic them nonetheless, feeless, in the Christian cause."

"Interesting," said Torquemada.

"In what can I serve Your Eminence?"

"I want more of your physic."

Benedict was taken aback

"Reverend sir, if you have consumed the entire contents of my vial in this short time you are dead and I am privileged to behold your ghost. Where did it all go?"

"You've a clever tongue, Dr. Benedict. I have made some enquiries about you; everyone says you have a clever tongue. I hope you keep it. As for the vial, my stupid bishop dropped and broke it. I took only the three drops daily, as prescribed. It did me a world of good. I want more."

"Your Eminence has only to command," Benedict said, and produced another vial.

"God wills me to command," Torquemada said.

Benedict repressed a frown. It was always ominous when patients spoke as if they were God. He was tempted to substitute a vial so potent that three drops would kill, but of course he did not. For every dead Torquemada there were a dozen more, perhaps worse, to rise and take his place. Benedict measured out a dosage, and Torquemada drank it.

"Show me again that interesting front-door key of yours," Torquemada said.

Benedict reached into his sleeve and handed it to him. Torquemada struck the servant's bell, and the bishop entered.

"Have this tested," he said; and he leaned back in his chair, fingertips to fingertips under his hawk nose, smiling unpleasantly at the doctor. Benedict prayed that they would not saw the key in two and find the pure gold under the skin of base metal.

"You look worried," Torquemada said.

Benedict said smoothly, "I am always worried about the health of my patients."

"A clever tongue, like that demon Isaac Abravanel, who hissed his way into the King's council and now is chief minister," Torquemada said, scowling fearfully. "A foul Christ-killer of a Jew."

Benedict said, "I have barely heard of this statesman, though

[53]

his name is known to all good Spaniards. I am only a poor practi-
tioner of the physician's craft, and I know nothing about the
great ones of this world."

"He is a Jew," Torquemada spat out, "but I cannot burn him
yet."

The three drops were taking effect. Under their influence the
Grand Inquisitor was speaking carelessly, revealing his true
character: spiteful, fearful, jealous, bigoted, insecure in his high
position.

Outside somewhere, someone was testing the golden key.
Shortly, after Benedict had mumbled some inconsequentialities
about the weather and the war, the bishop returned with it and
handed it to Torquemada.

"Well?" said the Grand Inquisitor.

"Brass," said the bishop. "It tarnishes."

"You amaze me," Torquemada said to the doctor. "That is not
what I expected. Not what I expected at all."

He blessed him Christian to Christian, and bade him be gone.
Pizarro took him home, saying, "I'm glad it was brass, Dr.
Benedict. He needs you, but he hoped it was gold."

"Why?"

"Perhaps he has found something about you that makes him
suspect you. Perhaps he thinks you are a crypto-Jew."

"My whole life is witness that I am a good Christian."

Pizarro laughed. "I am not the Grand Inquisitor, Dr. Benedict. By the saints, I believe you, especially since the key is
brass. And I am indebted to you, for this," he touched his
wound. Benedict sustained the unpleasant impression that
Pizarro was proud of it. He did not ask about the woman's
husband. "I thank God, Doctor, that you are in the clear."

So long as Torquemada needs me, Benedict thought; but fears

[54]

arose in his heart for Juan his son, for Maria his wife, and for his apprentices, especially for the one who had disappeared.

José's disappearance stretched out till Christmastime. There was no word of him. Dr. Benedict pursued his profession, faithfully making his rounds.

As for the war, the news was all good. The walls of Granada were breached; fire and cannonballs fell upon the Alhambra, and large contingents of Moors were surrendering. The end was close, after seven hundred years. But whether victory would usher in the golden age that the doctor had envisioned he now began to doubt.

Then a litter, accompanied by two black-robed friars, stopped at his door.

In the litter was a corpse.

WE believe this poor fellow was an apprentice of yours," one of the friars said, lifting the blanket that covered the corpse and revealing the blue and bloated face.

Benedict gazed for a moment at the lifeless countenance, still and alien in death. The quick intelligence, the hope and promise of youth, the love of life, the hatred of injustice, the devotion to the healing art, all that had stamped José as an individual, all that the doctor had inculcated into his personality, all were gone, all lost; and the body that had served for a few short years as the dwelling place of some small part of the living spirit of God now lay without breath, inert and empty. How pitifully similar all dead bodies looked once the soul had departed. To a doctor's eye the change was even more striking than to a layman's, for to a layman, moved by remembrance and love, the mask of death looks like a sleep. Dr. Benedict could see the lax musculature of the face and neck, already drooping toward the earth that soon would cover him, as if some ghostly, greedy hand had already risen from the earth to grip what once was clay and now was clay again, as if José were obediently trying to answer the call. This phenomenon appeared in all the dead; it never ceased to affect the doctor. The waste, the awful waste of death, so infinitely more wasteful in the young.

"Yes, reverend sirs, this is the body of José, my apprentice."

The doctor's face was stricken. The friar said in a kindly tone, "It is clear that you loved him. I give you my blessing and I offer my condolence. The Lord giveth, the Lord taketh away."

"Blessed be the name of the Lord," Benedict answered. "Is it known how the tragedy occurred?"

"A servant of the Holy Office happened upon him lying in the river at the foot of an embankment. No doubt he fell; his leg is broken."

"No doubt," said the doctor.

Servants carried José into the house. Benedict thanked the friars and gave them some pieces of silver, enough to appease their cupidity but not a sufficient gift to arouse suspicion that he might be a wealthy man.

"I will see to his burial," he said in a shaken voice. They blessed him and went their way, taking the blanket.

Later, despite what he found, Dr. Benedict was convinced that their friendly attitude was genuine, that they knew no more than they appeared to know, and that the act of returning José's body had actually been an act of Christian charity.

Little Juan and Maria peeked into the room where the servants had laid the body, and wept.

"He drowned," Benedict said. "Poor José! And I reproached him for missing supper."

Later the servants filed by and said good-bye to the silent form. José's death left a saddening gap in their close-knit family circle. They mourned as if a blood relative had been taken by this cruel and tragic accident. Benedict told them no more than that. But he knew more, and he was puzzled, and the vague apprehensions that lately had troubled him grew.

José's broken leg presented a clinical picture that Benedict never before had observed as the result of an accident. The bruises were not convincing. They did not penetrate the skin. They looked rather the result of pressure, as if powerful levers had wrought the damage. José's toes were especially suspect: here too were no wounds. Benedict felt his scalp creep. Few doctors, other than those employed by the Holy Office, ever examined the tortured bodies of the Inquisition's victims. But Benedict had an eerie illogical notion that that was precisely what he was doing now. But such a lapse of discretion on the part of that great and secretive organization would have been unprecedented and he doubted the evidence of his own eyes: perhaps José had actually met death in some freakish accident that had actually produced these freak results: perhaps, after all, José's death had been natural.

His first impulse was a strong one: to probe no further, to do nothing that might be construed as desecration of the body, but to arrange for its burial in all haste and hide the mystery underground. But a surge of anger arose in his heart and he made up his mind to get at the truth. They said José drowned? Very well, he would find out. Perhaps he could find out without leaving evidence of his examination.

The stomach was distended and obviously waterlogged. This was as it should be in a drowning, except that José seemed to have swallowed an unusually large amount. He pressed the chest firmly and bent his face close to the face of the corpse, but no air was expelled from nostrils or throat; he neither heard nor

felt upon his cheek the little sigh that should have resulted if the
lungs had been full of air. But neither was water expelled, as it
would have been if the lungs were full of water. He tapped the
chest sharply to hear what sound would be produced: if waterlogged it would give off a dull thump like a cask full of wine; if
filled with air it would sound hollow, empty like an empty cask.
It sounded empty. Benedict knitted his brow, perplexed. But his
examination had already disclosed the fact that, since there was
still air in the lungs, death had not been due to drowning.

Now he examined the throat to see what was obstructing the
passage of air from the lungs. He found the only wound on the
body. The throat was clogged with a tangle of shredded flesh
clotted together with congealed blood. He made an opening
through it, and José sighed and the rib cage settled slightly as
the dead breath was expelled. Already it stank of the charnel
house.

Now the doctor knew. José had not died a natural death. José
had been subjected to a rare and extreme form of torture,
designed, like all inquisitorial techniques, to force confessions
from reluctant witnesses. What had he been asked? What had he
told the black-robed questioners who took down every word in
writing, noted every gesture in their tablets as they watched,
grim-faced and efficient? Had José held fast to his faith? José
could not answer now. Had he kept the secret of the House of
Baruch — Miriam, Johann, the doctor himself? Clay could not
answer. When, one by one, his joints had cracked and his leg
bones snapped, had he talked? No, or his torturers would not
have gone on to do worse. In his last agony, when they took the
long-snouted metal funnel and forced water into his slowly
swelling body till his belly was nigh to bursting, had he nodded
a yes? — for that would have been enough, and brought down

[59]

upon Benedict and all his family the dread fury of Torquemada.

"I wouldn't have blamed you, lad," Benedict said to the silent form. "I could not have stood half of what you did."

But he deemed it more likely that José, who was young and strong and fanatically loyal, had confessed to nothing, not even when the funnel was pushed so far down that it tore the throat.

It was strictly forbidden to die under torture. The Grand Inquisitor himself sternly enforced the letter of the law, a law dating back a thousand years to the time when the Church first intervened to mitigate the savagery of the Roman judicial *De Quaestionibus,* a mitigation that had wrought much good in earlier days. Children under fourteen could not be tortured, nor could pregnant women, nor could torture be repeated nor could blood be shed. But now with the Spanish Inquisition all but divorced from the Church and firmly under the direction of the Spanish state, the good was habitually circumvented and only the letter of the law was obeyed. Thus, torture was often repeated by the pretext of calling each session a "continuance" of the last. In José's case it must have been continued several days. Greater care was taken about the shedding of blood, however, for that could be detected by the crowds who watched the executions, which were always carried out by the medium of fire, lest blood be shed even then. Only occasionally did someone die under the question, and then largely by accident. Benedict believed such an accident must have occurred to José through inexperienced manipulation of the funnel. The physical damage wrought by the funnel had probably choked his breath and suffocated him. Benedict hoped so, for that would have shortened his agony.

He closed José's mouth and prepared him for burial, murmuring, "Farewell, thou good, thou faithful to the end. Thou'rt a better Jew than I. May the psalm of our kinsman David come literally true for thee, as even the Christians believe, who look to it also when they mourn their dead: May you dwell in the house of the Lord forever. As for me, I do not know; I know only about the preservation of the body."

He gave him Christian burial and lighted candles for him in the church and gave the priest a donation for a hundred Masses for the repose of his soul.

Then, having fulfilled his duties and noting no evidence of suspicion on the part of the Holy Office, he took heart and worried less and read much in Isaiah. There he always found comfort in the words that seemed directly addressed to him and which justified his crypto-Jewishness; they certainly did not preach martyrdom: Come, my people, enter thou into thy chambers and shut thy doors about thee; hide thyself as it were for a little moment, until the indignation be overpast.

Nor did he worry overmuch when Torquemada sent for him again for treatment, for on January 2, 1492, Granada fell and the King and Queen marched at the head of a magnificent procession into the city and raised the lions of Leon and the castles of Castile on the heights of the Alhambra. They tore down all the crescents atop the mosques, purified the infidel places of worship with holy water and set up a multitude of crosses, rang thousands of bells long prepared for the purpose — bells were forbidden by Islam — and issued a proclamation promising no reprisals against the conquered. These promises soon were repudiated, but everyone believed them at the time, and Benedict's faith that tensions would now relax again took root.

The Grand Inquisitor was very thin, and there were fever spots on his cheek bones, the only color in his face, which was elsewhere pallid in the extreme. There was a nervous tremor in

[61]

his hands. But there was no indication of bodily weakness. He paced the room with a firm and rapid step, getting up from his chair and sitting down again constantly. His voice was strong and he talked incessantly, smiling, chuckling, rubbing his hands. Torquemada was in a state of near-to-manic exultation.

"Victory, victory for God, victory for me! At last I am done with half measures! The Lord hath visited and redeemed His people! For that mine enemies have blasphemed me the God of heaven, power is given me to scorch them with fire, and they shall gnaw their tongues for pain! Physic me, Dr. Benedict, for I am nigh to faint for joy."

Benedict felt no compassion for Torquemada now, but he was awed by his deep and agile intelligence. Torquemada could stand aside from himself and recognize his own symptoms. He gave him a bitter draught of camphor, mandrake and fennel, such as he often administered to hysterical women to calm them. It wasn't much, but it was the best he could do. The Grand Inquisitor's illness was not of the body.

Benedict rode slowly home alone on his mule, plunged in thought. The monster did not screw up his face at the bitter taste, he mused. He has iron control. He did not demand that I drink the draught; he trusts me; he did not ask to see the key. I am safe. José did not talk.

All around him church bells were pealing for joy, bonfires were burning in the streets in celebration of the victory, taverns were full and from them came happy sounds of singing and laughter. Even some Jews ventured out of their quarter and some Spaniards smiled at them in a friendly manner. But despite all these signs of the golden age Benedict felt depressed, and in every bonfire he saw a threat.

When he reached his home a blind beggar with a cane was sitting on his doorstep.

"What is it, my good man?" Benedict asked.

"I felt sick and hungry and faint, and they told me a doctor lived here," the beggar said.

"Come in and I will feed you, and if you are sick, God willing, I shall help you."

"No," said the man, "I knocked and no one opened. Let me but rest a moment."

The pride of the poor, thought Benedict.

"No doubt my household are out, taking part in the general rejoicing," Benedict said, "and if you cannot accept my help at least take this and offer it in a church in thanksgiving for our glorious victory."

The man held out his hand and Benedict gave him a coin of some value. Shortly he shuffled away.

Inside there was only Maria. Juan was in the streets with some friends busily feeding the bonfires, enjoying the holiday atmosphere, the servants were marketing or celebrating with other servants, the apprentice was making rounds among the sick, whose sickness took no account of the end of the war or the fall of Granada.

"Why did you not feed the beggar, Maria?"

"I was afraid to."

"It is right to be cautious, but surely one hungry blind old man poses no threat."

"I do not know why I was afraid. He tapped and tapped with his cane all around the door. Then he sat down."

Benedict said, "Perhaps you were right."

"I knew you'd reproach me. I'm sorry if I acted uncharitably."

"No, no, I do not reproach you. It is right to be cautious. Anyhow, I made it up to him. I gave him enough to buy lodging and food for a week, or drink for a day, which is probably how he will spend it." Benedict smiled.

"Yes, I saw. I was peeping through the grill. He certainly held out his hand in a hurry, didn't he?"

"He certainly did."

A sinister thought crossed his mind, bringing the ghost of a frown to his forehead, but he was preoccupied, and he did not dwell on it.

That night there was a crunching sound at the front door. Maria sat up in bed and said, "What was that?" Benedict turned over and muttered, "Oh, just some drunken revelers throwing things around, carousing in celebration. The watch will pick them up." How good that the house was stone! Within its solid protection he had lived all his life, worked, worshiped, loved and begotten a son to live in it after him. The house was his dearest possession.

Next morning, departing for his rounds, he saw the cause of the noise in the night. Someone had come with an iron bar and wrenched out the heart-high stone. The Hebrew scroll was missing from the cavity beneath.

Hurriedly the doctor reentered his house and closed and locked the door behind him.

"The beggar wasn't blind," he said in a tremulous voice that Maria had never heard in him before. "Nor was he a beggar. Miriam, our secret is out and we are in grave danger. I fear that you and the boy must leave Spain."

"Leave Spain?" There was total disbelief in her voice. She looked at him oddly, as if he had gone mad. Then she stood

[64]

silent, her face suddenly pale. He had not called her Miriam in a very long time.

"I am a doctor. I should have known. My mind was elsewhere. I gave him the coin carelessly, forgetting he was blind. I did not place it in his palm. His hand, *and his eyes,* followed my hand, and he took it in his fingers. I am undone. I am a fool, a *fool!*"

She passed her arm around his waist and noted with a lonely hopeless feeling that her husband, wont to be so strong, was shaking.

"Do not be afraid, Baruch," she said.

"I am terribly afraid."

"Even if it is known that we are Jews, the victory proclamation promised tolerance."

"Not to crypto-Jews, Miriam. We are in a special category: we are lapsed heretics."

"But a Jew is a Jew, a Christian is a Christian, a Moor is a Moor. *Los reyes católicos* promised protection to all."

"All but lapsed heretics, and they are classed as traitors."

"How do you know they are? How did they find out — if they did? Maybe the theft of the mezuzah was a prank, or maybe it fell out when the wall was struck by a stone during the revelry of the night."

"No, Miriam; there is something I have not told you."

He told her how José had been tortured. She shuddered. "He need only have let slip an intimate knowledge of Jewish customs to arouse suspicion; he need not have betrayed our secret and his own! I am convinced he did not or they would have held him for burning. It is an excellent time for an auto-da-fé, a time of victory, a time to release emotion! A time to pander to fanatical mobs. How well our persecutors understand all this. No, Miriam, even a hint of heresy is enough to warrant investigation

[65]

by the Holy Office at such a time, and if José happened to reveal, in answer to some subtle question, that it is customary for us to bless our homes and keep a little memorial of the commandments at our doors, that would have been enough to involve us. Then a beggar came, tapping on the stones, ear cocked for a hollow spot where the evidence might be hidden. And then last night the evidence was stolen. It fits the diabolical pattern of the manner in which they build up a case against a victim."

Miriam comforted him. "You are overwrought, Baruch. We would not be at large at all if these horrible things were true. Put your fears out of your mind."

He pressed her hand gratefully. But he saw she too was afraid.

"I do not fear for myself," he said. "Perhaps as you say we are safe. But I feel some apprehension for you and the boy."

Miriam said, "Nothing has happened yet; the King's prime minister is a Jew; the Grand Inquisitor's physician is a Jew; I am not at all worried about the Grand Inquisitor's doctor's wife and son."

Thus they cheered each other; but secretly each felt a sickening sinking sensation in the pit of the stomach whenever there was a knock at the door.

Benedict acted swiftly. Leaving the sick to their sicknesses he went at once to the shop of Tubal the alchemist. The old man met him with the usual subservient attitude that a Jew adopted in the presence of a Christian, but there was an unaccustomed glint in his eye — or perhaps he had just cleaned his spectacles.

"Yes? It is Dr. Benedict, is it not? Ah, it is. In what can I be of service, Doctor?"

"I came to sell, not to buy, Tubal."

[66]

The alchemist seemed to have grown in stature, or perhaps he seemed taller only because the roles were now reversed: Tubal was safe and Benedict was not; Benedict was the suppliant and Tubal had the power to deny.

"To sell? To sell what, Dr. Benedict?"

"Everything I possess. Except my home. Not my home, Tubal; do not take that away from me."

"Not your home, eh? I see. It is a very fine house, however. But you do not wish to sell it. Therefore you will not. Do you have other properties? Let me remember. I think I do remember. You own several houses and shops which you rent, though under another name. Are there not also some vineyards and orange groves? I seem to remember that there are. And a stable of excellent horses and mules. Yes, it comes back to me now. You are not a poor man, Dr. Benedict." Tubal's tone was bantering and unpleasant.

The terrible thought occurred to Benedict that if Tubal knew, Torquemada must know. Tubal saw the fears in his face.

"Many times you have cheated me, driving my prices down because you are a Christian."

"You have divined that I am a crypto-Jew."

"So you paid twice as much in the end," Tubal said, smiling. "Crypto-Jews pay even more than Christians. And now you are in trouble? I fear we all are, but you are one of the first to perceive it."

"Last night the mezuzah was stolen by an agent of the Holy Office from its hiding place at my door."

Tubal raised his white eyebrows. "Indeed? That I had not heard. Things are moving faster than I thought." His manner softened. "You had best not be seen in my shop, Dr. Benedict."

Benedict thought he was being sent away.

[67]

"I will sell on extremely favorable terms, Tubal."

"You will have to, Baruch," Tubal said grimly, not unkindly now. "Please come with me where you will not be seen."

He led him into a small room at the rear of the shop. Neatly arranged on shelves were rows of books and manuscripts in many languages. They sat down at a writing table.

"To tell the truth, I loathe all crypto-Jews," Tubal said. "There is an animal in Africa, a detestable hybrid, born of unnatural union between a lion and a tiger. It tries to be both, but it is neither the one nor the other. It is shunned by both lions and tigers. Both hate it. It lives alone. It is good for nothing. It deserves its fate.

"But you were born to your crypto-Jewishness, and so was your father, and his; so you are as you are, and it is not your fault."

"I did not know you knew so much about me."

Tubal said, "Do you not look into the background of your patients? I do the same in the case of my customers. Can I sell to a friar what I sell to a Dr. Benedict? Would you have me burn? If I am not for myself, who is for me; and if not now, when?"

Benedict recognized the quotation from an ancient rabbi, and bowed before the alchemist's great learning.

"Bad times are coming, Baruch, nay, they are here. Will you emigrate? It would be wise. Nothing prohibits it — yet."

"My wife and my son must go, and my remaining apprentice who is not yet murdered, and such of my servants as I can contrive to save. But as for myself, I do not know. There is much sickness, Tubal; it is hard to desert the dying. My heart is divided. Instinct bids me flee and I cannot make up my mind. But the young must be saved."

"Aye. And the young need mothers and mentors. And money,

Baruch, money. Money is armor against the world which hates us."

"So I have thought."

"Whither will you send them, and when?"

"To the nearest safest place, and at once."

"Portugal is near, and will be safe for a while. For a little while."

"I have thought of Portugal."

"But the way to Portugal is overland. Soon there will be roadblocks at every barrier, and at the roadblocks soldiers, still flushed with victory but with no enemies to fight, no duties other than to patrol the roads and worry and bully their Spanish countrymen, Moriscos, Marranos, us, Baruch. Portugal is but a temporary asylum and the way thither is hard."

"I have also considered Africa."

"There you consider wisely, Baruch."

"But Africa is a savage country."

"Weh!" said Tubal, casting up his eyes, shrugging, extending his palms, disgusted. "There speaks the supercivilized overeducated scientist, eyes bent to earthward, fleshward, vainglorious in his little learning, spurning the stars. I cast the horoscope of the Sultan of Granada, Boabdil, the Little King, and I saw in the configuration of the planets the fall of Granada. Is Granada fallen? Listen to the bells. Now I foretell you that Portugal is unsafe and Africa is not savage, and you have the effrontery to dispute me."

"I do not dispute you, Tubal. I am not conversant with the message of the stars."

"Do not affect humility," Tubal said. "You do dispute; but you want help, and so you pretend to agree with me."

"I think you are a deluded, superstitious old charlatan," Benedict said hotly, rising to go.

"Ah," Tubal said, grinning. "I respect you for that honest remark. Sit down. Now I will help you and not rob you." He clapped his hands in the Arabic fashion and the giant appeared with a handful of papers. Benedict was uneasily aware that they were already prepared, as if in anticipation of his visit.

"Did the planets tell you I would apply to you?" he asked.

"Did they deny it?" Tubal said.

The papers were in duplicate, in Spanish and Arabic. One was a bill of sale covering all Benedict's property, which was minutely described and covered some obscure holdings that Benedict had forgotten he possessed. It also included the house.

"Not my house," he said.

"You will never see it again, Baruch."

"Still, not my house."

Tubal struck it out.

The bill of sale was in an amount so large that the doctor said, "You allow yourself little profit when you resell, Tubal."

"Had I wanted a profit I'd have got it in some other manner."

"Without the house, which you have stricken out, I would willingly take less."

"Let it stand as it is, Baruch."

"You are overpaying."

"Others will benefit."

The doctor signed.

Now payment had to be made.

"You will want gold, of course, in smallish coins, will you not?"

"Some can be large, but the greater part, yes, should be small, lest I arouse suspicion." Tubal eyed him, for Benedict seemed to believe what he just had said.

"You innocent!" Tubal said. "Does a rich man ever consider how many muleloads of gold all his worldly goods might constitute? Do you actually suppose, Baruch, that you could get out of Spain with three strong beasts with saddlebags jingling with coin of the realm without being stopped, questioned and robbed? — you and your family — and buried in some lonely ditch, and neither King nor Queen nor Holy Office would ever see one coin of the treasure, one bone of your dead bodies!"

"Tubal, I beg you, do not distress me."

"You, who fancy yourself so clever; you do not know your own worth."

"I had never thought what my worth might weigh."

"Much. But I had meant it otherwise, or I would not be helping you. I have in this room a wondrous scroll, written ages ago by the Egyptians, called The Book of the Dead. In it I see you, me, many. Even I cannot read all the priestly writing but the pictures convey meaning to one who knows the old legends still whispered along the banks of the Nile. In the picture one sees a human heart and a feather, balanced in a scale held in the hand of the eternal judge, and the heart wins. No one will ever translate the hieroglyphs, but no one will ever dispute the goodwill that outweighs error. You are not comfortable, Dr. Benedict? You feel a chill? I should fancy it otherwise."

Benedict was clutching his cloak around his shoulders. "I am not at ease," he replied.

"Sign this," Tubal said, producing another paper. "This is payment."

The paper contained four lines of Arabic script. "It reads,"

Tubal said (since Benedict's knowledge of Arabic did not extend
to rapid reading of the script):

> *To Hassan,* son of Assiz, son of Hassan, of Marrakesh in Morocco,
> *Greeting:* On receipt of this present, pay to Baruch ben Baruch
> ben Baruch, known in Christendom as Benedict, son of Benedict,
> son of Benedict, a physician of the city of Seville in the kingdom
> of Spain, or to his son and heir, Johann ben Baruch, but to no
> assign, the sum of one thousand pounds, gold.

It was signed simply, "Tubal."

"It is a letter of credit," Tubal said, "an ancient device we
invented, though you Spaniards may never have heard of it. It
eliminates tedious transport of bullion, and many dangers."

"This Hassan will pay? For this scrap of paper?"

"That is why it is known as a letter of credit. Credit, credo,
faith, trust; it is all the same word. Yes, this Hassan will
pay."

"I do not know why I am signing these," Benedict said, signing
the deeds that transferred his land and properties. Then he
affixed his signature to the letter of credit, authorizing an unknown African to reimburse him for the labor and thrift of a
lifetime.

"Perhaps because you have greater faith than you know,"
Tubal said.

The giant servant sealed the letter in a waterproof packet,
reducing it by folding to a size about two inches-square, and
attached a loop of string to it. Tubal placed it on Benedict's
breast, the string around his neck, the packet hidden beneath
the black folds of his academic gown.

"Well, Baruch?" said the alchemist.

"Well, Tubal?"

"How does it feel to have all your worldly goods hung on your heart like an amulet, weighing no more than a snail?"

"Very strange, Tubal. But I believe it to be as you say."

"Have you no questions to ask?"

"No, Tubal."

"You did not ask one question I anticipated."

"What?"

"Why I stipulated, 'no assign.'"

"It never occurred to me that I would assign my wealth."

"Did it never occur to you that you might die before your son achieved wisdom and your son might sign away his birthright?"

"I may die, but my son will not sign away his birthright."

"Esau did."

"Johann is not Esau, and will not despise his birthright."

"We can so hope."

"He is subtle as Jacob."

"Let us so hope."

Suddenly Benedict said, "Cast his horoscope, Tubal."

"No."

"I wish to know if my seed will endure, and do good in the world."

"You would not believe the word of a charlatan."

"I spoke in anger."

"You should not have called me a charlatan."

"I half believe it still."

"It will do you no good to half believe what you half think you half want. But I will foretell you a loftier wonder: your key will endure and no unworthy hand will sully the burden of virtue it bears for so mighty a span of years that my science cannot see the end, for it ends in a flame that blinds me."

[73]

Benedict smiled. It was a cryptic cabalistic utterance designed, like the oracles of the Greeks, to cover every circumstance; but it was kindly meant, and Benedict thanked him.

"That is much comfort, Tubal."

The doctor bade him farewell and left the shop.

The giant shuffling servant said to the master, "I smell smoke."

"Oh, yes," Tubal said to the creature whom his enemies called a golem, "he is dead, quite dead."

"I am sorry. Can you not help him?"

Tubal shrugged. "No one can help him. It is in his stars. Oh, very dead indeed. I am sorry too. He was a good man."

CHAPTER 6

Now that he had made up his mind to send Miriam and the boy out of Spain he reflected how much he would miss them. Now that he had converted all his properties into a negotiable letter of credit he felt strong; the panic drained away; he could move at a moment's notice. He mused, I could put them aboard any ship in the harbor within the hour if I needed. I have assured their safety. He felt like a general who had outwitted the enemy. With this feeling came a confident conviction that the enemy posed no immediate threat.

Of course there was need for speed, he thought; but I have acted speedily, and now there is less need; nor must I act in a manner that would arouse suspicion by queer and unwonted behavior. What plausible excuse could I give for sending my wife and child into the wilds of Africa?

Every house on the street was familiar as he made his way home. Here he had saved the life of a child; there he had eased the passing pain of some elderly sufferer. All was intimate and dear that struck his eye. Spain and Seville and his art had

[75]

constituted his whole life, rich and rewarding, but without Maria and Juan such a life would be empty and bleak. Why should he send them today when he could delay the painful separation till tomorrow?

The need was no longer for speed but for thorough preparedness, he thought, and touched the packet beneath his gown.

The sight of his house, strong, stone, and fraught with memories from earliest childhood, stirred his heart and intensified his love, fortifying his longing to remain and keep his household close around him. Life would be lonesome and alien without them. On the lowest level it would also be vastly uncomfortable. Nothing would go right. Family habits would be upset and there would be no Miriam to act as chatelaine of his snug little castle. Who would manage the servants? Who would see to it that his sheets were warmed with a warming pan? Who would see to it that his fire was lighted, his favorite suppers prepared? Was he to live in a tomb among hired strangers who did not know his habits and cared nothing for his routine? He felt guilty about these small considerations, deeming them unworthy, but they added one more pang, one more deterrent to leaving Spain.

He noted with satisfaction that Maria had had the stone replaced, cemented in so cleverly that he had to look twice before he realized it was a new one. How competent she was. All was as it had been before, and his home cast upon him the old spell of security. He thought of the sick, who needed him. He knew he would *not* have thought of them if he had not been seeking for one more excuse to remain; but think of them now he did. Perhaps all this would pass, perhaps no one would emigrate. How blessed that would be.

A genial friar was collecting alms in the street near his door. Benedict knew him by sight and gave him a coin. "I wish I could give you more," he said. The friar thanked him and Benedict said, "I am a poor man and many of my patients never pay me at all." Anything was welcome in the present need, said the friar. "But I look for an amelioration in the present distress now that the war is over," Benedict said. "Our beloved King and Queen have promised better times," the friar said, and blessed him. It was comforting.

And yet, though I feel so safe, I must keep alert, the doctor thought, and let himself in with the golden key. "You are safe too," he chuckled, glancing fondly at the key. "You are brass."

But tonight I need not be alert, not tonight. Tonight there is no need for speed.

That night, which he cherished to his dying day, was the happiest of his life, with his family around him at supper where the wine tasted sweeter than he could ever remember. His wife smiled, "It is only the usual table wine." He said, "For a moment I thought you had broken into the Passover supply, for it tastes like the wine of deliverance into life."

"You were simply fatigued and thirsty, Baruch."

"Why is this night different from other nights?" Juan asked.

Both Maria and Benedict chuckled at the boy.

"Lad, that is a question asked on a special occasion, which this is not," Benedict said.

Next day the doctor returned to his rounds. It was good to be at peace again and working. One patient was a rough-and-ready sea captain, a friendly man whose name was Pinzón. Benedict gave him a strong alcoholic infusion of orange and lemon for the sniffles, and remarked casually, "How goes the shipping business these days, Señor Pinzón?"

"Booming," said the captain. "I never saw it so good."

"Yet I should have thought it might be depressed now that the war is over and there is less military traffic."

"Oh, it's the Moors, Dr. Benedict. They are getting out while the getting is good. I am taking them over to Africa in droves, the rich ones at any rate. Those putrid scum fear the wrath of their conqueror, as well they should. Some go to Rome, some as far as Constantinople, but most go to Africa. Well, say I, let the rascals go."

"I am glad that the end of the war brings you no depression in business," Benedict said.

"Quite the contrary, at least for the moment. It is impossible even to rent a bunk; they are sleeping on the deck, down in the bilges, anywhere, them and their turbans and their kneeling toward a spot on the horizon where they think Mecca is. I make circles sometimes just to confuse them." He laughed.

"We are well rid of these infidels," Benedict said.

"Amen to that, Doctor; amen."

"But their exodus may prove a loss to the medical craft. It cannot be denied that the Moors have many medical secrets that we Christian doctors have attempted to fathom in vain, herbs and the like, probably imported from Africa."

"Well, let the damned herbs stay in Africa for all I care. We don't need them."

"Still, I have always been curious about them. It is a scientist's nature to be curious. In what manner could a poor doctor, like me, for example, gather knowledge of such herbs?"

"By taking a trip to Africa, I'd suppose, on a ship. Then go poking around in a Moorish garden. I only sail the ships, you know; I don't fly them overland into the interior."

"I have considered such a trip, a very short trip of course, since my duties keep me here."

"Idiotic notion," said Pinzón.

"Or I might send my wife and son or my apprentice and let them go gathering flowers, as it were. They might be able to buy herbs in the market, where I would be suspect. An exploratory mission."

The navigator threw up his hands and exclaimed, "Do not talk to me of explorations! Some crazy Italian adventurer from Genoa has been pestering Their Majesties to outfit a fleet of ships to go exploring. He says he has positive knowledge that by sailing west across the Atlantic he will end up in the East! He has powerful backing for his scheme and there's a rumor that the Queen will finance the expedition. Well, a commission's a commission. I have put in a bid to supply the ships and maybe I'll sail one myself. And maybe I'll just take him around in a great big circle and bring him back again. I'll have to keep busy. This Moor emigration won't last forever."

"The Moors will be forbidden to emigrate?"

"No, worse, later I expect they'll be forcibly ejected, all of them. Torquemada will see to that. There must be over a hundred thousand of them. When that day comes and they have to go, a ship captain won't make a penny ferrying them over the sea. Ha! But what a day that will be! Some say the Jews will go too."

"Do you anticipate this soon? Shipping will be crowded even more than now. Perhaps I should speed up my small exploration in the matter of the African herbs, lest I cannot get passage later."

"If you are sending someone to Africa I'd advise you to do so at once." Pinzón said.

"How soon?"

Pinzón laughed. "I've a ship leaving tonight."

"Tonight is too soon."

"It wouldn't be comfortable anyhow. She's only half decked, low slung, narrow, and wet in foul weather, though she's my smartest sailer for her size, only forty tons. She'll be loaded to the gunwales with rich Moors."

"When is the next?"

"Oh, maybe three months, maybe four, maybe longer, depending on whether or not I get the royal commission for this Italian fellow."

In four months who knew what the state of the Moors, the Moriscos, the Jews, the Marannos, the infidels of Spain and the crypto-infidels might be? Benedict remembered the ominous words of Tubal, "Things are moving faster than I thought," the specter of the Grand Inquisitor suddenly dominated the pleasant Pinzón house, and Benedict heard again the hysterical muttering of Torquemada, "I am done with half measures; they shall gnaw their tongues for pain." Alarm clutched at the doctor's heart.

"When does tonight's ship return, Señor Pinzón? Perhaps, if it makes a quick trip, I could go over and back on the African mission without neglecting my practice."

"Wait, Doctor. You're not really going, are you? I cannot spare my physician so long."

"A month, two months?"

"I have instructed the master to make a quick turnabout. About a month, I'd say."

"In your excellent state of health, Señor Pinzón, you will require no physician for one short month. Could you book me a place on this vessel tonight? For three of us, my wife, my son, myself, four if you have place for my apprentice. It will be a holiday for them, an education for him."

"I see no reason why not, if you are serious and if you think I am well enough. I will give you a note to the master. But mind you don't get lost in some harem garden admiring the flowers, and come back in time to physic me if I do not get rid of this confounded — whatever it is."

"Nothing but a cold, Señor Pinzón."

Pinzón scribbled a note on a scrap of paper. "This will take you over and bring you back," he said. "Maybe you'll actually pick up some dogbane or henbane or wolfbane to dry up a cold. I get it every winter. I too have heard it said that the Moors know things about medicine you Christian doctors never think of. One thing I like about you, Dr. Benedict, you never pretend to know more than you really do. Candor is rare in a physician; most are contemptible quacks, but you never hide anything. Well, here you are, and God prosper your search."

Benedict reached out and took the paper. It was an order to a Master Diego de Solis of the caravel *Niña* to take him and his party aboard.

"Have you ever sailed before, Dr. Benedict?"

"I have never set foot out of Spain."

"Well, you'll be crowded. But eleven Moors will have to move out to make place for you in the cabin. Master de Solis will afford you every accommodation the ship permits of."

Benedict said, "I will pay my passage now."

Pinzón was offended; he blushed scarlet.

"How long has it been since I paid you a fee, Dr. Benedict?"

"Sir, I do not keep my own accounts."

"It is over a year. You will understand that I do not wish to speak of passage money. Your ship will be your home while you are my guest away on your holiday."

[81]

The pride of the Spanish rich, thought Benedict, as haughty as the pride of the Spanish poor.

"God prospering, I shall return in a month," Benedict said, bowing in exit, "to call upon Your Excellency and report how Your Excellency's beneficence has helped the healing art."

"If it helps," Pinzón said, smiling.

Benedict left, thinking, He owes me more than anybody except Torquemada. Now he has paid, but Torquemada will never pay.

Benedict could not curse. To conjure down the wrath of God upon a fellow human being was beyond his capacity, even upon so monstrous a being as Torquemada; he could not bring his tongue even to form the words of such a curse, which, in a little corner of his fifteenth-century mind, he half believed might wield some dire irrevocable potency: often he had witnessed a hopelessly sick patient get well when he simply said, "You are going to be all right." Words might work the other way round and do murder, and he, who had sworn to preserve life, would be guilty of taking it. But in so near as he could come to cursing, just that near he came to cursing Torquemada, the dread of whose fury was clogging the escape routes out of Spain. "And my family and I when we flee must displace eleven others, who must tarry behind and, God forbid, face the flames." But he never considered doing anything else in his personal peril: the House of Baruch must go, and now, and by night, as it had happened in Egypt.

"It will be but a little while," he told his wife, "and then we shall return."

"If you say we must go, Baruch, why of course we must."

"We shall not starve in Africa," he said, tapping the packet under his gown. "I have sold all my property, and carry it here in a quintessential distillate that only a Jew could have thought of."

She looked at him, bewildered.

He placed it around her neck. "Wear it next to your heart, my dear. It is safer there than on me."

"You sold everything? *Everything?*"

"Not the house, of course, since we'll be coming back."

"We will do as you say, Baruch. I am glad you did not sell the house."

Juan piped up, eyes big, in a voice not yet a man's, "Sell the house? Leave our home?"

Benedict rumpled his hair fondly. "No, Juanito mío; this is the House of Baruch; it is dear; it has sheltered us and our sires; it will always be home, and we have its key and it will always be ours, and we shall come back and live in it always, just as we always have."

Juan said, wrinkling his smooth young brow, "I am glad we're not going to leave it for long."

"Your papa and I will be with you," Maria said. "Wherever we are, that is also home."

"I wouldn't like another house," the boy said.

"Here," said Benedict, on a sudden impulse, for there was fear in the child's eyes. "You shall carry this while we're away, but mind you don't lose it." It would make him feel better. It would teach him a sense of responsibility. Soon he would be a man, with responsibilities to burden and later to bend his shoulders. It was well to start them young. It was the golden key.

Juan straightened his back and squared his shoulders, not yet full breadth, and said with the solemnity of new and sudden trust, quite formally, "I will keep it by me, safe, till we come

[83]

back, my father." He tied it to a leather thong that laced his doublet.

"Better stick it inside," Benedict said, grinning. "It's not an order of knighthood, you know."

"Oh," said the boy, and tucked it into a pocket where he kept other treasures, like shiny pebbles from the street, bits of string and a pocketknife for whittling sticks.

"Much better," said Benedict.

Nothing was required for the voyage, save cloaks against the sea winds, and money. All else could be purchased in Africa, or, depending on the length of their stay, dispensed with. There was no need to transport furniture or belongings to the ship, nor would there have been room. But Benedict could not bring himself to leave his surgical instruments behind, no more than a limb of his body. He sent the apprentice early to the ship with the order from Pinzón, bidding him take the chest of tools, in which he placed a bag of money. "Say you are summoned to treat some sailor or other; sailors are always getting banged up or falling down drunk and injuring themselves; give this paper of passage to the master, and await our coming till nightfall. And do not, as you value your place, show yourself upon the deck, but stay out of sight till we come."

The apprentice said, "Shall I ride?"

"Aye, take a mule, and hitch it to the quayside; it will look more convincing. Does a doctor send his learner on foot to physic the sick?"

"What will become of the mule?"

"It will be stolen, you dolt, the minute the ship leaves."

Short-breathed and flushed, the apprentice rode off. Benedict sighed: He is stupider than José, but behold, the stupid are alive and inherit the earth, and José is carrion.

As dusk approached they left the house. Juan locked it and automatically, there being no one in sight, raised his hand to his lips and transferred a benediction to the place where the stone had been. Benedict boxed his ears. "Fool, it is gone." Maria passed a protecting arm around Juan's shoulders, looked at the doctor reproachfully, but said nothing. Juan bit his lip.

"There is nothing there anymore," Benedict muttered. "Nothing at all."

At the quayside they hitched their mules. Eleven Moors were on their knees, dusting their turbans in the waterfront filth, praising Allah and weeping, for these were the displaced ones. They were remarkably well dressed. Benedict, Juan and Maria elbowed their way through them.

The ship tugged at the ropes and Master de Silva paced back and forth impatiently, watching the ebbing tide. It would cost Pinzón a day's delay, and him a reproach, if he did not sail on it.

"You are Dr. Benedict?"

"I am, Master de Silva."

"Kindly come aboard at once. We are almost too late as it is."

"Hurry, boy; hurry, my dearest," Benedict whispered. He would not feel safe till they were out of sight. "Go below, make no noise and do not speak loudly. We must not show ourselves till we are out at sea." They quickly obeyed, for his haste and fear were contagious. He saw the hatch close over their heads. Benedict smiled and breathed easier. It was accomplished.

He hesitated for a moment at the quay. The Moors, having abandoned all hope, slipped silently away, no longer weeping but accepting what Allah had sent them with the strange resignation that characterized their faith: when all was lost they did not complain.

[85]

"Come aboard, Dr. Benedict," de Silva cried. Sailors were already casting off the lines.

Lights were appearing in the windows of houses. Against the darkening sky the silhouette of Seville, every building of which was familiar and dear, stood like the face of a loved one, as beautiful in darkness as in light since the heart can see and remember long after the light has failed. The soil of Seville was still under his feet, and he was reluctant to step from it.

"I am coming," he called.

A figure appeared, black gowned, cowled, and its face in the shadow looked like a skull remembered from a dream. It was the beggar.

"One moment," it said softly.

De Silva called, "If you do not come aboard, Dr. Benedict, I will sail without you."

"So you are Dr. Benedict," said the friar.

"I am."

"My master wishes to see you."

"Who is your master, Reverend sir?"

"You have physicked him. You will know."

De Silva called, "Are you coming aboard or not?"

In the confusion and heart-clenching terror of the moment Benedict had only one purpose: to get the ship away from the quay as soon as possible. He must say nothing that might delay it; on the contrary he must speak so as to speed it away. Miriam and Johann were out of sight. Probably they were already in the cabin. They would be safe. All other considerations paled before that simple blessed fact.

Benedict called, "I am summoned to the bedside of a patient. I will take the next ship. Go without me. Go!"

"But your wife — "

Benedict shouted to drown out any reference to her and Johann. "Yes, she will accompany me on the next trip. Perhaps we shall all go on the holiday, but not this trip."

"He is crazed or drunk," muttered the master. "He forgets they're already aboard. Ah well. It is none of my affair."

"Adios, Dr. Benedict."

"Don't lose the tide, Master de Silva, and a prosperous voyage!"

The little ship cast off and floated down the tide of the Guadalquivir. The distance widened and with it a widening margin of safety for Juan and Maria. Benedict breathed deeply and smiled. He turned to the friar. "Your master is sick? He could not find me at home, so he sent you to seek for me? I am honored. And now that you have found me you need not seek me further or break into my house to summon me, for my wife and child are sleeping."

"We will see if they are," the friar said. From this Benedict knew that his house would not be searched for some hours; Miriam and Johann would have cleared the estuary; Spain and the Holy Office would be far behind them. A sense of fulfillment warmed him like a blanket, though he had to clench his teeth to keep them from chattering; again he was desperately afraid, for a hope was trickling back into his heart, the hope of personal safety now that his seed was safe and would endure. Perhaps Torquemada was really sick.

He was ridden on a fast horse beside the friar surrounded by a guard which appeared suddenly out of the shadows. Among them was young Pizarro, but the youth's face was hard and contemptuous. Benedict directed a glance at him, a glance full of terror, appealing for some sign of recognition. Pizarro turned his head. Benedict thought, "He knows. The scroll has betrayed

[87]

me, and there is no help from Pizarro. But perhaps in his place I should act the same, for I displaced the Moors."

He took one quick glance at the Grand Inquisitor, to whose presence he was instantly taken. Torquemada looked, to a doctor's eye, which diagnosed out of habit, like a man who had never been sick a day in his life.

Benedict mustered the courage to say, "I am happy to see Your Eminence in such health."

A soldier struck him on the mouth. "Do not speak till you are spoken to."

"None of that here," Torquemada said, scowling at the soldier, who seemed to shrink into himself.

Torquemada directed his eyes toward Benedict, whose lip was bleeding. "What is this?" he asked, holding up the mezuzah that had been stolen from beneath the stone.

The doctor had heard tales and gathered some evidence in his own practice that persons who nearly drowned, but who were partially resuscitated before they quite died, sustained, before they finally lost consciousness, a queer feeling of serenity. Such a serenity settled upon him now. "That is a Hebrew scroll, Reverend sir. In it is written the *Shema*, which affirms the unity of God, and usually, as in this case, the two great commandments."

"Whose is this scroll?"

"It is mine, as you know."

"It is enough," Torquemada said. "Take him away, and do not put him to the question."

A secretary in a corner was busily writing this down. "Not to be questioned?" he asked. His face was unpleasant and visibly disappointed, for he would have been at the questioning. The

Grand Inquisitor turned and withered him with a glare from burning eyes. "To what purpose? He has already confessed."

"I shall put down, 'Confessed, Lapsed Heretic,' Your Reverence," the secretary said and snapped shut the tablet.

Next day it was cloudy and Benedict awoke fearing that a storm might be troubling the passage to Africa.

Not a hand had been laid on him in his cell. He was fed a hot supper and given a warm coverlet for his pallet. He awoke refreshed, all his senses keen and alive. The air smelled good, and he felt adequate for twenty calls. Then he saw the fog through the bars and remembered where he was and the doom that overhung him. But at least he had not been tortured as poor José had been. He rose and peered through the bars and looked down upon the marketplace. During the night workmen had been busy. There, before his eyes, in the middle of the square was a stake with faggots piled at its foot. People already were gathering, though as yet it was early. In that part of his mind which made him so excellent a diagnostician a hideous realization burst through: they did not throw me into a dungeon with no view, lest I miss the sight of their preparations.

He collapsed in a corner of his cell, quaking and covering his eyes with his hands, but still he could see the stake and the gathering crowd. Some of the crowd were familiar. Many he had treated, some he had saved. Is it nothing to you, all ye that pass by? Behold and see if there be any sorrow like unto my sorrow. No, he muttered, shivering, It is nothing to them.

The lock shot back with a firm click and the door swung open on well-oiled hinges. Meticulous care had been taken in this luxury cell to avoid the lugubrious theatricalities of a prison. Benedict's lip trembled and he felt his body suddenly wet with cold sweat. They are coming to burn me, he thought. He did not want to burn; he did not want to die at all.

It was only a jailor with his breakfast.

"They're going to burn a Jew," the jailor said by way of greeting. "We've not had a burning for six months. You'll get a good view from here. You're a doctor, aren't you? I can tell by the gown. I don't get many doctors; just noblemen and rich Moriscos on this floor. You're very lucky. You ought to see what it's like underneath. When will you be leaving us, Doctor?"

"Soon, I expect."

"Aye, that's how it is. Only grandees and the rich get these cells and they always leave soon. Well, here is your breakfast."

He waited as if he expected something. Benedict gave him a gold coin. The jailor's eyes widened at its worth.

"I thank you, Señor Doctor! I thank your Excellency! Will you have wine with your supper? I can arrange it. Meat too, if you want, though it's Friday." It was Friday, the thirteenth of January, and the year was 1492.

"I am not sure where I shall be taking supper," Benedict said.

"Released so soon? I'd have liked to keep you longer. I've a bad cough, Doctor. Maybe, when you leave, if it's not too much to ask, I could come to you and you'd physic me. Can you get rid of my cough?"

The jailor was pasty-faced and alarmingly thin. Benedict looked at him, and saw what was wrong, and sighed. "I expect we shall meet again not too long hence."

"That is kind of you, Doctor. It hits me especially bad in the winter."

"It will soon cease to trouble you."

Under other circumstances Benedict would have told him to seek some other means of livelihood and go to a higher, dryer

[90]

elevation, perhaps as a forester in the vicinity of Madrid, where the King had a hunting lodge in the woods, for here in Seville he would face the certainty of dying of consumption. But it was too late to save others; there were only two persons he wanted to save.

"This Jew, jailor, this Jew that they're going to burn, did he have a family?"

"Oh sure, a wife, they say, and a son. You know these Jews. They always have sons."

"Yes, I know them."

"Well, he had 'em, but he got them away. He sold his property and smuggled them out of the country."

"Will they be followed?"

"No, nobody can get at them anymore. By now they're in Portuguese waters off Africa. That Jew was smart. But of course they always are. Outwitted the king and queen and the Holy Office! Never been done before, they say. Spain can't collect a penny, the rascal. Oh well, there'll be others."

"What did he do so bad that they're going to burn him?"

"Isn't just being a Jew enough? And this one pretended to be a Christian. That's the worst kind. They want it both ways. Accursed be all crypto-Jews!" The jailor spat. Benedict noted that the spittle was streaked with red.

"That came on just recently," the jailor said, staring at it on the floor. "Is it a bad sign?"

"It will not last," Benedict said. "Soon it will stop. Do you spit around the house?"

"Where else would I spit? Of course I do."

"Do you have children?"

"Two little girls."

"Spit outside when you're home," Benedict said.

[91]

"You talk just like my wife. That's what she always says. I will spit where I like."

"Would you like your little girls to spit blood too?"

"Dear Jesus, no! Will they? Just because I do?"

"They might." Benedict said, "Better spit outside when you have to. It's neater, anyhow."

"Well, my wife will certainly thank you if I stop," the jailor said, grinning. "I'll tell her about this. I cannot afford doctors very often, so mostly I just pray. I will take your advice; it must be good or it wouldn't come from anybody on this floor. I can't pay you a fee, but I'll light a candle for you."

The doctor saw the candle; the flame grew in his mind's eye till it blazed like a furnace, consuming.

"The advice was freely offered, jailor. Do not light a candle for me."

The image of the stake arose in imagination, high as a mountain, flaming like Tubal's alembics. Benedict did not look out. He was afraid to. The interim with the jailor had been but a ghost of his lifelong work, returning absurdly out of context, like a remembrance of things that happened so often at social gatherings where perfect strangers would come up and talk about their ills and try to get free medical advice. But it had given him a moment's respite from the terror of the marketplace. Now the terror returned.

"This Jew that they're going to burn, suppose they had caught his family. Would they have been burned too?"

"Who knows? I don't think so. People don't like to see women burn, children even less. But a man burning, that's something else. People like that."

"Do you?"

"I'm different. I work in a prison. But I'd rather see them burn than some of the things I see down there." He pointed his finger to the floor and the dungeons underneath. "I used to work down there, but I asked to be transferred when my cough got bad. I breathe easier up here. Your breakfast is getting cold."

It was a smoked fish, and under other circumstances Benedict would have eaten it with relish.

"I am not very hungry," he said.

"You reproach me, Doctor. A thousand pardons. I have talked too long and it got cold. I will call a man with a brazier and he'll heat it up for you."

"No, no brazier. Do not trouble. I shall eat it later. It has been gratifying to talk to you. You have taken my mind off my troubles. Come to me whenever you wish and we shall talk again."

"Thank you, Doctor," the jailor said, picking a key from his ring, sensing that his important prisoner was dismissing him. He opened the door. As he left he said, "My name is Martin. May one ask the name of the distinguished doctor to whom he will come for advice in the future?"

"My name is Benedict," Benedict said.

The jailor gave him a startled look and glanced around to make sure they had not been overheard, crossed himself and hurriedly left the cell.

He knows who I am, Benedict thought. The secrecy of the operation of the Holy Office amazed him. He thought, He did not know before. Now he fears for himself, only for himself, as who does not?

But there was consolation, too. He thought, Before he knew who I was he assured me my wife and Johann were safe, so it must be common knowledge, and it must be true. I hope he is not questioned. But even if he is, his days are numbered; he is

[93]

doomed by disease. I am doomed only by the ignorance around me, the bigotry and the political expedience that requires an auto-da-fé.

It was small comfort. How readily he would have changed places with the sick jailor.

Now he ate the cold smoked fish, and wondered, as often he had, at the cravings of the healthy body, which seemed to function like forces outside oneself: he was actually hungry. In his mouth it tasted as it would have on any other day, salt, vivifying, delicious. But he ate only half and then his stomach revolted, and he threw it up; and again the cold sweat of fear oozed out of him, soaking his palms and the nape of his neck and running down his back, till his gown was wet and clung to him.

I never knew terror could produce these symptoms, he thought. Soldiers have told me they did not feel their wounds when they sustained them during battle; they felt no fear till afterwards. But here I sit, experiencing no pain as yet, and I am limp with terror. Terror of what? Of death? Of God? Of extinction? Not of death, for death comes a few short years before it would have if I had lived with a long white beard; no, not of death. Nor of God, for God is love, or so the Christians say, and I know of nothing in my faith that denies it. Nor of oblivion, for I cannot remember the eternity of oblivion through which I slept before my mother bore me. Nor is it terror for Miriam and my seed, for they are safe. So it is terror for myself and my body, which is going to hurt terribly.

I could climb up to the window, he thought, and place my feet upon that narrow sill and, with luck, contrive to throw myself down so as to break my neck and end the torture before it begins.

He made an attempt to climb up, but he was shaking and

uncoordinated, he could not make his limbs work as he wanted, the wall was smooth and he slipped back. Panting, his mouth dry, he gazed out beyond the bars.

Outside the crowd now jammed the square; vendors of sweet-meats circulated among them; the children were in a holiday mood. "Dear God, had I only a drug!" Benedict moaned. He heard himself moaning, and a queer thing happened, the beginning of strength. He was ashamed. He was ashamed of his whole life. He had tried to get more than was his due. He thought, I wish I had lived a better Jew.

But he did not feel ashamed, nor did he reflect on the good or the bad in his life, nor was he strong when they came for him. He cowered and crouched and made himself small in a corner and said, "I am not Benedict. You are in the wrong cell. Benedict is down the hall."

Guards reached for him. He squirmed and tried to wedge himself into a crack in the stone floor. Then they roughly jerked him to his feet and ripped off his clothes and shoes till he stood naked. Over him they placed a long coarse tunic of cloth, originally white but now yellow by reason of an impregnation of brimstone, on which crude letters were scrawled, Lapsed Heretic. It fell off as he struggled and was not replaced till later.

The guards finished, and Benedict stood between them. They supported him because his legs shook and could not bear his weight. Then two personages entered the cell. One was clerical, one was secular. The secular person was an army officer in parade armor, representing Ferdinand and Isabella; the clerical person was the beggar again, representing the Holy Office, in his friar's black cowl and habit.

The beggar spoke first.

"You are going to be questioned."

[95]

A wild hope rose in Benedict's heart. Perhaps he was going to be tortured. Perhaps he could contrive to give the right answers. Perhaps he would live to see the morrow, and the morrow thereafter, and many tomorrows; and perhaps he would be released at the end.

A secretary drew near with a tablet to write down the answers.

"I did not say 'put to the question,' Dr. Benedict. I merely said 'questioned.' "

"I will answer," Benedict said. His voice was low and hope was gone. He would not even live to be tortured.

The beggar interrupted, "I will conduct the inquisition, Señor Capitán, if you please."

He and the captain exchanged hostile glances. Benedict looked on in wonder, and saw in imagination, which was oddly stimulated and beginning to confuse reality with unreality and today with tomorrow, a vision of Church and State in conflict, snarling like dogs over a bone, his bones, the goods and the souls of men. He shook off the guards who supported him, and stood firmly on his two feet. His head had been bowed; he had seen his feet on the floor. He would have diagnosed them as strong competent feet, belonging to a man who walked solidly on the face of the earth.

He raised his eyes and said, "I will answer the truth."

"What is your name?" the beggar said.

"I am Baruch ben Baruch ben Baruch."

The captain said, "No gibberish! What is your real name?"

The friar repeated sternly, "I will conduct the inquisition."

"Well, it's beginning to rain outside, and the crowd will get wet and go home."

"That is his real name," the friar said. "But I had to hear it from him. What are you known as in Christendom, Dr. Benedict?"

"Benedict, physician of Seville."

It was, in fact, beginning to rain, but the implication was lost on the prisoner: it would slow the fire, but that did not frighten him now. The tremendous event of pronouncing his ancient name as the head of the House of Baruch upheld and sustained him.

"Is it true that you have lived all your life outwardly as a Christian, but inwardly and secretly you have practiced the heresy of Judaism?"

"I am a Jew."

"Do you detest and abhor your Jewishness and renounce your lifelong deception and will you in true faith of your own accord be reconciled to Holy Mother Church, who waits with yearning arms open to receive you, for the benefit of your soul and for promise of Heaven? There is still time. Say but the word, say yes, and your soul shall be healed, and your punishment will be easier."

"No."

Yet Benedict said it reluctantly, not because of himself, for he knew this was only a formality before sentence of death; they were going to burn him whatever he said. He said it reluctantly now because he disliked hurting people. All his life he had alleviated pain, hating it with his soul and working with his art to banish it from mankind. The friar was pitifully sincere, genuinely hoping he would say the right thing, and he had said the wrong thing, and the friar was pained.

The friar sighed. The clerk took down the answer.

"No," Benedict repeated. "No, to all you asked. I am sorry for you."

The clerk wrote it again.

"I release this lapsed heretic to you, the secular arm, bidding you in chastisement of his faults to show mercy, Christian charity and shed no blood," the friar said to the captain.

"And high time, too!" the captain said. "Guards! Take him out before they all go home."

Benedict did not see his feet as he strode over the cobble-stones of the marketplace, for he held his head high.

He mounted the faggots and leaned against the stake, and felt the chain pass around his neck. He wondered idly if someone would tighten it. No one did.

A dozen soldiers with torches came and tried to light the faggots, which took fire but went out. Then someone came with a bucket of oil of some sort or melted wax, perhaps from the butts of candles; it smelled like candlewax.

The friar stood in the rain holding a crucifix tied to a long pole of green wood and thrust it close to Benedict's face, crying, "Repent, repent; abjure, abjure; recant, recant! There is still time."

Oh, you silly man, Benedict said, or thought he said, for the fire was touching his feet and he did not know whether he spoke or screamed. The crowd yelled, he noted, so probably he screamed.

Then something odd happened, and fixed his thoughts on a medical matter. The sulphur-impregnated sanbenito took fire and blazed up in a yellow flame that hid him from sight for a moment; the witch's cap they had thrust on his head also flared up. In that moment he was a torch, and his body was invisible under the blinding fire. Then the sulphur consumed itself and the chemical fire subsided and Benedict emerged again to view, his body blackened except for his beard in which red sparks could be seen and from which smoke arose.

He slumped, and only the loose neck chain kept him from falling.

"There is something in sulphurous fumes that narcotizes a person," he marveled. "I will ask Tubal the alchemist about this. What a blessing it would be if by a whiff of sulphur I could put my patients to sleep when I perform operations."

Tubal was in the crowd, but Benedict did not see him.

"That is the smoke you smelled," Tubal said to his servant.

"He is brave," the servant said.

But Benedict did not feel brave. He did not feel anything. As the sodden faggots took fiercer fire, smoke choked him. Between rifts in the billows of smoke, as his head drooped lower, he saw his feet again. They were burned through, and the blackened bones were beginning to separate and fall.

"I will get at the secret of this gaseous anesthetic," he thought, before his eyes burned away and he could not see his feet.

Then he dozed off, and his life was done.

BOOK II

SHORTLY before Christmas in the year 1657 a prominent Dutch physician in the prime of life skated over one of Amsterdam's frozen canals in answer to a patient's urgent call. Like all native-born Dutchmen Dr. Jan van Benedict liked to skate: it filled the lungs with good fresh air and kept the muscles strong and it roused the blood to more vigorous circulation. What an exquisite mechanism, the circulation of the blood. What an unconscionable time it had been in the discovering. From the dawn of history to this present generation it had baffled physicians, yet how simple it was, how inevitable, how logical. What a pity the great English physician, Harvey, who had solved the mystery, had just died in June of this very year, he who might have lived to solve so much more; yet how much greater a pity it would have been if he had never lived at all, to bestow upon mankind the priceless fruit of his genius.

Neighbors and friends waved greetings or raised their hats respectfully to Dr. Benedict. Many he had known since his university days at Leyden; some of the oldsters had even known his father, who also had been a native-born Dutchman. They all knew that Dr. Benedict was a Jew and of course could not vote in the city council like a full-fledged citizen nor could he hold public office; but no one looked upon him as an alien and no one remembered his immigrant grandfather who had come from Africa and built a house in Amsterdam for his son and his son's sons.

Nor did Benedict consider himself an alien. In the free air of the Netherlands where no one thought it wrong or odd that a Hebrew synagogue should exist alongside their churches, where a thriving community of Jews lived in dignity and friendliness with their Christian neighbors of many sects, Dr. Jan van Benedict was proud to be a Dutchman and proud to be a Jew, and he saw therein neither divided nor double loyalty, for it was one of the rare and happy countries in a rare and happy period for his religion.

At the moment he was frowning. His mind was not occupied with abstract sociological niceties. He had grown up in the Dutch air of near-equality which he assumed would endure, though he did not take it for granted: a Jew could take nothing for granted, or so the rabbi said in the synagogue. But he was so made that he seldom thought about abstractions. Practicality was in his blood, and practicality was in the long tradition of his family, strengthened by his training as a physician and surgeon.

The thought that brought the frown to his face and set him to sucking angrily on his tobacco pipe, till the bowl glowed fiercely under a perforated silver windguard, was a purely professional and practical one.

Skating in step beside him was his son, tall as himself and home from the University for the festival of Hanukkah, which came very close to the Christian Christmas.

[104]

"What are you angry at, Father? You've got that same scowl you used to have when you whipped me when I was a boy."

"Whipped you, Baruch? I never whipped you."

"This," the son said, laughing and slapping his backside, "remembers it clearly. Ouch! I can feel it now."

Benedict glanced at him and the frown faded. The young man made a handsome picture, with his high intelligent forehead, his remarkably white teeth exposed in a hearty laugh and an exhalation of athletic breath blowing white from his mouth like a plume from a bird of paradise. He was soberly dressed, as befitted a candidate for a doctor's diploma, but the sober clothes were expensive and Benedict's heart swelled with pride that he could afford them for such a son.

"I never chastised you with a whip, Baruch. Whips are for dogs."

"Then it was a wooden shoe; I cannot remember. But it was some devilish instrument of torture."

"And never unless you thoroughly deserved it."

"At Leyden the schoolmasters were worse."

"Then you were an inattentive student and deserved their chastisement."

"I am attentive, Father. But sometimes I talk too much. I was telling a friend that you had a thermometer —"

"Talking during a lecture? Gossiping during a *lecture?*"

"Well, yes. It was during a lecture."

"One does not talk when the master is lecturing."

"And my friend said there wasn't any such thing. Then the master stopped lecturing and came down to where I was sitting and rapped me smartly on the ears with his wand."

"Did he rap the other student too?"

"Oh no. He was a Christian."

"You should both have been rapped."

"Well, we weren't."

"Who started the talking during the lecture?"

"I'm afraid I did."

"Nevertheless, you should both have been rapped. But the Jew took the brunt as usual. That is why we must be twice as attentive, twice as diplomatic, Baruch. Listen, lad: I will teach you something you can never learn from your masters. Cast down your eyes and look at the ice beneath our feet. Tell me, is the canal on which we skate frozen thick or is it frozen thin?"

"Thick. It is very cold."

"And easy to skate on, is it not?"

"As easy as walking."

"And perfectly safe?"

"Perfectly, since it's thick."

"So. So! You diagnose the ice as thick, my fine young student doctor. Very good. I might agree with you, since the weather is frigid and everything in my experience bears evidence that frigid weather produces thick ice. But bear in mind that we see only the top. What is happening underneath? A warm sewer may be venting from some nearby house and may be melting it unseen and slowly eroding a thin and treacherous spot. Or a sudden change in the weather, while we sleep, may rot the whole sheet overnight. Who knows when an ill wind may blow, even in Holland, even in December? Therefore, as a doctor, you must always be chary of making diagnoses and, as a Jew, always be prepared to skate on thin ice."

"Even if it looks thick?"

"Especially then."

His son was thoughtful. Seldom had he heard his father speak of danger. The frown had returned to his father's face.

[106]

They skated some moments in silence, and then his father said, "I wish it were any other patient. I wish it were a rich Christian or a rich Jew, or even a poor Christian or a poor Jew; that would be simpler; simple things are always preferable, in life and in the practice of medicine. I tell you frankly that the reason I am frowning and out of temper is that, in a sense, I am the one who is skating on thin ice. I am bothered. Perhaps I shall send you home. We need not both suffer the scandal of this call. Perhaps I shall even turn back myself."

But the doctor had actually lengthened his stride and was skating faster.

"Yesterday I received this call. I delayed a whole day, debating in my mind whether to answer it, whether it would not be prudent to send a servant with word that I was out of town. I was disquieted at the nature of the information, and prudence dictated that I get the apprentice to issue a quick disclaimer lest I become involved in a patient's death and be held responsible; for we are taught, If I am not for myself, who will be for me? Then, hard on the heels of the first summons came a second, in writing, and the patient wrote, 'I spit blood.' But still I delayed till this hour."

It was not for the son to answer the father's questioning of conscience, but he passed his arm through the crook of his father's and lengthened his stride to keep pace with the father's rapid skating. Behind them, carrying the doctor's bag, the apprentice looked on and smiled knowingly. Never yet had he known Dr. Benedict to turn back from a call, fee or no fee.

Benedict continued, "I could not delay then. He would not have sent me a second appeal if he could have found any other doctor to tend him. He is wretchedly poor. He cannot afford a competent Christian physician. He is far too intelligent to hire a quack. And no decent Jew will approach within six feet of him."

"Is he a leper then?"

"No, I have treated lepers. They pose no danger if you wash carefully afterwards. No. Far worse. This patient is Benedict Spinoza, a heretic Jew. Last year the Elders of the Synagogue tried him, found him guilty and cast him into anathema, with such terrible curses and execrations as I hope never to hear again, for I was there till the very last candle was extinguished and all was darkness within the house of worship, and I could not help but pity the man. I cannot permit him to die if it lies within my power to save him, for we are also taught, and here is the rest of the same text from our sages, If I am for myself only, what am I, what good to God or the world? So willy-nilly," Benedict said, "I face the problem that by treating him I lose my whole practice, both Christian and Jewish, since Spinoza's heresy offends both, and perhaps go bankrupt and you, Baruch, may never finish your schooling." The doctor smiled, as if it were an exaggeration, which in Holland it was; but the smile was wry.

"No, Father, you cannot let him die."

"You need not come with me, you know."

For answer Baruch tightened his arm in the crook of his father's.

"God bless you, my son," Benedict said.

Benedict knew that his son also realized the risk they ran in attending this renegade from Israel. All Jews were familiar with the dread formula of anathema, which was feared the more because it was so ancient, so little employed and so deprecated as legendary in a tolerant religious climate where Christians too hesitated to employ their ancient rite of excommunication. In sunny and equable weather the gods withhold their thunder.

But in Spinoza's case the terrifying curse had been spoken, and the Jews of Holland were uncomfortably reminded that the jealous Lord of Sinai might still be as jealous of His people on the shores of the cold North Sea as He had been of them in the wastes of the desert. It went thus:

> With the judgment of the angels we anathematize, execrate, curse and cast thee out, in the presence of the Sacred Scriptures with the six-hundred-and-thirteen precepts written therein and with all the maledictions written in The Law: be accursed by day and accursed by night; be accursed in thy lying down and in thy rising up; accursed in thy going out and in thy coming in. May the Lord never pardon thee; may the wrath of the Lord burn forever against thee and blot out thy name; may the Lord sever thee from all the tribes of Israel. And hereby all persons are publicly admonished never to converse with thee by word of mouth or by writing, never to do thee any service, nor abide under thy roof, nor to approach within six feet of thy person; nor may anyone read anything written by thy hand or dictated by thy mouth.

In earlier times such a curse had constituted a virtual sentence of death. Even in Protestant Holland it was a severe and dangerous social censure. But the Benedicts did not turn back.

Spinoza's house was shabby, small and sorely in need of paint. The shutters were closed, though the sun shone brightly. No smoke came from the dilapidated chimney. On the door was a nameplate: BENEDICT SPINOZA. Like most of the Jews of Amsterdam Spinoza had changed his name. Christians tangled their tongues ludicrously over Baruch, which he simply translated into Benedict, and as for De Espinoza, which bespoke his Portuguese ancestry, it sounded foreign. Similarly, though

[109]

Dr. Jan van Benedict was listed in the roster of the synagogue as Johann ben Baruch and his son as Baruch ben Baruch, the easier, Christian version of their names was Jan van Benedict and Benedict van Benedict. The custom was common and in no wise reprehensible, nor did the Amsterdam Jews seek to hide their Jewishness, for the roster of the synagogue was open for anyone with the curiosity or education to read the Hebrew script and many could. It was a joke among the Elders that half the congregation could not properly pronounce their real names. No one cared, not in Holland, not at that time.

"Spinoza must have spent hours polishing that nameplate," the doctor said. "A stubborn man. Despite his disgrace he does not propose that his name be blotted out."

"How does he make his living, such as it is?" his son said, glancing at the house.

"I do not know. He used to teach Hebrew, but of course his pupils go to other teachers now."

Spinoza met them at the door, shielding a candle against the wind and blinking his eyes at the sudden sunlight. Behind him all was dark. He was dressed in a smock such as portrait painters wore at work; but this, though scrupulously clean, was full length, much worn from many launderings, and heavily quilted, as if to serve also for warmth. His complexion was dark, yet he looked pale. He was noticeably thin. Through the doctor's mind flashed the tentative diagnosis: Starvation, asceticism or consumption.

"You are obviously Dr. Benedict," Spinoza said pleasantly. "I did not think you would come. I should not have blamed you."

"And this is my son," the doctor said, "who receives his own doctorate next year." The apprentice was obviously a servant and needed no introduction.

"Kindly come in," Spinoza said.

They entered; and in the semidarkness the apprentice clumsily shuffled his feet, raising a cloud of dust.

"Step carefully!" Spinoza said irritably, and added immediately in a softer tone, "But of course you could not know. Gentlemen, it is important not to contaminate the air of this place."

The interior of the house was as cold as the outside. Dr. Benedict could see his breath.

"I am sorry," the servant said.

Spinoza hurried to a shiny circular object about six inches in diameter, upended on a shelf at the far end of the room; it looked much like a pie plate. He covered it with a silk scarf, lovingly, like a mother tucking the covers around an infant who has just fallen asleep and must be protected from drafts.

"Now the dust won't fall on it and spoil it," Spinoza said, and opened the shutters, and the sun shone in. "I was just finishing a test. It mustn't be scratched, you know. The floor is gritty."

Benedict reached down and tested a pinch of dust between finger and thumb: it was viciously abrasive and so fine he could not see the individual grains.

"Do you breathe this stuff?" he asked.

"When I am at the grinding the air is full of it," Spinoza said. "But one cannot stop or the work will be spoiled. When I polish, of course, I wait till the grit settles to the floor. I had finished polishing; that is why I was rude. Polishing is the most critical part and one must be careful to avoid letting the grinding grit fall on the surface."

They looked around and saw that they were in a workshop of some sort, certainly a place where a man labored, not where a man lived: no bed, no chair, no books — and Spinoza was a great reader. No table, no light, no stove, and the month was December. There was a workbench with a rack of tools as delicate and clean as the doctor's own, but smaller in size, as small as a watchmaker's, which they greatly resembled.

Spinoza raised a velvet cloth on the workbench and pointed with pride to several glass lenses, shining with diamondlike brilliance. "For spectacles," he said, "and every one a perfect sphere."

"Spheres?" said Benedict. "Globes?"

"No, no, Doctor; sections of spheres. As if you were to cut a small slice from the skin of a large, perfectly globular melon. Then the shape of the lens would be what the lensmaker calls a sphere. Are they not beautiful? Perfection is always beautiful."

"They are indeed. I never saw spectacles in the making before."

"This is how I mount them," Spinoza said, showing him several empty spectacle frames. "This part of the work is tedious and mechanical, but without it no one would get the benefit of my beautiful lenses."

"That is what you use all these little tools for? They are ingenious."

The servant looked bored, but Baruch realized that his father was simply letting the patient talk, learning all he could about him, gaining his confidence before making a diagnosis or suggesting a treatment. "A man must surely have a steady hand to do all that delicate work with such small tools as these," he said.

"I suppose I have," Spinoza said idly. "I never thought much about it." So, thought Bendict, there is no tremor; my patient accepts his steady hand without question, to be taken for granted, ignorant that a hand can be otherwise.

"How do you decide which glasses to prescribe for them?" Benedict asked.

"Why, I merely try on a series of test spectacles, each with more magnifying power than the last; and when the client says, 'Now the print is clear,' then I grind him a pair like those he saw best with. Such testing is not really necessary if you can afford to own many pairs of the various powers, but I must make my own. These, for example — he held up a test pair from a separate compartment — are for a man forty-five years of age, these for a man of fifty, these for a man of fifty-five, and so on up to the age of seventy. After seventy the eyes do not change until death."

It was an innocent and accepted profession, Baruch thought. Surely no one was anathematized for plying so useful a craft.

"Do you fit many spectacles to women?" Benedict asked.

Spinoza chuckled. "I cannot remember a single case, and a pity it is, for it would double my business. But women consider them disfiguring and never employ them."

Adopting his mood, Benedict chuckled also, and said, "Yet in my practice of medicine I have often observed that the ladies become farsighted too as they get older, and indeed some can scarcely thread a needle."

"There is always a daughter or a servant to thread them for them," Spinoza said, "or they do it by force of habit. And so few know how to read. That is the real necessity. Come. Let me show you something amusing."

He took a strong lens, one fit for a man of seventy, and went to the window. He crumpled a scrap of paper and held the lens to the sunlight, which was streaming in. A dot of light of intense brilliance focused upon the paper, which shortly smoked, then burst into flame with a tiny pop and consumed itself. "In this manner I economize on tinder, flint and steel," Spinoza said smiling. "With the wizardry of my glass I have conjured down the fire of the sun to the earth, or so it looks till one comprehends. One would not perform such an experiment in Germany, of course; one would be burned for a witch. Here in enlightened Holland it is safe." Benedict noted that Spinoza stressed the word "enlightened" with a tone of sarcasm, remembered Spinoza's anathematization and kept his face straight, sustaining a feeling of sorrow and pity. But he was already taking a chance, and it was no part of his duty to commiserate with the scientist, who mused a moment, then said:

"You will find it more comfortable in my kitchen. Kindly follow me."

He took them to another room, just as cold, where everything lacking in the workshop was provided: Spinoza's narrow bed, some chairs, a table, his many books, and a large Dutch fireplace with its hanging pot where he prepared his bachelor meals. "I'm afraid I let the fire go out," he said. "I was busy with my candle test and I let it die. The candle test must be performed in a stable atmosphere, without air turbulence."

"I see," Benedict said.

Spinoza looked at him. "You do not, Doctor. Do not patronize me."

Lamely the doctor rejoined, "I do not know the details, but it is obviously a delicate test."

Spinoza took a bellows in his hand, directed a jet of air upon the near-dead embers, cast upon them a handful of charcoal and soon there was a fire on the hearth; and slowly the kitchen-bedroom, much smaller than the workshop, grew tolerably warm.

"Heat in the workshop while I am testing distorts the shape of the speculum," Spinoza said. Benedict thought, He is a gentleman, sensitive, sorry that he reproached me for patronizing him, conscious also that he needs me when no one else will treat him.

Spinoza said, "I was engaged in the test when you were kind enough to visit me. And do you know, Dr. Benedict, I found the speculum perfectly spherical!" He smiled proudly.

Sphericity pleases him, Benedict thought. It is the perfection he demands. Perfection! As if it were possible! Still, one had to admire a man who reached for it and believed it existed.

Spinoza said, "Now I can provide you with your accustomed temperature, though if it had *not* been spherical I should have sent you away. The speculum is finished now."

"How long were you in the grinding and polishing of this speculum?" Benedict asked.

"Three weeks in the grinding, one week in the polishing. Why?"

"It is a large piece of work. Was there much of the gritty dust in the air while you were working?"

Spinoza said, "There is always grit in the air when you grind. The coarser grits that you use at the beginning aren't troublesome because they are heavy and settle to the floor; but as the finer grinding progresses the grits hang in the air and get into the cracks in the walls and even in my hair, and then some invisible impalpable grains can fall onto the work and scratch it; then it all has to be done over."

"Does this happen when you grind spectacle lenses too?"

"They do not differ; whenever you grind there is dust."

"And do you bend over and breathe the dust? And when you test do you always test in so cold a room?"

"Such is the procedure, Doctor. Testing must always be done

[115]

in the dark with the light of a single candle in an absolutely even temperature."

"And for that temperature you choose the temperature outside," Benedict said.

Spinoza said, "I think I know what you are going to say."

"There is no question that there is some connection between your work and your illness," Benedict said.

"I know no other work, nor would I enjoy any other. I will continue it."

The doctor had seen similar symptoms in the diamond polishers of Amsterdam, among jewel engravers and among blacksmiths who inhaled the metallic smoke from the red hot irons they wrought upon their anvils.

On the hearth Spinoza's pot began to simmer and the aroma of a nourishing soup filled the room. The doctor detected pork, chicken, cabbage, fish that never had known scales, carrots and turnips. He was dealing with no aesthete; here was not a man who mortified the flesh out of rigid adherence to the dietary rules; here was an anathematized Jew, who ate pork like a Christian and did not fast if he could help it and probably never had. Here was a free thinker, neither Christian nor Jew but capable of uttermost devotion to a dangerous art. What else was he?

"Let me see your hands," Benedict said. Spinoza held them out to be examined.

They were strong and the joints were supple. They resembled Benedict's own: sensitive, scrupulously clean, even the fingernails. But there was an irritation at the roots of the fingers, red and inflamed.

"Do you always have this?" Benedict asked.

"It comes and goes," Spinoza said.

"When does it come, and when does it go?"

"It comes when I grind, goes when I stop. It itches, but it never bothers me or keeps me from my work."

The doctor nodded. The son, Baruch, had not noted the minor inflammation between the patient's fingers and looked at his father with question and admiration in his glance.

"It is probable," Benedict said, "that the weakness in your chest is aggravated by your deplorable housekeeping."

Spinoza frowned. His thick black eyebrows twitched and his thin lips set in a hard line.

"I keep my rooms kosher," he said with some asperity.

"You summoned me, I did not summon you," Benedict said, half rising to depart.

"Do not go!" Spinoza said. "Had I been able to physic myself I should not have called the doctors. You were my last hope."

"Nobody else answered your call, eh?" Benedict said.

"I concede that I called others. Your fees are well known. I cannot afford you. But no one else would come. And therefore I said to myself, 'Since I cannot stomach the common I shall try for the best,' for even I know that the spitting of blood is a warning of death. Is it wrong of me that I endeavor to stave off that inevitable day? I have much work to do before I die. To say nothing of the natural reluctance an organism experiences at the prospect of extinction."

"No, it was not wrong," Benedict said, smiling kindly and with some admiration. It was something new in his experience to speak with so brave and frank a patient. "No sensible man wants to die. Do not worry yourself unduly about my fee. What do you drink?"

"Water," Spinoza said. "Naturally I prefer wine, but wine does not fit my present budget."

"Drink beer," Benedict said.

"I detest the taste of beer."

"That is your Portuguese heritage. Drink it as a medicine then, like a good Hollander; and the scale between your fingers will disappear."

"I shall have to cut down on food." There was a dubious note in Spinoza's voice.

"Charge more for your spectacles then. You must eat plenty of food. But drink three pints of beer per day. Let me see your tongue."

Beer, as all Dutch doctors knew, sweetened the breath, aided digestion, flushed the bladder, eliminated toxins, firmed the liver, strengthened the muscles and put on flesh among those too nervous to digest properly even if they ate enough. It put roses in the cheeks of girls and enabled mothers to nurse their children. To these healthful properties of the national brew could be added the strange but undoubted skin-cleansing effect of curing stubborn cases of eczema, from which Spinoza suffered in the creases of his hands. Taken in excess, of course, beer produced a hideous red nose; but Benedict did not think Spinoza would do anything to excess except work and think.

Spinoza stuck out his tongue. It was coated.

"Let me feel your pulse."

Spinoza extended his wrist, pulling back the sleeve of his morning gown. The flesh was cold but the heartbeat was strong, albeit a bit rapid.

"Now I must see if you have a fever."

Spinoza brushed back his hair, which he wore long, from his forehead. Shoulder-length hair was fashionable among men, and, with those whose hair was sparse or who were old and bald, wigs were beginning to be worn in the style of Louis XIV, who

set the fashion for Europe. Spinoza, Benedict believed, would
have worn his hair long regardless of fashion, since it was
tiresome to have one's hair cut.

He applied his forearm to the patient's forehead. Then, in
what looked like a kiss, he applied his lips thereto as a mother
does to an infant, lips being very sensitive to slight changes in
temperature. Spinoza's forehead was feverish. The doctor was
already satisfied that his patient had a severe cold and was
suffering from a rise of body heat. But Benedict was thorough.

He motioned to the servant, who took the thermometer from
the bag. It was a small spherical bottle of blown glass with a
slender closed pipe extending from the body of the instrument, a
delicate thing and a tribute to the glassblower's art. On the pipe
were white ceramic dots at spaced intervals, applied by the
glassblower when the glass was still sticky and hot and adhesive.
Each division represented one-thousandth of the capacity of the
bottle. As the temperature rose, so rose the level of the alcohol
in the transparent glass pipe. The alcohol was stained yellow for
better visibility; the yellow rise in the pipe measured the patient's temperature.

Benedict placed the bulb of the thermometer under Spinoza's
armpit.

"What is that thing?" Spinoza said.

"It is called a thermometer."

"It measures heat?"

"Yes."

"Heat anywhere?"

"Body heat."

"But would it work in a room?"

"I should think so."

[119]

Spinoza mused, *'therm,'* heat; *'metrein,'* to measure. From the Greek. Yes; it would be called a thermometer. Fascinating.

The yellow-stained alcohol rose three divisions in the reading pipe.

"What does the thermometer say?"

"It says you are sick," Benedict said, "which I already knew; my arm and my lips had already informed me that you had a fever. You should keep your house warmer."

"But I cannot. Not while I work."

An even temperature was not so important when he was working on mere spectacles, he said; but for a speculum? Oh, that was another matter. The shining disc he had covered, lest it be scratched, the slightest change in temperature deformed its sensitive surface. One could not test it if the temperature changed. It expanded, it contracted, it actually changed focus. The surface rose and fell like a tide; it rose and fell like the breast of a breathing body; it rose and fell like a cake when the oven is opened. Reflecting surfaces were four times as sensitive to changes of temperature as mere lenses. The glass disc was the mirror of a reflecting telescope, with which one gazed at the moon, at the plants, the stars. Isaac Newton had invented it. He was constructing this one for Christian Huygens, the Dutch mathematician and astronomer, whose commission was a great honor. With it Huygens would view the depths of the heavens and search out its secrets. How could one work without perfect tools? How could the toolmaker consider the comfort of his body if it vitiated the integrity of so superb an instrument?

"A sunnier climate would be better for you," Benedict said. "Clean air and sunlight are the only sure cure for the weakness of the lungs when the weakness has advanced to the point where one spits blood."

"Now you will counsel me to go to Italy," Spinoza said, "where even a heretic Jew is safe in the Papal States of the Christian Church and where the sun is warm."

"Such a suggestion was on the tip of my tongue," Benedict said.

"For two reasons I will not go," Spinoza said. "First, my honor is involved, and I will not retreat under fire. Secondly, my work: it is here; here, I am close to the great scientists of Europe whom I serve and from whose trust I draw my inspiration. Therefore, I shall stay, though I spit blood till I die." Spinoza spoke this decision with the detachment of a mathematician, and a lesser man than the doctor would have taken it at face value and probed no further; but Spinoza's tone betrayed him. Spinoza was a very young man, and the doctor said, smiling:

"Is there not a third person, Baruch?"

Spinoza winced at the familiar Hebrew version of his name. Only another Jew would have used it and only in intimacy, from which Spinoza's proud nature instinctively recoiled.

"No one that concerns you, Doctor," he said.

So it was a girl, thought the doctor.

Well, there was one encouraging sign in the multiple twists and turns of the patient's complex nature. In all Benedict's practice he had never run across so intense and contrary a character. It was known in the Jewish community that Spinoza's father had left him a comfortable legacy, enough to give him a handsome income for the rest of his life. Spinoza's sister had contested the will through the Dutch courts. Spinoza had fought for his legal rights and he had won. On which he had turned everything over to the sister, who took it, and retained nothing for himself, giving up even the affection of the sister who, from that time forward, had neglected him. Had he taken her every penny, justly his right, she could not have hated him more, and he would have been better off. How odd, thought Benedict, that Spinoza had acted with humane compassion toward her after winning the lawsuit in cold mathematical precision. To be mathematically right was apparently important in Spinoza's mind. Such a patient was not easy to diagnose.

Benedict said, "In Italy, where your lungs will heal, an optician of your skill will always find employment. Italy is full of weak eyes, both among the elderly clergy who congregate in Rome and the lower classes, whose blood is mixed with all the Byzantine disease of the Oriental refugees. Yes, in Italy there are weaker eyes than anywhere. From my own observation I know that my patients who require spectacles are inordinately proud of Venetian glasses, which are more readily procurable in Italy. If you emigrate thither and settle there you will never want for a living; and, unless I err, you will live twice as long."

"No," said Spinoza, "and you knew I'd say no."

"Is it of total indifference to you whether you die young or die old?" Dr. Benedict said.

"You postulate a host of unacceptable assumptions in that question, which you think so simple to answer," Spinoza said. "On the crude low level of your question I answer yes, I am totally indifferent. On the higher level I answer no; no man dies, since each man was always alive; his life simply takes on varying modes of its innate infinity."

Clearly the fever has unsettled his mind, thought Benedict, who had seen feverish patients talk nonsense before.

So he said kindly, "In that case, since you will stay here for reasons which seem good to you, I will tell you what must be done to preserve your present mode of infinite life."

"I will listen," Spinoza said.

"Eat solid, drink beer in the amount prescribed and marry soon."

"Ah, that I might," Spinoza said.

"To a woman who is a good housekeeper."

"Yes, she should be."

"Who will mop the dust from your floors. It is that dust that you breathe that is lodging in your lungs and grinding them raw."

"Meanwhile," said Spinoza, "till the lady accepts me or if, as might be, she will not have me, what then?"

"Then, sir, require of your servant that he sweep the floor thoroughly each day and let the wind blow in and remove the noxious substance from your home."

"I have no servant."

"Then do it yourself, Baruch, for as the Lord liveth, that dust will be your doom as surely as a hangman's noose."

"Sweeping daily is out of the question. It raises the grit and it settles on my work."

"Better there than in your lungs."

"That must be for me to judge, Dr. Benedict, since they are my lungs."

There was no moving him. Benedict compromised.

"Then wet your floors with oil and lay the dust."

Spinoza's face brightened; it was obvious he had never thought of it. "*Konam!*" he said, soberly, nodding his head, a word which in Hebrew meant sacred and which the Jews of Talmudic times had employed to introduce a solemn vow. "I swear I will bind the grit to the floor." He knew exactly how to do it without interrupting his work, he said. There was an oil that solidified on exposure to the air. He would sprinkle his floors with it. He wrung the doctor's hand.

[123]

Like everyone else, the doctor thought, he longs to live and he fears to die, despite his outward indifference. He is too stubborn, too proud, he is pitiful. But are not all sick people?

"I have calculated the time you have spent in my house," Spinoza said, "and I know exactly what I owe you for your visit, including the fee of your son and the cost involved in that portion of your servant's wages justly attributable to me. I cannot pay at the moment."

"I did not ask you to."

"But I have set it down in my mind and I will not default. I am no charity patient."

The doctor nodded, shrugged.

"I *could* pay you in kind. My spectacles. Your patients. Many must need them."

"Many do."

"I will give them to you free if you will continue to physic me. You, in turn, will charge them the going price; and so, in a circular manner, your fees will be paid by me and I shall not be ashamed and you will not be out of pocket."

The time had not yet come when a doctor spurned payment in kind and insisted on coin. "In such an arrangement no one will suffer and all will be helped," Benedict said amiably.

"And you will continue to tend me?"

"I will, Baruch. But mind your floors."

"I will, Baruch," Spinoza said.

"That was the most human thing he said in the entire interview," the son said to the father. "He called you by name, and he actually smiled. You gave him hope."

"He had hope all along, my son. The art is to bring it out and render it acceptable to the patient. Too often they resign and take selfish pride in the martyrdom of their resignation. But what was the real hope in the burning eyes of Benedict Spinoza?"

"Why, the hope of not dying. Nobody wants to die."

"At your age you speak so? No; it was the girl. I will find out who she is."

"Why bother?"

"For all those spectacles, the best in Amsterdam? Why not?"

In this manner Benedict van Benedict, candidate licentiate of the University of Leyden, learned, and not all from his books.

CHAPTER 2

S HORTLY after the visit to Spinoza a minor tussle occurred between Dr. Benedict and his son, the student doctor, now in midstream in his university career. He had seen at firsthand how his father, the most prominent physician of Amsterdam, treated his patients. Not unnaturally the thought came to him: Can I not learn more from him and faster than from all the professors at the university? He wavered in his belief that a return to Leyden was necessary. He broached the subject to his father, stating, with much truth, that most physicians merely served an apprenticeship and then set up practice on their own. "If the state required a license," he said, "then of course I would continue my schooling. But it doesn't."

Dr. Benedict was distressed and he spoke severely.

"In the many lands where our family have lived, Baruch, the sons of our House have always sought and always achieved the best medical education the time and place could provide. That is why we have prospered. Study is a family tradition. Study is the highest tradition of the whole worldwide family of Jews. That is why we have survived, few as we are."

"I meant only, my father, that I can learn faster from you, as I did today when we called on Spinoza."

"Faster, you say!" Benedict spoke with contempt. "Like doctors who only pull teeth and only cut hair? They save no lives when they operate and they doom a patient when they diagnose. It is lazy and dangerous to think that fast learning alone is good, even if you happen to be sufficiently bright to learn fast. Did you listen, my son, with both ears when the rabbi spoke recently in the synagogue how the Scripture classified students in the old days? Believe me, they are just the same today."

"The four types?"

"The four types."

"Of course I listened," Baruch said confidently.

"Name me those four types, Baruch."

"Why, they were: Quick to absorb and quick to forget; Slow to absorb and slow to forget; Quick to absorb and slow to forget; and the slow to absorb and quick to forget."

"Was that all?"

"Yes, there were only four."

"Do you really remember so little? Was there no commentary? Did not the Scripture also foretell the fate of each type?"

"Yes," Baruch said, wrinkling his brow, "I seem to remember —"

"Do not seem to remember. Remember! Let the wise old words sink into your soul. Only one type of student was praised: The quick to absorb and slow to forget; and the praise was, 'He is smart.' And bear in mind that the Talmudic word 'smart' does not mean crafty or self-serving or cunning or, above all, smart-alecky. It is simply the only word we have to translate the wary self-awareness expressed by the compact old tongue in which our Scriptures were written. So be smart, Baruch, and talk to me no more of the God-given gift that you merely learn fast." Looking less severe and smiling, he added, "I'll concede that you do, and it makes me proud, but it takes a lot more to make a Doctor Benedict than that."

With this injunction the student returned to Leyden, somewhat sobered, proud to be the son of such a father and firmly determined to become a type-three student, the only type that the Talmud praised; though it puzzled his free Dutch mind how so ancient a Scripture, written in the Orient and alien to Western Europe, could be so profoundly modern and applicable. He thought perhaps he might read it one day. There was a dusty copy in the university library in a Dutch translation. It might be instructive. It certainly sounded practical.

After his son's departure Dr. Benedict returned to the routine of his rounds, treating the sick. He was surprised to find how he had neglected his ordinary work. But he grinned and stuffed his pipe and talked with his medical colleagues, who said, "We too fall behind when our sons come home from college," and he worked twice as hard, musing occasionally (though somewhat casually, as was his wont) on the wonderful cryptic words of Hillel, who said, "If I am only for myself, what good am I?" Sons certainly did take time to shape, to mold, to prepare to carry on. Loss of time was loss of income, but for Baruch to continue his study seemed to justify everything. And work as such for Benedict was stimulating.

Benedict removed from the left ear of John de Witt, the burgomaster of Dort, a growth called a "turbinate," which threatened his hearing. De Witt was a wealthy man, an overseas trader with interests in many Dutch shipping lines; he was a free-thinking statesman and, in addition, an extremely able mathematician. In a political atmosphere of federal patronage and deficit municipal spending, he had balanced the Dort city budget. The Prince of Orange, head of the Dutch government, Stadholder of the Netherlands — "as if he held the state in the palm of his hand!" grumbled De Witt — cordially disliked him, because, when the Prince asked, "Does Dort need money?" De Witt answered, "No, Dort does not," and refused both the government aid and the controls that inevitably would follow if he accepted.

"I will not be bought!" De Witt said vehemently, as Dr. Benedict dipped a scalpel in alcohol and burned it off the blade in the blue flame of a spirit lamp.

"Why did you ask for me?" Benedict asked, calculating the fee. It would be substantial. It would pay for many a costly lecture for Baruch to attend at the University of Leyden. It would pay for many a charity call.

"I need both my ears to hear what is happening," the burgomaster of Dort replied. "Besides, you won't torture me with your surgery."

Benedict knew that De Witt was a very brave man. He knew also, from long experience, that cowards boasted of bravery they did not possess, and some actually seemed to ask for the pain of the knife so as to boast of their fortitude afterwards; but these the doctor always narcotized with opium first.

Benedict said, "It's a very large turbinate."

"I would rather be whole," De Witt said staunchly, "the better to do my work. Will you strap me down?" He extended his limbs for the straps.

Benedict purred, "That is the normal procedure in turbinates of this size, my lord burgomaster; but search as you will, send your men, rifle my surgery chest, you will find no straps."

[129]

"I might wince and spoil your aim."

"I think not."

Benedict took a lump of ice and applied it to the burgo-master's ear. Then he swabbed the area with alcohol and, with a tiny bellows, directed a strong jet of air against it, till the patient shivered with the intense localized numbing cold. Then with a swift sure circular motion of the razor-sharp scalpel he cut out the growth.

"*Lieve God!*" swore De Witt. "I shall wince and spoil your aim, for I feel you beginning."

"I've finished," Benedict said, and showed him the turbinate, having first wiped off the redness so that it looked like a nicely cleaned baby shrimp.

"It's over?"

"All over," Benedict said.

Benedict knew that the fear of pain is worse than pain itself; he knew also that there would be some discomfort for ten days as the ear healed; but the pain of healing, ending in itching, could be easily borne. It was always wise, however, just after an operation, when the patient was feeling good, to warn him of the aftereffects. "Your ear will swell a bit, and feel feverish and hot for a few days," Benedict said, "but your hearing is restored. I shall leave a soothing ointment for you to apply."

He had already packed the ear with cotton impregnated with poppy, and prepared a small flask of the narcotic fluid, in which was incorporated an astringent alum to stop the bleeding.

"Renew the dressing if the ear pains you," he said. "How is your hearing?"

"Sharp like a spy!" De Witt said. "Every word. I shall need no dressings.

"Such will be the sharpness of your hearing from now on," Benedict told him, "and even better as time goes on."

Then Benedict said (for the relief on the face of his patient was tinged with the ghost of the fear of pain, and the patient needed sleep), "Would my lord burgomaster have in the house a small glass of brandy? I have treated many patients today and I am somewhat fatigued." Benedict did not need it. De Witt did, and would be glad of the excuse.

"Gallons! A cellar full!" cried De Witt.

When a servant brought it De Witt quaffed a grateful throatful, and he rested well that night. But next day and for several days thereafter he secretly applied Benedict's soothing ointment. Benedict's heavy fee was promptly rendered and promptly paid, and John de Witt charged it to the municipality of Dort as an administrative expense, thus reducing somewhat the fiscal surplus that so irked the Prince of Orange, and eased for the moment the strained relationship between them, but only for the moment.*

Dr. Benedict had other calls that day, and during all the forthcoming months. He continued to be Amsterdam's most sought-after physician. Some patients were as rich as De Witt, and those he charged heavily. Some were as poor as Spinoza. But he treated all alike. He would say to himself, "The sick rich are as sick as the sick poor, and the fortunate must subsidize the unfortunate; for they all possess identical human bodies and identical human souls and I cannot in conscience differentiate. Who can, but God?" Then in his questing Dutch mind and in the free, Protestant Dutch air, he would question even God and

---

* Some years later, when the political wind veered and blew against him, John de Witt, the sturdy Dutchman, was torn limb from limb by a mob of fanatics; and what remained of him was strung up by the heels in a public square. His tragic end is, however, no part of this story.

bethink himself, "If six thousand years of my Jewish Scriptures contain so many contradictions and so many accounts of honest intellectual controversy — the Midrashim on the Torah, the Gemara on the Midrashim, commentary piled upon commentary — shall I not sympathize with my Christian brethren as they begin to question their own Scriptures, to probe, to interpret, to seek after the tolerance we've long since achieved, and try in their own way to better themselves? They are latecomers, but I cannot believe they are totally barbarian, in spite of Spain. Holland is proof that they are not all barbarian bigots. Anyhow, we need each other. Can Spinoza pay me, sick as he is? Cannot De Witt, sick as he isn't? How I would it were vouchsafed me to touch them with my finger, Jew, Gentile, Turk, all suffering patients, as God touched Adam, *while Adam slept* — what a fantastic surgical procedure the good Lord must have employed! — and while Adam slept, He made Eve! One day, perhaps, so Godlike a gift shall lie within the skill of human physicians. I shall not live to see it, nor my son. But I shall teach him to strive for so shining a goal; for it is in the blood of our House to hate pain and yearn to conquer it."

It was in the blood of all the physicians of the House of Baruch. Benedict would exert all his art to ease the pain of a chimney sweep as earnestly as he had eased John De Witt's, though the chimney sweep could pay nothing and De Witt paid like a prince.

Not all the doctor's visits were successful. A charity patient, a bargeman from the canals of Amsterdam, whose leg had caught in the kink of the towrope and become gangrenous, died howling. Opium dulled the terminal agony for a while, but in the end Benedict could only stand helplessly by when the drug lost effect. The widow, a gentile, spat on the heels of the Jewish doctor, whom she had called at the last moment when her own Christian quack could offer nothing but prayers; and she threw into the street the food Benedict sent her afterwards in lieu of the fee he could have charged her. When he was gone she sneaked out and gathered it up and took it into her house, keening, "This for my man? This garbage? Damned Jew." Later she ate of his charity, complaining to the neighbors, "You see what a guilty conscience he had."

Benedict sighed, shrugged and puffed his pipe, musing, "When in my flasks I mix a strong caustic with a strong acid there is much smoke, much heat and a furious strife among the elements; but when it is spent the liquid is neutral, tasteless, neither sweet nor sour, I have drunk it. Nothing. Nothing but water. In controversy there is progress and progress brings an end to strife. This too I must teach Baruch. Nothing that accomplishes anything, anything, is ever neutral. But how pleasant this world would be if it were and if, in God's time, it ever is."

His musings were tugging at him, like the bargeman's tow-rope, out of the familiar. "These are not my concerns. All I desire is that Baruch become a good doctor." Such musings belonged to the philosophers, not to physicians.

Shortly the time arrived when Spinoza summoned Benedict again to his home.

To the doctor the time had seemed short, so busy had been his days; but now the canals of Amsterdam were liquid again and he went by barge, marveling at each year's swifter passage. Spring flowers were in bloom on the banks of the waterways. It was for him a less bustling time since at this season most people were healthy except for some innocuous sniffles brought on by the west wind from the cold North Sea sweeping over the flatlands of Holland, whirling the sails of the windmills, pumping enormous quantities of excess water into the ocean and preparing the fields for the perpetually bountiful harvests that were the essence of Holland's economy and the wonder and envy of the world. In Spinoza's house there was a man of distinguished appearance and a most beautiful girl.

Spinoza himself could not be the patient, for Dr. Benedict observed his hands and saw no trace of the scaly condition that had manifested itself in the creases between his fingers, and his facial color was good. The floors looked like black marble. The optician had been better than his word. He had not only kept down the dust but he had contrived to make it beautiful. It shone. Spinoza was in excellent spirits. No, patently, Spinoza was not the patient. But long training counseled the doctor to pretend that he was: nothing rendered a doctor so suspect and so lessened the fee as to chase after new trade. Let the trade come by referral.

"My dear friend," Benedict said, "much time has passed since you did me the honor to call me, and I had begun to hope you would never again need my art; so I cannot say I am happy to be here, honor though it be, to serve you; but here I am."

"I am quite well, Dr. Benedict," Spinoza said, "but I have a friend who has come to me for advice."

Benedict bowed to the man, who wore a scholar's gown to hide his ordinary dress, which was threadbare.

"Mynheer," said the doctor. (The respectful title had not yet lost, as it was to lose in his son's time, its overtones of high status.) The man seemed to accept the title as his due.

He was Professor van den Enden, Spinoza said, introducing him: a doctor of law, a teacher of languages, and a most

[134]

treasured friend. Spinoza did not add, but Benedict, who knew Van den Enden's reputation, knew also that he was a Doctor of The Sacred Theology, a defrocked Jesuit and an intellectual rebel who, forsaking the Old Religion, had turned agnostic or atheist or worse, who had married and who now eked out a precarious living by acting as tutor in Greek, Latin, and Hebrew to such pupils as would have him. The girl was his daughter, Klaara.

CHAPTER 3

PROFESSOR van den Enden was a difficult patient. In a rapid voice, without being asked, he described all his symptoms, and after each symptom immediately prescribed the procedure that Benedict should employ.

These were always the worst kind, Benedict mused, puffing on his pipe. If they knew so much, why didn't they physic themselves? As the professor spoke, Benedict was increasingly aware of an outmoded trend in Van den Enden's medical notions: imbalance of the humors was still indeed an acceptable theory of disease, very easy, all-embracing; but could any man so highly educated as this patient still remain ignorant of the circulation of the blood? Professor van den Enden had actually referred at one point to the air in his arteries, an error that Galen had exploded seventeen centuries before. "But old errors die hard," Benedict remembered, and here was Van den Enden resurrecting one of the silliest.

But Dr. Benedict knew better than to argue with his talkative patient and simply nodded, "indeed," or "how significant, Mynheer," studying the man.

Van den Enden stood up and removed his academic gown and rolled up his sleeves, baring an arm on which there were numerous minute scalpel wounds. "Now you may perform your examination," he said, adding with excruciating condescension, "Our Jewish friend over there failed to mention in presenting you to me —" The introduction had been distinctly the other way around, Benedict remembered. "— that I am not in the least averse to being physicked by a Jewish doctor."

Spinoza and Klaara were still in the room. But Spinoza had eyes only for the girl and Klaara seemed oblivious of her father's pomposity.

"I have always taken pride," Van den Enden said, "in my position as a Liberal. Liberal in politics, liberal in religion, liberal in the arts — in which I have received some recognition — liberal in medicine. You will be advised, Dr. Benedict, though he —" jerking a thumb in Spinoza's direction "— did not apprise you of the fact, that one of my doctorates is Doctor of Medicine."

"Incredible."

"I beg your pardon?"

"That one should achieve such distinction in so many disciplines," Benedict said. "And at so early an age."

Van den Enden frowned slightly and glanced sideways, and lowered his voice. "You do not deceive me with your covert medical query, Dr. Benedict; but your point is well taken and perfectly legitimate. I am fifty-eight years old."

"No one would ever believe you."

Van den Enden beamed and complacently added, "Indeed, before you query me further, I will state that my vital powers have not diminished nor my natural forces abated. Like Moses,

you know. *You* would remember the Biblical diagnosis of Moses'
extraordinary health, of course."

"Of course. He was one hundred and twenty years old, as I
remember. I congratulate you, sir."

"I really believe I could still hold my own with a lad of
twenty."

If such was actually the case, Dr. Benedict thought privately,
Professor van den Enden was in serious trouble. But as so often
in elderly intellectuals, it was probably just a bit of harmless
braggadocio.

Benedict said, beginning to feel uncomfortable, "I assure you
I had no intention of querying you further. Would it not be wise
to continue our conversation out of earshot of the young people?"

"My daughter, Klaartje," Van den Enden chuckled. "I have
brought her up to be liberal too, Dr. Benedict. Liberal and
realistic. I pride myself on my greatest accomplishment, my
little Klaartje."

Klaara heard her pet name, and paused to direct her clear
blue eyes, blue as sapphires, with a pretty smile toward her
father, and returned them, wide and shining, again to Spinoza,
who was hypnotized by her beauty.

He was thinking, "Her skin is fair and soft as a white rose
petal; her lips are red and soft as a red rose petal; and her lovely
eyes shine like blue stars that never are seen in their fullness of
beauty save only in telescopes."

Often, in his hours of contemplating the heavens as he gazed
through the telescopes that he had lovingly made with his own
hands, he had felt himself drawn almost bodily upward and
inward toward the beckoning depths of the circumambient
infinite; he had sensed a oneness of himself with infinity; and

simile modo, as he himself would have expressed it, he now felt drawn by the sapphire of Klaara van den Enden's eyes.

Spinoza was saved from a concluding thought. He was a meticulous thinker. He would follow a line of reasoning, razor-sharp as a geometrical line, from its beginning to its end, with mathematical precision. He heard his name mentioned and was spared the inevitable comparison of Klaara's sapphire-blue eyes with stars, for the inexorable logic of the progression of thought would have been this: eyes, a speculum, the grinding of the speculum — alas! His best glasses were ground with sapphire. Sapphire was the hardest thing in the world except diamond.

Therefore, for him, since he was spared the concluding thought, Klaara van den Enden's eyes were not sapphire, were not hard — just beckoning.

"As for Spinoza," Van den Enden was saying, "he never hears anything when he's concentrating on something."

"Nevertheless, I would like to examine you in privacy," Benedict said.

"You two can go into the kitchen," Klaara said brightly.

Spinoza nodded and smiled.

"The doctors are dismissed," Van den Enden said amiably. "Oh well, that is the fate of doctors."

In the kitchen Benedict took his temperature, and found it normal, plus, perhaps, one degree, a rise that could be attributable to the inadequacy of the thermometer or to the normal increase of body temperature when a sensitive patient undergoes a searching examination. How often did not the heartbeat of a female patient rise three or four beats simply by reason of the physician's presence! It could equally rise by reason of soft music, or the presence of an interesting young man, or a sudden thunderstorm. Nothing, nothing significant in Van den Enden's temperature, and especially no fever.

Van den Enden's pulse was loud but normal, neither skipping a beat nor irregular nor hesitant. The loudness, Benedict felt, was again attributable to the tension that normally accompanies an examination.

Thus, item one, item two: both normal.

"Any cough?" Benedict asked.

"No."

In this he was better than Spinoza.

"Headaches?"

"Ah there," said Van den Enden enthusiastically. "Yes, many."

"Often?"

"Often."

Increasingly the doctor's diagnosis was taking shape.

"What do you do for your headaches?"

"Nothing. I suffer, and next day they go away."

"Nothing?" For he had smelled brandy on his breath.

"Brandy helps," Van den Enden said. "In moderation, of course. A finger or two in a glass when they get bad."

Benedict nodded. It was not, after all, an unusual remedy nor was it necessarily bad. He thought he himself might have prescribed brandy to narcotize the headaches that afflicted this high-strung patient, who, Benedict believed, was far too intelligent to overdo the brandy. Jesuit training, for all that it had first drawn the patient to the pain killer, would by its very discipline save him from excess.

Purging, in that day of overeating in the affluent Netherlands, when a lean countenance was a reproach and a paunch a symbol of status, was not only fashionable but often a necessity. No country ate so well. No country ate so heavily. But there was a limit to the number of meals composed of cheese, meat, fowl, swine, mutton and fatty sauces that the human stomach could tolerate — plus massive servings of those starchy tubers, new from the New World, called potatoes, drowned in spicy gravies, and copious sweet desserts to finish the meal.

"I eat sparsely," Van den Enden said.

But when the doctor asked what he ate and Van den Enden honestly enumerated his dietary, Benedict could only diagnose him as a glutton.

How, then, was he so thin?

"Purges?" the doctor asked.

"Normal frequency. Twice, thrice a week, perhaps."

Yes, that was normal frequency.

"And the headaches then disappear, till the next purge, Mynheer?"

"I regret that I cannot say so. I know they should, but they do not."

"It sometimes happens," Benedict said, "that there is minor bleeding in the ventranal orifice when a costive situation supervenes, and I wonder if you have had any indication —"

Van den Enden burst into a hearty laugh. "My dear colleague, circumlocution is beneath the dignity of doctors. Let us speak plainly . . . " on which he proceeded to do the opposite. "If you refer to the emerods with which the Lord smote them of Ashdod, I admit, submit, concede and stipulate that I have suffered from them since the age of my youth."

"Yes," Dr. Benedict said, "pray go on."

"But," said Van den Enden, "I am not a Philistine, and Ashdod concerns me not in the least."

It was odd how Van den Enden sought a correlation between his perfectly understandable physical symptom and an ancient legend which neither of them took seriously or understood to be scientific. In spite of his medical doctorate, Van den Enden seemed pathetically eager to attach some mystic significance to his need for frequent purgings. It irked Benedict's factual mind. There sprang to his tongue a denouncement: "Mynheer van den Enden, you are making yourself sick with a silly concern for yourself. For your own health, stop it."

But one does not talk so to a patient. Straight-faced, he went on to another subject.

"Do you at times have griping pains, like dagger thrusts in the belly?" It was a safe question. Everybody had. They were seldom serious.

"Ah there!" said Van den Enden, smiling happily. "What an excellent doctor you are! Who else would have known? Who could have known? Indeed, sir, I suffer the tortures of the damned from those very symptoms. But I do not permit my pain to show." In a spate of words he quoted a dozen authorities, all of them hopelessly out of date, who had much to say on belly pains. It was as if he were lecturing a roomful of students; it was as if he were trying to teach his doctor. His doctor listened patiently, unimpressed.

"The pains," Benedict said. "Which side?"

"Which side?" Van den Enden said. "This will require a complete answer."

There were only, thought Benedict, two sides; but he listened, and for a reason. If they were on the right side, or across the region of the navel a competent physician might suspect inflammation of the bowels. Two out of five would die in excruciating agony within twenty-four hours; three out of five would recover. There was no treatment.

"You ask me which side," Van den Enden said. "I will answer in a word."

In twenty words, where one would have done, he answered.

"In a word," Benedict said, "diffuse?"

"Yes. Diffuse."

Benedict shook his head slowly, wisely, while Van den Enden thought, "This man understands me," and preened himself on a colleague's accurate and unbiased relation of symptoms. He could not know that Benedict was forming in his own mind one word: flatulence.

He could not know that Benedict had diagnosed him far better than he himself could have wished, who wanted something mysterious. "He is not," Benedict now knew, "in the slightest danger of inflammation of the bowels. The poor man has managed to achieve for himself a case of chronic indigestion, heartburn, gas on the stomach and, probably, a gaping rent in his stomach or gut."

Age-old theories, so easy, so specious, so all-explanatory, tugged at Benedict's heart: Splenetic, bilious, humoral imbalance, the heat drying up the moist, the desiccation of the body dross. No Christian doctor would have demurred, and, had he so spoken, Van den Enden would have approved. But Benedict could not subscribe to so silly a diagnosis, and what irked him most was that he could not in honesty provide a better. "There is so much," he thought, "that we do not know; but his pain is real and I am sorry." Would there ever come a time when pain could be conquered?

"If I cannot cure the cause," he mused, "which I do not know, I can treat the symptoms."

"I would suggest," Benedict said, "a slightly smaller daily intake of brandy."

[143]

"I felt sure you would. You Jews never drink. It is all very easy for you. Yet I am prepared to suffer through the deprivation if, as you stipulate, the intake be only slightly smaller."

"And two or three glasses of milk per day, either goat's or cow's, but preferably goat's."

"Milk? Doctor!"

"Milk."

"Milk is for babies."

"Milk might be rendered more potable if laced with a finger of brandy."

"In that case I shall certainly consider it."

"Pray do so, if you desire to live."

Van den Enden said, "When the angel of death brushes you with his wing, be it ever so gently, every man desires to live."*

During this diagnostic colloquy in the kitchen, Spinoza and Klaara were talking alone in the bare, almost monastic, workshop.

Spinoza had finished his labor for the day; the long summer twilight of the northern latitudes was beginning to descend. He lighted some candles, of which he had a quantity for his optical work, and brought her a chair, which she found hard and uncomfortable. But there was only one and it was the best he had in the workshop and it did not occur to him to offer her one from the kitchen.

---

* He lived for a long while, but in the end he was hanged. His demise will strike the modern reader as regrettable. Sensing a shift in the theological winds that began to blow over Holland, he emigrated to France where, by reason of his skill in the medical profession, he became Surgeon in Chief to King Louis XIV. Louis, one of whose titles was Most Christian Majesty, suffering an anal fistula which another doctor was fortunate enough to operate on and cure, underwent a drastic change in deportment and became inordinately devout. He found in Francis van den Enden a convenient scapegoat for his own libidinous past and sentenced him to be hanged "for erroneous religious beliefs." The execution was carried out in Paris on November 27, 1674.

He stood.

In the candlelight and the gathering dusk Klaara was exquisite, and her eyes shone like sapphires and her hair like gold, and she smiled.

The pull upon him was overpowering, for Spinoza was a very young man, with a very young man's physical inclinations; and Klaara was at no pains to deny them, though she cleverly denied him the full power of her eyes. For if he was acceptable, might there not be someone more acceptable still? And perhaps richer?

For some weeks Benedict physicked Spinoza and Van den Enden was often there and always brought his daughter. Spinoza's love grew, and Klaara did not thwart it.

It was then that Spinoza proposed marriage, in balanced periods and with many a disclaimer, but with deep and heartfelt intensity, mixing, as he could not help but do, his profound physical attraction toward the exquisite girl so close to him with a burning compulsion to be absolutely honest and straightforward with her and his ideals. The effort failed, but the effort was honest. Klaara said neither yea nor nay.

This was the method — he would have called it the "mode" — of his proposal.

"Dear Klaara," he said, and there was a frog in his throat. "I am aware that I have little to offer; I am aware that, in your eyes, you must view me as an anathematized Jew; I am equally aware that as a Jew I am perhaps abhorrent to you —"

"Not abhorrent, Benedict."

"— or at least, the least of the least, for you sprang from the loins of a Christian."

"Father was defrocked, you know, else I'd not be here. But I'm so glad I am." She smiled archly and lowered her eyes. "You are charming," she said.

Spinoza continued almost as if she had not spoken. Once a logical argument gripped his methodical mind he could brook no interruption, even from the girl to whom he proposed honorable marriage, even when she flirted, till the words were out, precisely articulated, as only he could have voiced them. This naturally disconcerted Klaara.

"Such as I am," he said, "I feel for you a most honorable desire to have you to wife; such as my name is, I long to bestow it upon you, to love you and cherish you all my life long, and, if God wills, or if there be no God but what the world calls God, namely, the universe and all that ever was or ever will be, we being modes of it and not ignoble, to have by you children, yours and mine, to love and adore and bring up to a good education and healthy appreciation of all you are and all I am."

To Klaara it was a peculiar proposal, and much of it she did not understand, though her father did when she told him about it later.

"He's a good man," said Francis van den Enden.

"He mixes me up."

"Do you love him?"

"I don't love anybody."

"There is no hurry to marry, at your age."

"But I feel —"

"Then marry. You could do worse than this Spinoza."

"I don't know what to do."

"And I cannot advise you, except to say you could do worse. He will make a name for himself in this world."

"I don't want a name and I don't want a philosopher."

"What do you want?"

She could not tell, but he half knew and more than half feared.

"You'd better go to bed, child, and have a good rest," and she did; but before she kissed him goodnight she said "There's Kerkering."

"Kerkering? Graf Ritter von Kerkering? That rich young German from Hamburg?"

"I don't know where he comes from."

"He comes from Hamburg."

"Is that bad?"

"No, dear. It's the man, not the province he comes from that counts."

"I like Spinoza too, but he mixes me up."

"Sleep tight, child."

"Good night, Father."

So it's Kerkering, thought Van den Enden. He shrugged his shoulders and smiled. "There is no accounting for women," he thought to himself and lay back on his bed and went to sleep.

In the middle of the night Francis van den Enden developed excruciating pain in the small of his back, and sought medical advice.

A young man in a student's raggedy garb knocked noisily at Dr. Benedict's door.

"I have come," he said, "to beseech your attendance upon my master —"

"Yes, son?"

"— my master, Affinius van den Enden."

"In what is he your master, young man?"

"In Latin, sir."

"And that is why you designate him 'Affinius' instead of our good Dutch 'Francis' "?

"Yes, Doctor: Amo, Amas, Amat," and the raggedy lad lapsed into first-year Latin.

Benedict chuckled.

"An excellent verb to conjugate, especially at your age. Without it, indeed, where would one be?"

Mistaking the reference, the student replied, "He is at home."

"Not at Spinoza's?"

"No, at home, sir, and in great pain."

"I'll come at once."

Here goes another fee down the drain, thought Benedict. But it was not in his nature to deny a patient, especially one who was in pain. He let himself be led by the lad to a small house in a fashionable part of town. "No, rather on the fringe of fashion," Benedict corrected in his mind. "It's a good address, but actually somewhat run-down."

At the door he gave the student a gold piece for his pains, which the student promptly tested with his teeth and found that his teeth would dent it, on which he grinned and said, "It can be hoped that my Latin master gets sick often and summons the same generous doctor."

"That is an unworthy thought," Benedict said severely.

In Van den Enden's bedroom he found the patient propped up on pillows, poor color in his face and a brandy on his night table. But Van den Enden did not look *in extremis.*

"I was summoned," Benedict said gravely, "by a most engaging student of yours. If they are all as intelligent and, hm-m, as competent, your name as a Latin master is made."

"Did he say *Pax huic domui?*" Van den Enden asked.

"If he had I'd not have known what he meant, so rusty, alas, is my college Latin."

"It means 'Peace to this house.' "

[148]

"I could wish no more."

"And your answer would have been, *Et omnibus habitantibus in ea*. I suppose you don't know what that means either."

"I'm afraid I don't," Benedict said, eyeing him clinically.

"It means, 'And to all those who dwell herein.'"

"Had I known the proper reply I'd have made it with a full heart."

"You're a good doctor," Van den Enden sighed, and in the sigh Benedict caught the note of self-pity. Was he trying to prepare the ground for weaseling out of the doctor's fee?

The answer came: "I am somewhat embarrassed financially for the moment," Van den Enden said. "Oh, it is only temporarily; a great opportunity appears opening up for me — it is not in this country," he added cryptically. "But I shall never forget your services, wherever I am."

Benedict had a notion that he would indeed forget, but he said, "My services are not based on gold, Mynheer van den Enden, but on the alleviation of pain, and so, if it lies in my power, shall they always be." Well, thought Benedict, it's half true anyhow. "Now, Mynheer, where do you hurt?"

"Here." Van den Enden rolled over in bed with an effort and pointed to the small of his back.

Benedict watched every motion. There was no hesitation in the hands, no tremor. That ruled out many serious diagnoses including the tremor caused by continual and heavy drinking. But the motion of the patient's legs was an obvious effort and seemed to exaggerate the pain in the back.

Van den Enden said, "I think it's my gall bladder."

Benedict let him diagnose himself, patiently, smiling.

Van den Enden asked, "Do you know what a gall bladder is?"

"I have seen some," Benedict answered.

[149]

"Ha! You rascal! Then you have attended autopsies?"

"Yes."

Van den Enden said, "We frown upon autopsies, even in Holland though of course they're legal. Unchristian. You Jews wouldn't worry about that."

"On the contrary, we Jews frown upon them even more than you Christians, and our laws strictly forbid them; but I'm not a very good Jew —"

"And I'm a defrocked Jesuit."

"— and I deem it better to study the body and cure it, if I can, than to worship it and let it die for lack of care. Yes, I have seen the human gall bladder, queer yellow thing, when a corpse was anatomized. The man was a criminal, but I doubt if that affected his gall bladder. In his case the cause of death was hanging."

Van den Enden shuddered ever so slightly. "You will never see mine anatomized."

"Of course not. You are not a criminal. Why are you so sure it's your gall bladder?"

"Because the pain is situated there."

Again his steady hands pointed to the small of his back.

Benedict took his temperature with the bulb that he inserted into his mouth. It was only a degree or so above normal.

He put his ear to his chest and listened to the heartbeat. It was a bit fast, but that could have been caused by anything — the excitement of a doctor's visit, the pride and joy of diagnosing his own ailment, fear that something mysterious might be wrong, anything, even the voices from the other room.

"Does the pain stay in one place?" Benedict asked.

"No, it does not. What a curious question. How did you know?"

"I didn't for sure. I only suspected." Benedict had run across strangely traveling pains lately in other patients. He had no explanation for them. They always went away and the patients never died.

"Only yesterday," Van den Enden said, "it was in my left shoulder."

"Was it? Did it shoot down your arm?"

"My dear Dr. Benedict, do not patronize me. We both know that symptom. It did not shoot down my arm and it did not constrict my chest and I did not feel as if I had indigestion. Ergo, it is not heart trouble. In fact, the pain then appeared in my right leg."

"Did you limp?"

"Like a cripple. I was walking up a flight of stairs. Then suddenly the pain left my right leg and settled in my left leg. The right leg felt just fine, but the left was just as painful as the right had been."

"Just as bad?"

"Just as bad, but reversed."

Like a mirror image, Benedict thought, and was reminded of Spinoza's optics.

"Did the pain stay?"

"No, now it's in my gall bladder."

Benedict sighed and looked thoughtfully at his patient, who appeared genuinely frightened. Will the time ever come, the doctor was wondering, when disease will pose no mystery? How convenient it would be to have a medicine chest full of little bottles, each neatly labeled, a separate one for every single ailment under the sun! Of course there would be no doctors; anyone could buy the medicines at the nearest apothecary and physic himself. Perhaps that would not be so bad. Other artisans had had their day and disappeared from the face of the earth.

Where were the fletchers? — those marvelous pluckers of goose quills so important for arrows in war, when arrows were shot from bows. Gone. Gone since the invention of gunpowder three centuries before, and the very name was forgotten.

He lowered his gaze from the vision of the future and smiled at its sheer impossibility. There would be new diseases when the old ones were conquered, just as these mysterious traveling pains were new.

Van den Enden turned his head and saw the smile. Benedict's eyes happened to be resting on the night table where the brandy was.

"What are you laughing at?" Van den Enden demanded unpleasantly. "Do you find something amusing in my pain?"

Benedict shook his head no.

"Perhaps you will prescribe goat's milk or some other fraud out of your Jewish bag of tricks."

All patients in pain were likely to be abusive, Benedict knew, and did not take offense.

"Brandy is all that helps," Van den Enden said defensively.

The doctor reached over and handed him the glass.

"I do not counterprescribe it in this case," he said quietly. Van den Enden took a generous gulp, somewhat appeased, and continued, "I know of nothing in Galen or Bombastus von Hohenheim to account for the peregrination of these pains. And if Galen and Bombast don't know, who does?"

"Who indeed, Mynheer van den Enden? Take another sip of brandy."

"Do you mean that?" He looked at him suspiciously.

Benedict nodded, and Van den Enden took a cautious swallow.

"You knew I would anyhow as soon as you were gone, you cabalistic rascal." His color was better now and he moved his feet with considerably less effort than before. "I did ill to call you a Jew, Doctor; my conscience smites me."

"Defrock your conscience also, Mynheer. That's what I am. Does your gall bladder still hurt?"

"Yes, but not so much."

"You could have physicked yourself equally well, you know — brandy, poppy, mandragora . . ."

"Oh yes, I have all the common pain relievers, but what I really wanted —"

"Yes, Mynheer van den Enden?"

"I confess that I was frightened; it is bad to be frightened alone. What I really wanted was the company and the opinion of the most famous physician in Amsterdam."

Benedict accepted the compliment as he had the abuse, gravely and noncommittally. It was not unusual for a frightened patient to be cheered by the mere presence of a doctor, particularly when the patient was another doctor. Doctors always made the worst patients. They knew too much and their imaginations ran away with them.

Benedict said, "I can tell my distinguished colleague that I have seen many cases of these flitting aches and pains in the last few months. They portend nothing serious, distressing as they are, and in time they always go away. For them one pain reliever is as good as another. Ah, Mynheer van den Enden, would God there were no pain in the world!"

No longer frightened, Van den Enden grew sleepy. Laughter and voices came from the other room and annoyed him.

"Klaara!" he shouted. "I'd be greatly obliged if you and the Count made a little less noise. I am trying to get some rest."

To Benedict he said in a low, proud voice, "My little Klaartje is with her betrothed, the Graf Ritter von Kerkering, from

Hamburg. The Count-Knight has large estates and important mercantile interests."

"I congratulate you, sir," Benedict said.

Klaara tapped at the door and stuck in her golden head. "I'm so sorry, Father."

Behind her loomed a handsome blond animal straight out of the Rhineland. He wore his own hair, the French fashion of the periwig not yet having penetrated into Germany, and his golden curls and hard blue eyes were curiously like Klaara's.

Klaara said, "I beg your pardon, Doctor. I did not know you were here."

"Striking couple, aren't they?" whispered Van den Enden fondly.

"Indeed they are, Mynheer," Benedict whispered in return.

"Now you two," Van den Enden said aloud in a caressing voice, "be off with you."

"I think I shall be going also," Benedict said.

In the other room the Count-Knight said to Klaara, "Who was the physician attending your father?"

"Oh, one of Spinoza's friends. His Dutch name is Benedict, but everyone knows his real name is Baruch, just like Spinoza's."

"I see," said the German. "Another Jew."

"Father says Dr. Benedict is the best physician in Amsterdam," Klaara said loyally. "At any rate, he's the most expensive."

"They always are," said the German.

Then they forgot Spinoza and Dr. Benedict-Baruch and talked about something very much more important — themselves.

D<small>R.</small> Benedict, the most sought-after physician of Amsterdam, had never been sick a day in his life. Now, to his chagrin and astonishment, he awoke after a troubled sleep with a pain in his chest, as if ropes were tightening around it, constricting his breathing.

"Did I eat something that disagreed with me?" he wondered.

And his left arm. A hot pain shot down it from shoulder to fingertips.

"Did I sleep on my arm and impede the circulation?" It hurt, it tingled, and yet it was curiously numb.

He came wide awake and knew what had happened.

"Azrael, Azrael," he murmured to the presence in the room, "Why me, O Angel of Death? Why so soon? There are sick people who need me, people in pain, *I have so much to do!*"

Then he remembered a legend.

King Solomon was sitting on his throne, speaking with a friend, when Azrael, the Angel of Death, appeared in visible form. The friend said, quaking with fear, "He seems to want me, so balefully does he glare at me! Call the wind, O King, for the whole world obeys thee, and bid the wind carry me hence into India that I may outwit him!" King Solomon very kindly obliged, and instantly the wind came and carried his frightened friend out of the throne room and set him down in India.

On which the Angel of Death said to Solomon, "Imagine my astonishment when I saw this man here in thy presence. For I was commanded to take his soul in India, and I found him here in Palestine." After which Azrael disappeared and went to India, where he accomplished his mission.

"No man knoweth the hour of his death," Benedict murmured. "I suppose it always comes as a surprise."

But it occurred to him that he was by no means dead yet, and the presence in his room was not the dread angel but merely the solicitous form of his apprentice who was bending over him with a goblet of liquid in his hand.

"I had some difficulty arousing you, Master," the apprentice said in a shaking voice.

"So you should have had under the circumstances," Benedict said; and, nodding to the goblet, "What is that?"

"Foxglove, Master."

Benedict smiled approvingly. "I have trained you up well. Give it to me." He drained it at a gulp, and soon, almost too soon, the pain vanished from his arm and he breathed without effort. He slept deeply all night.

Next morning a curious phenomenon supervened. To Benedict's eyes everything took on a bluish tinge. The face of the apprentice looked blue, blue as the fruit of the beach plum ripening in the wastelands of the dikes and sand dunes. Or maybe blue as an amethyst. Benedict felt a little light-headed. He remembered that some silly doctors still recommended the

[156]

wearing of amethysts to ward off drunkenness. Probably Van den Enden would do just that. He chuckled.

"You made it too strong," he said to the apprentice. "Do you want to kill me."

"God forbid, Master!"

Benedict drank some of the draught. "Reduce the strength by half," he ordered, "or you will have no patients of your own when you come to set up practice without me."

Thereafter the doctor mended, and whenever the apprentice saw him dozing peacefully he would leave him for a short while, answering calls.

But the thought of the heart attack was much in Benedict's mind. Never to be certain that he would see the next sunrise; always to observe the restriction of activity that his symptoms demanded: these considerations depressed him. Never to skate again over the frozen canals, never to link his arm again with his son's, never to smoke his pipe as he looked up at the glorious stars, never knowing how much time remained to him to teach his son! That was the hardest thought of all. The first warning had come; Azrael had brushed him with the grandeur of his wing; how many more warnings would be vouchsafed him before the final summons came? There were seldom many.

Had he been one of his own patients he would have prescribed a bland diet, little or no exercise, and he would have hurled his pipe into a canal.

But he was not his own patient. Generations of Dutch stubbornness coursed in his veins; and he remembered how recently he had thought, Doctors make the worst patients. "Even to themselves," he now realized. For he would *not* give up his pipe and, save for the daily draught of foxglove, he would not alter his way of life. Above all he would not tell Baruch about his little ailment. Baruch was about to come home from the University of Leyden with his doctorate. "I *will* live to see that," Benedict determined, "and that is a very great deal."

As he mended, his joyful apprentice was able to tell him, "There have been many calls, Master. I said you were out of town."

"You did well. Did they call again? It is amazing how often patients get well without me."

"A few. I physicked them."

"Any fatalities?"

"I had no fatalities. Indeed, I had several cures — on pink sugar water and just enough gall to make it nasty to the taste and hence more efficacious, as they thought. Their ailments were largely imaginary. They were mostly rich widows."

Benedict nodded approval. "When I was young and handsome like you they would chatter at me, too, by the hour, and I would prescribe the same. And the fees?"

"Princely. I have them all here in a purse, all saved for you, not a penny missing. It is something to be the apprentice of Dr. Jan van Benedict."

"Take them for yourself, my boy. You have earned them just listening to the creatures."

Nothing loath, the apprentice took them.

"There was one patient I dared not physic."

"Who?"

"Spinoza."

"He has summoned me?"

"Several times."

"Why did you not tend him? He needs a doctor far more than the widows."

The apprentice did not answer directly; he made excuses; he

said he did not wish to leave his master so long; he said Spinoza lived far away on the other side of town.

"Come, come," Benedict said sternly. "It's not so far as all that."

"I was not sure you would get a fee."

"Then I have taught you badly. And I do not believe you."

"Master, the real reason is that I was fearful for your good name. Spinoza is avoided by everyone. I did indeed go across town and I enquired among his neighbors. They say he has become more and more eccentric. He shuts himself up for days at a time. Letters are delivered to his door, but he will not open the door to receive them. When he does go out he buys himself a bit of bread and hurries home and shuts the door again. He speaks to no one, not even when, occasionally, someone greets him on the street. His appearance is said to be that of a madman, unkempt, unshaven, gaunt as a skeleton, wild-eyed. And he keeps muttering to himself. They say he mumbles 'Klaara, Klaara, Klaara,' like a dirge."

"Poor man." Benedict sighed. "Of course he knows by now. I shall go to him at once."

The apprentice protested.

Benedict said vehemently, "And get me my pipe!"

Repeated knocking at Spinoza's door brought no response. Noting that the door was ajar Benedict pushed it open and, stepping over an accumulation of letters that had been thrust under it, penetrated into Spinoza's workshop. It was dusty; it had never been dusty before; the curtains were drawn.

There in the gloom sat Spinoza huddled in a chair, his head bowed, his hands resting limp upon his thighs and a half-munched loaf of bread on the table beside him. He held some-

thing white in his hand. Benedict opened the curtains and let in
the light. The white thing was a handkerchief, stained with
blood.

Spinoza raised his head languidly and looked at the doctor
with sunken lackluster eyes.

"Dr. Benedict!" he said. "It was good of you to come."
Spinoza's innate courtesy caused him to make a motion as if to
rise, but Benedict laid a hand on his shoulder and said, "Stay
where you are, my friend."

Reports of Spinoza's appearance had not been exaggerated.
There was a week's growth of beard on his sunken cheeks and he
was ghastly thin. He seemed incapable of the slightest exertion.

Benedict pointed to one of the bottles in the medicine chest,
which the apprentice had opened. The apprentice raised his
eyebrows in disbelief. The doctor poured a dram into a small
glass and held it to Spinoza's lips. "Drink this," he said, and
Spinoza obeyed like a child. Like a child? Perhaps, thought
Benedict, more like a man who, had it been hemlock, would not
have cared. "When they lose the will to live," thought Benedict,
"alas." It was a fiery restorative composed of nightshade in a
decoction of brandy and aloes. In criminal hands it had been
used to murder, and so deserved the name "deadly nightshade."
In compassionate hands it could be used to cure.

Benedict then gave a staccato series of orders to the apprentice. "Go to the kitchen and make a fire and put a pot on to boil.
Go to the market and buy some clams, some lobster tails and a
gutted fish ready to stew and a fowl cut up in pieces. Make
haste."

Into Spinoza's cheeks had crept a bit of color and his eyes lit
up briefly with a trace of amusement.

"Not a particularly kosher stew, Dr. Benedict."

"We can talk about the dietary laws some other time," Benedict said.

Spinoza yawned lengthily. The doctor smiled. The years rolled away and he remembered how he and his wife had watched for just such a yawn when Baruch was a tiny baby. For if he yawned, then whatever childhood ailment had troubled him was past, the fever would go down and the boy would be well the next day.

Spinoza was dozing when the apprentice returned. They picked him up, chair and all, and set him down beside the roaring fire in the kitchen, while the fish stew bubbled and filled the empty house with a delightful enticing aroma. When it was done Benedict spoon-fed him.

Wide awake and stronger now, Spinoza said, "I can do it myself, Doctor."

"I hate to leave you alone all night," Benedict said doubtfully.

"I am always alone," Spinoza said. "I shall be quite all right."

As they left they heard him murmuring, as if to himself, "And yet one is never alone, since all that ever was or ever will be is one with one, and is God."

"Is he in a delirium?" the apprentice asked in a whisper.

Benedict said, "I don't think so. He's probably just philosophizing. It's a good sign."

The apprentice scratched his head and shook it simultaneously, totally bewildered.

Benedict said, "I've always felt the same way about Spinoza."

They saw him again next day. To their surprise smoke was rising from Spinoza's chimney. The patient was apparently up and around.

In answer to Benedict's knock the door swung open and there

stood the raggedy student who had carried the summons from Van den Enden.

"What are you doing here?" Benedict asked.

"I'm taking care of Mynheer Spinoza," the lad said unhappily.

"Where is Mynheer van den Enden?"

"Gone to France," the student said with a grimace. "That son of Satan, that devil defrocked, that wicked, selfish, miserly . . ." and he launched into a string of abusive epithets that would have done justice to a bargeman.

Benedict wanted to smile, but he put on a truly menacing face. "Cleanse your foul mouth or I'll wash it out with a medicine that will wither your tongue like a prune and you'll never be able to speak again!"

There were witches in the world; Van den Enden had told the boy so, and every year a dozen or so were burned in Germany for the glory of God, the discomfiture of the Devil and the edification and amusement of the Germans. The lad took a terrified step backwards. "Oh no, Dr. Benedict, wonderful, kind, wise, generous Dr. Benedict, do not do that!"

"If you behave yourself perhaps I shall reconsider," Benedict said. "How are you called?"

"Benjamin, Mynheer."

"Benjamin what?"

"Just Benjamin, sir."

"What does your father call you?"

The student blushed red as a beet. "I never knew my father. He died before I was born, or so my mother said."

"And where is your mother?"

"I — I don't know. That miserly son-of — I mean my late master Affinius van den Enden, said she ran away with a shoemaker. Then he took me in, to do work around the house and said he would teach me Latin so I would become a fine scholar like himself and make money. But when he went to France he left me without a penny, to wander up and down the canals and eat what garbage the bargemen threw out. Then I remembered you and I went to your house, but there was no one there."

While I was sick, thought Benedict. Poor lad.

"And then I remembered that you were Spinoza's friend, and this morning I came to his house. The door was open. I didn't break in, I swear I didn't. You will not wither my tongue like a prune?"

"No, since it speaks the truth, Benjamin. Now I would see Mynheer Spinoza."

But Spinoza was standing behind him, smiling. He still looked far from well, but he no longer looked as if he wanted to die. "You have learned more about this boy than I did, Dr. Benedict. I didn't even know his name. I found him in the kitchen scooping up the remains of the fish stew. I hope you didn't put anything magic in it, like that amazing restorative of yours."

"Magic!" thought Benjamin, shuddering inwardly. "Maybe he *is* a witch. I'd better be careful."

"I put nothing in the stew except everything forbidden by the dietary laws," Benedict said with a chuckle.

They went into the kitchen. An empty pot stood on the hob by the dying fire. Benjamin hung his head. Spinoza patted him on the shoulder and said, "I am hungry too; go to the market and buy some bread and cheese." He gave him a small coin.

"And meat and a good fat duck and a flask of wine," said Benedict, "for I am hungry too," and gave him a larger coin. "And bear in mind, young man, that I expect you to return with the exact amount of change, for I will know exactly what everything costs."

"I am sure you will, sir," Benjamin said, and scurried off, his tattered students' garb flying behind him like a distress signal, his wooden shoes clattering over the cobbles.

"Perhaps I shall keep him by me," Spinoza mused. "If Van den Enden didn't spoil him nothing can."

Benedict was surprised that Spinoza could bring himself to pronounce Van den Enden's name. What amazing recuperative power the man must have! Whence did it spring? Not surely from so frail and emaciated a body.

Spinoza rubbed his stubble beard. "I have not been quite myself since Klaara left," he said calmly, "but I feel better now." Benedict noted that he could not bring himself to say "married."

It was not beneath the dignity of a doctor to pull teeth, cut hair or give a patient a shave, and Benedict said, "I scarcely knew you under that beard; you're getting to look positively patriarchal." The assistant fairly leapt for the honor. "May I, Dr. Benedict?" Benedict nodded.

He threw a sheet around Spinoza's shoulders and lathered his face, holding the bowl with the notched rim under his chin, his fingers gentle as a woman's; and he wielded the wicked-looking razor with the skill of a master surgeon. Benedict looked on with a critical eye and had reason to be content with his apprentice. His work would live on, in Baruch, in this aspiring young man, perhaps in the lives and the work of all those he had tried to help in his long professional life. "I am getting dismal in my thoughts," he reproached himself. "This will never do." He stuffed his pipe and puffed it contentedly and made plans for Baruch's homecoming, while the assistant, having smoothed Spinoza's chin to the texture of a baby's, set about with a pair of scissors to trim Spinoza's hair, till he looked quite the man of fashion. "Now, Mynheer Spinoza, all the girls will turn their heads when you pass them on the street," he cried, exultant over his own handiwork.

Benedict shot him a warning glance.

But Spinoza merely said wryly, "You may rest assured that I will certainly pass them."

Benjamin returned with the food and set about cooking it as if he were used to such chores, but first he gave into Benedict's hand the exact amount of change. "I can tell you the cost of every item —" he began.

"Thank you, Benjamin. That won't be necessary."

Then he spread places for them at two small tables, one for Spinoza and Benedict, one for himself and the apprentice. He was neat and he worked quietly. Spinoza thought, "He'd be useful to have around." Spinoza did not have many students nowadays and he could not afford a servant. Perhaps he would even get him a pair of leather shoes — when he sold some more spectacles. Wooden shoes were worn only by country people and, in the towns, by the lower classes. Benedict could not read his thoughts, but there was animation in his face, as if interest in life had returned.

While they dined, Spinoza reverted to the dietary laws. "I followed them of course," he said, "before it was seen fit to cast me out of Jewry, but I never could square them with reason."

"I never followed them at all," Benedict said. "I never could square them with what I knew of nutrition."

Spinoza said, "The prohibition against pork seemed especially unreasonable."

Benedict answered, "As I remember, the Talmud lists a host of dispensations, even to traveling on the Sabbath and eating on

Yom Kippur if there is a greater obligation. I remember several."

But Spinoza was not listening. His mathematical mind was intent on proving a thesis and would not be drawn aside. "I know of course the classic arguments, the unsanitary conditions, the rapidity with which meat spoiled in the hot climate of Palestine where there was no ice at any time of the year. But would not good scaly finny fish spoil just as rapidly? But fish, if properly equipped with fins and scales, are kosher, and swine are not." He sipped his wine with relish, and asked the doctor, "Have you ever read the New Testament of the Christians?"

It was a rhetorical question; he did not expect an answer and Benedict gave him none.

"In it there is the parable of the Prodigal Son. It concerns a young man who went away from his father's house and spent his substance in riotous living while his brother remained at home and did all the work. Eventually this Prodigal was penniless and hungry, and he went home again. His father, the Christian Testament relates, saw him when he was yet afar off, and ran, and fell on his neck and kissed him, and bade servants bring the best robe and put it on him, and placed a ring on his hand and shoes on his feet, and killed a fatted calf; he made a great feast for him and honored him at a gathering of all the neighbors. That always struck me as grossly unfair to the faithful hard-working son who had stayed behind, and who in the parable is represented as being so furious that he would not even go into the house.

"The Christians say that this story emphasizes a cardinal point in their doctrine, namely, that one sheep which is lost and found again is worth a whole flock of sheep who do not get lost. I had always dismissed the parable as one of those hyperbolic paradoxes so frequent in Christian theology till I asked myself,

[166]

Where was this far country? How far was it? The Prodigal had returned on foot, very rapidly, practically between meals. What was the Prodigal doing there, besides squandering his substance in riotous living with harlots?

"And then I found the answer, and it bears directly on the dietary laws. When the Prodigal Son was penniless and hungry he obtained employment as a swineherd. He tended pigs. If there were pigs they served some useful purpose. If there were great herds of pigs that useful purpose was to breed them in quantity for food. If they were bred in quantity for food they were unquestionably sacrificed to some local god, since the best food always is, witness our Paschal lamb. It follows as a mathematical certainty that the pig, being a sacred animal to some god not very far from Palestine, became an abomination to the Jew.

"I submit that my thesis is demonstrated."

Benedict thought, "No wonder they threw you out," but aloud he said, "I am not a philosopher, but I can find no fault with your reasoning — if reason is all there is."

"Isn't it, Dr. Benedict? Isn't reason all there is?"

"God knows."

But it was heartening to see Spinoza so well.

Indeed he grew better daily, but the cough still remained. He put on little flesh and often Benedict would see red stains on his handkerchief. Spinoza seemed not to care; he had thrown himself with frenetic energy into his optical work and into the formulation of his philosophy. He kept long hours, he answered his correspondence, he filled countless orders for spectacles, and, always sparing of money, he found himself in easier circumstances.

Into his letters began to creep echoes of his philosophy. They were passed around among the learned; they shocked everyone by their complete break with all the comfortable traditions but they were so utterly honest and fearless that they demanded respect. One worthy Catholic convert tried to save his soul. "The Jews won't have you, Benedict; they've proven that. But we Christians will welcome you with open arms if you come home to the true fold of Mother Church. Have you ever read the parable of the Prodigal Son?"

The memory of Klaara no longer rankled, but Amsterdam was full of her ghost and the terrible hurt she had inflicted upon him. He sold his modest house at a modest profit and removed to Rijnsburg, three miles from Leyden, "so as to be nearer the scholarly atmosphere of the University," he tried to convince himself, and laughed at his own self-deception. That was only part of it.

One of Spinoza's most respected scientific colleagues was Christiaan Huygens, a fellow mathematician, astronomer, and a physicist. He had sent Spinoza the optical prescription for a telescopic eyepiece that he had invented. Spinoza made the lenses, mounted them and tried the eyepiece on his own telescope.

The heavens leapt down to meet him, closer and more distinct than he had ever beheld them. Clear, near and unutterably beautiful, the pull of the entire universe gripped him, called him to be one with all that was. He gazed for hours, infused with a rapture almost like a revelation. There, shining in glory, was white Saturn with his rings and the satellite, both of which Huygens had discovered. There was the constellation of Orion with the faint nebulosity clearly aglow and the multiple star that made it shine. He tore himself from the majestic celestial vision only when dawn paled the stars.

No greater contrast could be imagined than the contrast between Benedict Spinoza and Christiaan Huygens. Spinoza was known to everyone as an outcast, a philosopher rejected by Jews and Christians alike. Ominous winds from abroad were beginning to blow over Holland. Both sides now wanted to reclaim him. Come back, come back, Baruch, said the Jews. Said the Christians, Benedict, Benedict, the one true Church will welcome you; say but the word.

Both sides had practical self-interest at heart, for the Jews thought, This man will cause us trouble with the Dutch authorities, who have hitherto been so tolerant. Soon we ourselves may cease to be tolerated, since one of our number has philosophized too much and raised embarrassing questions that can ruin the welcome the Dutch so graciously give us. The Christians thought, If we can snare this unquestionably gifted man we can use him as a makeweight against the Lutheran heresy that now is rearing its hideous head over the whole of Northern Europe.

In physical appearance, too, Spinoza and Huygens were at total variance: Spinoza emaciated, vividly intense, dark of complexion and burning with interior fires; Huygens portly, fair of skin and wearing like an invisible mantle the cloak of self-assurance to which he had been born: scion of a noble family, high in diplomatic circles, widely traveled, possessed of an independent fortune and a princely mansion in The Hague.

In Leyden the two met.

"I had expected a much older man," Spinoza thought. "This man is so famous."

Huygens thought, "So this is the free-thinking, trouble-making, tradition-shattering philosopher that everyone is talking about," and was delighted to extend his hand in greeting; for Huygens was a free-thinker, too.

They were about of an age, though Huygens looked much younger.

The occasion was an important one. Christiaan Huygens had just invented the first pendulum clock. It was the outgrowth of a moment of reverie that Galileo Galilei, another astronomer, had experienced a few years before, during a Mass in the cathedral of Pisa. Galileo was idly watching a swinging lamp, and he observed that no matter how wide or how narrowly the lamp swung, its oscillations were invariably accomplished in equal times; he knew because he timed them with his pulse.

Huygens, with his fertile mind and mathematical bent, reading about the incident, thought, "This can be applied to a horologium," and forthwith he did so.

The occasion was his presentation of a superbly accurate pendulum clock to the Dutch States General, who accepted it with acclamation and honored its inventor and bethought themselves how they could put it to commercial use. No one understood better than the Dutch that time was money.

After the presentation of the clock these two dissimilar mathematicians met face to face. Their cordial talk would have been incomprehensible to the common run of men. It dealt with the theory of evolutes; it dealt with the shape of the earth, which they deemed probably oblate; it touched on the properties of the catenary curve such as cables which hold up bridges cannot help but assume. Neither man had ever met anyone like the other. Each felt at ease, talking in a quick specialized vocabulary that the other instantly comprehended, and they warmed to each other.

Huygens said, "Do you gamble?"

Spinoza said, "No. Why do you ask?"

"I don't either," Huygens said, "but many do."

"I know."

"At dice."

"I think the game dates from the Romans."

"One can learn much from dice."

Huygens went on to describe how he had taken a pair of dice and thrown them several hundred times in the privacy of his study, noting and marking down the number of dots that came up at each throw. From that experiment he had written and published a treatise *De ratiociniis in ludo aleae*. "It is the first formal treatise on the theory of probabilities," Huygens said.

The term probabilities was technical, new in mathematics. It was destined to inspire far-reaching research in a generation of mathematicians yet unborn. Spinoza had not heard it before but he was quick to sense its incalculable possibilities, not only in mathematics but in philosophy.

Spinoza said, "Do you think, Mynheer, that we are all that ever was or ever will be?"

"We cannot be both things at one and the same time," Huygens said thoughtfully. "Time moves. My clock proves it. One cannot be what was, what is and what is to be, simultaneously, or my clock is a cheat and a fraud. No, Mynheer Spinoza. Time moves inexorably forward."

"Saint Augustine would differ with you. If I remember my reading of the Christian theology, the good saint declared that time is ever one in the mind of God, past, present and future simultaneously."

"I have read the passage," Huygens said with a shrug. "But Augustine is not my notion of a very good timekeeper. I wish I could have given him my pendulum clock. I haven't much use for these mystics, Mynheer Spinoza. They're a little too much like you."

"No, sir; I am not a mystic. I am just an anathematized Jew, still seeking what is reasonable and real."

Huygens said with a comfortable chuckle, "I have observed one thing, Mynheer; they all now seem to want you on their side."

Spinoza asked, "Do you think, Mynheer, that we earthly humans are the only creatures possessed of the power to reason?"

It was as if Spinoza had touched a spark to tinder.

Huygens instantly launched into an extraordinary monologue.

"By no means!" he said vehemently. "I am convinced, indeed I have just written a treatise on the subject, we are not alone. There exist sentient inhabitants on the other planets. How absurd, how self-coddling, how utterly paltry to suppose that we are the only ones! No, Mynheer, there are others. Some are mere worms; some are mere vegetables; some are nothing but lichens. Some are angelic, as far superior to us as we are superior to ants and apes and anthropophagi. I do not expect to be praised by the orthodox. Pontius Pilate, who wrote the legend at the head of the Cross, said *Quod scripsi, scripsi,* I have written what I have written. And so have I. You will read it in God's good time. By God!" he ejaculated, "you will read it in God's good time!"

Spinoza smiled wryly. "Beware lest you suffer my fate, Mynheer."

Huygens became thoughtful. "I too have detected a subtle change in our liberal Dutch atmosphere. There is a whiff of fear in the air. We are not quite so free to speculate as we were. Perhaps I shall delay publication of my little treatise."*

They never lost track of each other, but they never saw each other again. Their intercourse was limited to the exchange of frequent letters. Their mutual esteem continued unabated. Huygens went back to his estate at The Hague where, time conscious as always, he invented the spiral watch spring and checked it against his pendulum clock, delighted with the new accuracy now possible in watches, making meticulous notes, as if each tick of eternity were important to set down on paper.

Spinoza ground and polished his lenses, bloodied into his handkerchief, and wrote in a journal that he kept, "I have a new friend, Mynheer Christiaan Huygens, a fellow mathematician; I have an old friend, a fellow Jew, a doctor Benedict, who wishes me to live and physics me, taking spectacles for his fee. I experience an unwonted desire to live, to continue to exist, whereas formerly I wanted to die. I have elaborated a philosophy."

His journal was factual. It was written without thought of who might read it. It was the private outpouring of a soul secure in its own integrity. When he set it down on paper it became crisply and personally his own.

This is the philosophy of Benedict Spinoza as he wrote it himself, to himself, a mathematician:

"I synthesize the whole of reality, bridging the chasm between the natural and the supernatural, the human and the divine. There is nothing capricious. Everything happens in an orderly manner according to mathematical law. There has always existed an eternal, self-subsisting absolute Being.

---

* It was not published for many years. Not until 1698, three years after Huygens' death, did it appear in printed form as *Cosmotheoros*.

"What is the relation between this absolute Being and the little world of Man? It is believed by the commonalty that God is an omnipotent entity who created something out of nothing, which is a mathematical absurdity; that He stands aside for the most part, but occasionally interferes in miraculous ways; that He stops the sun in its course and sets back the shadow on the sundial, and turns poor weak women into pillars of salt. I deem such vagaries incompatible with the dignity of God. I posit a world of reality. There is Nature; there is God; but there is no room for the supernatural. I do not degrade God. I elevate Nature to the stature of God.

"God and Nature thus become identical: God is the Universe, the Universe is God. The one cannot exist without the other, nor ever could, nor ever did; and thus the body of God is the Universe and the Universe is the body of God; and I, Baruch Spinoza, am one with all that ever was or ever will be, a bit of God and a bit of the body of God, one with Him and the glorious Universe of stars."

This was the Pantheism of Spinoza.

Everyone castigated him because of it, for pantheism was an abomination to every respectable religion under the sun: to Jews, to Protestants of all sects, Lutherans, Anglicans, Puritans in New England and Hollanders in New Amsterdam; to Nestorians in the wild forgotten isolation of Cathay; to Zoroastrians who kept alight the perpetual fire on their altars in India; to turbaned Turks who spread their gorgeous prayer rugs and faced toward Mecca to pray — not one, no not one would have condoned the forbidden pantheism of Spinoza.

☙☙☙☙☙☙☙☙☙☙☙☙

C H A P T E R 5

☙☙☙☙☙☙☙☙☙☙☙☙

BENEDICT allowed no hint of the threat to his health to creep into his letters to his son, and yet their tenor had subtly changed.

At the University, Baruch sensed the change: there seemed in them a certain weariness, an impatience for his University days to be over and done with. "Almost," thought Baruch, "as if my graduation were a sort of end instead of just the beginning of a doctor's career."

For Benedict, though he tried, could not quite disguise his yearning for his son to return.

Baruch was equally impatient. The day the University Chancellor had handed him the scroll of his doctorate, which qualified him to practice the craft of a full-fledged physician, had been the proudest moment of his life. Congratulating him with a gracious smile, the Chancellor had said, "Your father, Dr. Jan van Benedict, is a worthy example of the height to which Jews can aspire in the free air of Holland. You will honor him and our craft, yourself and your race, if you follow in his footsteps." With these words Baruch became Dr. Benedict van Benedict.

[175]

In actual fact, though he was first in his class, he had followed
in the footsteps of all the graduating Christians, even those who
had just squeaked by. But he was first among the Jews, none of
whom felt particularly discriminated against; they had been
born and grown up in a special status, which they accepted as
normal, without bitterness; they were respected and sought for
their skill, but they were socially apart; they could no more stand
in line with the Christians during the ceremony than they could
vote in the States General. But the Chancellor himself was not
without disabilities, which he too considered normal: he could
not wear a sword, the distinguishing mark of a gentleman, being
only a physician and craftsman himself.

The day Baruch came home from the University was an
exciting one for Dr. Benedict. He canceled all his calls. He was
up at dawn and spent a good deal of time peeking furtively out
of the shutters, "like an old woman," he growled at himself,
"wondering what the neighbors will be up to next." He knew
that his pulse was fast; he could hear it in his ears. He was
breathing more rapidly than usual, and he fancied he felt a
tightening in his chest. "Just imagination," he muttered. "It is
normal to be a bit excited on a happy occasion like this."

He hoped Baruch would wear his doctor's gown. What an
impressive picture they would make: the two Doctors Benedict
sallying forth in their long physicians' gowns, their tall physicians' hats, their apprentices following in their wake with the
tools of their trade. He even permitted himself a bit of fantasy:
they would be calling on a particularly difficult case; for the
benefit of the patient he would pretend to defer to his son's
opinion; he would say, in his gravest professional voice, "It
would be best to be guided by the advice of Dr. Benedict van

Benedict. Dr. Benedict van Benedict has just completed a long and intensive course of research at the University, where he specialized in precisely the very esoteric ailment from which you suffer." Later they would chuckle and he would tell Baruch, "Everyone feels very important when a specialist is called in for consultation, especially when it's esoteric, which sounds expensive. Did you notice that she paid the double fee without batting an eye?"

The fantasy was pleasant. But it was only a fantasy. The reality was the joyous homecoming of Baruch, and that in itself was pleasure enough for one day and to spare.

But he did not like the effect the excitement was having upon him, and he took a second draught of the foxglove. "I got up early," he thought, excusing himself. "This is really tomorrow's draught." Within a few minutes he felt calmer. He filled his pipe and puffed it contentedly, waiting.

Then, through the shutters, he descried the tall figure of his son approaching the house. He was wearing his ordinary dress. Benedict did not know it, but Baruch had actually been anxious to make a dramatic appearance in his brand-new doctor's garb, but at the last minute a feeling of delicacy restrained him: his father might think he was showing off.

Behind his son, loaded with bags, boxes and bundles, followed a husky youth who might be an apprentice — Baruch's doctorate entitled him to one — or might be a servant. Baruch's allowance had always been ample to pay for a servant all during his University career.

Not wishing to be found peeking out of the shutters, Benedict retired to his study and pretended to busy himself among some medical books, half expecting Baruch to come bounding into the house as he always had as a boy.

[177]

But the new doctor knocked decorously; Benedict's apprentice admitted him before he had a chance to get to the door. But there the formality ended.

Father and son threw their arms around each other and kissed on the mouth (as Christians never did) muttering welcome and congratulations all in a breath. Benedict's eyes were moist with joy. "Smoke must have got into my eye," he muttered. But Baruch had no pipe and his eyes were also moist. "Must have got into mine too, Father. Must be contagious. We must find an antidote." Then they burst out laughing from sheer outflowing of happiness, while the youth with Baruch's luggage looked on in astonishment.

"Your apprentice?" Benedict asked, indicating the stranger.

"In clog boots? Father!"

Benedict had been so intent on the face of his son that he had not noticed the wooden-soled footgear worn by Baruch's porter, which was all he was, a servant.

Shortly Baruch's dunnage was all deposited upstairs in his old room. All but one piece, something in a mahogany box that Baruch held under his arm and would not let be touched.

"He's only a street porter, Father. But he's greatly in need, strong, and anxious to please. He says he's poor as a church mouse. I told him that in that case Christian mice must be very poor indeed, and it's been a joke between us ever since he attached himself to me in Leyden."

"Will you keep him on? There's plenty of room for him here."

Baruch frowned slightly. "I'm afraid he wouldn't be comfortable here, Father. Anyhow, he says he can make more money on the streets of Leyden." Baruch seemed oddly anxious to change the subject. "Now let me show you something that Anton van Leeuwenhoek made. It's for you."

"From him? I don't even know him."

"No. From me."

Baruch opened the mahogany box and Benedict found himself looking down at a shiny brass instrument cradled on a cushion of blue velvet. It was the most superb example of a microscope he had ever seen. Indeed, he had seen only one before in his life, and deemed it far too costly for any use he might have for it. This was made by the master himself, van Leeuwenhoek.

"Baruch, Baruch, you will beggar yourself."

But Baruch just smiled, and said, "I doubt it. And if I do I can always start again, thanks to our craft and thanks to you, who made *this* possible." He unrolled the vellum scroll of his doctorate. "Unless you've cured all the sick people from here to America, as long as I have this I can never be a beggar. Not for long, anyhow."

Benedict smiled contentedly. He assured Baruch that there were plenty of sick people left all over the world. How mature his son had grown. He had even developed the subtle art of flattery, so essential in a physician. "Yes, I've left you a few sick ones, Baruch." How quickly Baruch had grasped the essential of education: Greater than heaped bags of gold, greater than sterile chests of jewels, the physician's art was a perpetually salable commodity, wherever poor humans were suffering and frightened. It was greater even than a rich legacy, though of course Baruch would have that too — not too soon, Benedict hoped.

Glancing at the microscope Baruch continued, "And I want to learn more. Of course, I can put on a grave wise face in front of a patient. Indeed it would do him a disservice if the doctor looked as bewildered and frightened as he is. But there are so many mysteries. Van Leeuwenhoek told me he found little animals in a drop of ditch water and little flowers growing in moldy cheese. Why? What good are they? Or are they harmful?"

"I have never suffered any ill effects from good ripe cheese. In fact, I like it," Benedict said, shrugging. "And only a fool would drink ditch water or even wash in it." But he admired Baruch's intellectual curiosity, even though it struck him as somewhat impractical. Perhaps he too had had it when he was Baruch's age. Perhaps he had grown too practical over the years of hard work.

"And I want to learn why the Christian Host bleeds when wicked Jews steal it and torture it by thrusting knives into it."

Horrified, Benedict cried, "Oh no! Not that old wives' tale again! Not in these modern days!"

"I am assured by my porter," Baruch said, lowering his voice, for there was a sound of clog boots on the stairs, "that the phenomenon has only recently been repeated and well authenticated by unimpeachable ecclesiastical authorities."

"Not here in Holland!"

"No, not here, not yet. It is supposed to have happened in France."

"Then God help France."

"Maybe the microscope would help clear up the delusion. If I could only get my hands on a nice red rotting Christian Host —"

It was the oldest of accusations against the Jews: That every Passover they stole and tortured a consecrated wafer from a Christian altar, having first, of course, abducted, slaughtered and drained all the blood out of a small Christian boy to moisten the dough for their unleavened Passover breads.

Benedict shook his head sadly. "Will they never learn, these Christians? Do old hatreds never die? Are the old hatreds still abroad in the world? Don't they even read their own Bible? All our Jewish prohibitions against the eating of blood are clearly set forth in the Old Testament. And we never tortured anybody; even when we stoned them we deadened their feeling first with a pain killer. As for crucifixion, we left that to the Romans. Alas! And the Good Man was one of our own!

"But no, they will not learn, since it is easier to hate than to love, to be cruel than to show compassion, and to find a scapegoat than to mend your ways."

Wagging an admonitory finger at his son, he warned, "I adjure you, Baruch, give up your quixotic notion of putting a Christian wafer under the microscope. If four thousand years of Scripture, ours and their own, have not taught the absurdity of these hideous ravings of madmen, a young Jewish scientist with a shiny new optical device cannot do so either. And you would get into trouble. There are still stakes to burn witches at. Not here in free Holland, but in Germany —"

"Free Holland!" Baruch muttered.

"Patience, lad, patience." Benedict soothed him.

The porter clattered toward the door. "Have you paid him?" Benedict whispered. "He doesn't look as if he's going to stay."

"More than he deserves."

But Benedict rose and thrust a gold piece into the porter's hand and bade him farewell with many expressions of thanks for his services.

"Tribute!" Baruch growled.

"Caution, just caution, son. I am much disturbed by what you tell me."

With the departure of the porter a shadow seemed to lift from the house. Some days later, out of curiosity, Baruch wrote to a schoolmate in Leyden, "Have you heard anything of my porter?" and received in reply, "Nothing of consequence, except that the babble-tongue has spread abroad the story that Jewish fathers and sons kiss each other on the mouth in the privacy of their homes. The bargemen and garbage collectors are said to be pruriently amused."

It seemed to Baruch that his father looked older and often preoccupied. He spent long hours closeted with his lawyer, or among the books in his study going over old papers. "I'm afraid I have shamefully neglected my business affairs, Baruch. Now be a good lad and make my calls for me again today. It gives you experience and saves me untold amounts of expensive shoe leather."

Baruch would return, sometimes late at night, usually with a fat purse jingling with fees. But Benedict, who had a keen ear, often observed, "An unwonted amount of silver these days, Dr. Benedict; gold makes a heavier, heartier, happier thump." But he knew that money was scarce this year. His lawyer continually told him so. Overseas wars had cut deeply into Dutch trade and severely reduced the copious flow of gold that had made Holland the richest commercial nation in the world for a hundred years. Now the sea lanes were becoming unsafe, piracy was rife, marine insurance rates were skyrocketing and the Bank of Amsterdam, though still rated the soundest financial institution in Europe, began asking embarrassing questions whenever some solid Amsterdam businessman would apply for an extension of the mortgage on his house or the loan of a few hundred guilders to tide him over till his tulip crop was ready for market.

Once Baruch returned and found his father in the study peering intently through the microscope at a piece of bread. So absorbed was he that he did not hear his son enter. Pushing the instrument away with a grunt of disgust, he said, "Nothing. Nothing but a harmless green fungus — Oh, it's you, Baruch." He flushed as if he had been caught in the act of rifling the pantry. Indeed, he had been doing just that.

"The cook must be getting old, Baruch. She knows very well that she shouldn't keep spoiled food in the house."

"Is it ergot, Father? It's rye bread."

"No, ergot is black or purplish, and deadly, as you know. You have purified decoction of ergot in your chest. You will be asked for it often by erring women who desire to be relieved of their burden."

"I know. I already have been, even when I was a student."

"Use it sparingly, if ever, and only in case of hemorrhage uncontrollable by other means."

"I've never used it."

"But this stuff!" Benedict snorted, indicating the bread under the microscope. "It's nothing but a harmless green fungus. It's a scald, it's decidedly unwholesome, the cook should have thrown it out. And yet, Baruch, I have known poor hungry people to eat such bread, and they never were the worse. Indeed, I have known some ignorant patients to use it as a poultice for sores and ulcers and wounds. Of course they use spider webs too, and moss and even mud. I suspect this unattractive green fungus is no better and no worse."

"I think I know what you were really looking for, Father."

Benedict nodded. "Yes, Baruch, I was. Red bread, infected bread that might look as if it were bleeding. Well, there simply isn't any such thing. But as long as bigots think there is there's always the Jew to blame. By the way, are we supposed to have poisoned any wells lately?"

[183]

"That only comes in the midst of a plague, Father."

They both laughed heartily.

Another night Baruch came home without a penny in his purse.

"Surely the times can't be as bad as all that," Benedict said.

Baruch was sober faced. "I did receive a few guilders, quite a few actually. But on my last call I spent them all for an etching."

"For a *what?*" Incredulity and reproach were in Benedict's voice.

"Here it is."

He drew from his sleeve a beautifully executed but rather uninspired etching of a Dutch pastoral landscape.

"You had better start at the beginning," Benedict said, wondering what drug could possibly be prescribed for sentimental young doctors who bought etchings. Etchings!

"Do you know Harmenszoon van Rijn?"

"Who signs his pictures Rembrandt? Of course I do — at least I know about his work. Though I never could stomach that revolting *Anatomy Lesson of Dr. Tulp.* You can almost smell the cadaver. Besides, it's full of inaccuracies. I used to know Nicolaas Tulp. He was a superb anatomist. He dissected like a true surgeon, with understanding and loving care, up to his elbows in his work, with all his tools around him; not like the theatrical mountebank that Rembrandt portrays holding a single pair of fastidious forceps at arm's length. And yet," Benedict mused, "there must be a power in the thing or I'd never have remembered it so long, and I must say it's an excellent portrait of Professor Tulp. But come now, Baruch; Rembrandt has always been strong as a bull and never has needed a doctor in his life. How does it happen that he called you? Does he still live in that beautiful big house on Broad Street?"

"Not anymore."

And he had not called Dr. Benedict van Benedict. His mistress had.

Rembrandt's beloved wife had been dead fifteen years. Scandal now descended upon him. He had taken for his comfort a plump little housekeeper named Hendrickje Stoffels and begotten upon her warm, willing and dimpled body a charming little bastard named Cornelia, now just cutting her first molar.

"It is causing the child some discomfort," Baruch said, "and the mother was frantic with worry, for little Cornelia's head was really very hot."

"What did Rembrandt say?"

"He wasn't there. So I left a small vial of Van der Heyden's Peruvian Bark —"

"I hope you didn't label it with such a formidable name."

"Oh no. I simply labeled it 'Jesuit Febrifuge,' which is also its name, as you know. Mevrouw Hendrickje was properly awed and perfectly delighted. I told her to use it a drop at a time, once every four hours only, since any medicine with 'Jesuit' on it was certain to be very powerful, as well as very expensive."

Benedict chuckled. "The child will get well without it, of course, as soon as the tooth erupts fully. But the bark will break the fever and ease her discomfort. Poor little thing."

"When I said it was very expensive Mevrouw Hendrickje saw I was waiting for my fee and began to cry. She said I would have to see Rembrandt about that."

Rembrandt was at the Keizerskroon Hotel, glowering at the auctioneer, who was selling off everything he possessed. His fine house in Broad Street, every stick of furniture, every pot, every pan, every knife, every fork, every plate, every table, every bed, down to his bed sheets and table linen; and all, all his life's work of paintings and etchings, everything, everything was to go. For Rembrandt had just been declared bankrupt.

"In England they'd have left him a bed and the tools of his trade," Baruch said. "But we Dutch are more thorough."

He sought out Rembrandt among the crowd of bargain hunters and told him why he was there.

"What a tragedy, Baruch! How was he taking it?"

"Oddly, I thought. First he expressed deep and honest concern over little Cornelia, but I reassured him. Then he was at great pains to tell me that he had acknowledged paternity as soon as the child was born. So proud he was of her that he had her christened Cornelia in memory of his own dear mother, so the baptismal records in the Reformed Church here in Amsterdam show. And then — you will not believe your ears — he said I looked peaked and wanted to buy me a glass of geneva. I told him I seldom drank anything stronger than beer, and he said, 'Oh, I forgot. You're a Jew, aren't you. You know, Van Benedict, you don't look like a Jew.' I was so incensed at the remark that I'd have bought the confounded schnapps myself. What is a Jew supposed to look like, Father?"

Benedict looked at his tall angry son, whose hair was as fair as a sand dune in the sun and whose eyes were as blue as the cold North Sea on a wintry day, now blazing with fire and ice.

"We are supposed to be short and fat, Baruch; to look like pediculous Armenian peddlers, black of hair, hooked of nose, with shifty coal black eyes, and lots and lots of nice lace and rugs, for sale cheap, gracious lady, in a battered old leather bag that we've probably stolen."

"But the Armenians —"

"I know, lad. They're Christian. Did Rembrandt buy you the glass of geneva?"

He had wanted to, Baruch said; but suddenly he caught himself up with a jerk, swore a resounding oath and remembered that he could buy nothing; it would not be legal while the auction was in progress. He possessed not a penny. There, before his eyes, friends and neighbors he had known for years, were bidding for his possessions. They were polite enough, Baruch said, but their faces were set and expressionless and their eyes were not on Rembrandt but on the bargains.

In Hendrickje's name Rembrandt made a bid and bought back one large chest of which she was particularly fond. "The entire sale netted him less than five thousand guilders, a fraction of its value," Baruch said. "It was then that I bought the etching. The auctioneer said the price was adequate; Rembrandt said I overpaid. Then we left the auction, and I bought him his glass of geneva. I had a glass too, and I'm frank to admit it went down like water and proved grateful to my stomach. I think I was more overwrought than Rembrandt himself. He took everything quite calmly and said he could now look forward to painting again, since he had no more worries. Maybe all artists are queer."

Rembrandt moved from his mansion on Broad Street, without friends, without enemies, forgotten, thrown entirely on his own. He retired to the Rosengracht, a cheap and obscure quarter at the western extremity of the city. There he lived for many years and did work that was to make him more famous than all the works he had lost to the buyers at the auction. But there was a sadness in them that was not there before, a depth that was lacking in the lusty exuberance of his early painting. Serene and self-confident he continued to paint self-portraits, which aged as he aged. But he never limned another etching.

[187]

You were right to buy Rembrandt his glass of schnapps," Benedict said. "He undoubtedly needed it. It is a dire thing to be penniless, old, forgotten, finished." Benedict repeated the sentiment often in the coming weeks.

In his father's tone Baruch detected the same weariness that had characterized the letters he had received at the University. He supposed his father had fallen into some of the habits that usually afflict elderly men: of repeating themselves and of a strange fear that seems to grip them as youth and strength recede — an irrational fear of poverty never justified by their substantial bank accounts.

Benedict's joy at his son's return did not flag; indeed, it grew day by day as Baruch took over more and more of his calls. Baruch demonstrated just the right sense of balance between dedication and a healthy commercialism. Dedicated he was, for he would spend hours with his father describing an interesting case, even when the patient could not pay. Commercial he could be also, especially when some rich patient took half a day bewailing some imaginary ailment simply because she wanted attention — and some of the men were just as bad. Such patients paid handsomely, and seldom boggled at the fee. "Sometimes I think they're just lonesome, Father," he would say.

Benedict would nod assent and envelop his head in fragrant clouds of pipe smoke, proud of his son's maturity. The pipe, indeed, did not taste as good as it had aforetime; but he knew that Baruch would be quick to note any change in his habits; so he smoked as much as ever, even though tobacco had lost its taste.

Occasionally they would make a call together, thus bringing to reality Benedict's dream; the two doctors, father and son, tall and impressive in their physicians' gowns, sallying forth to fight the world of disease and pain. But the fantasy of the "esoteric ailment" was never quite realized, for Benedict became aware that Baruch had to shorten his stride to his; and even then the exertion caused him to breathe faster than he could easily hide, and he could hear an uncomfortable pulse in his ears like the sound of an intermittent water pump venting into a canal: he calculated the pump's periodicity at over a hundred. It should have been seventy-two.

One factor in Baruch's character was especially pleasing, though it caused a tug at Benedict's heartstrings. The young man had itchy feet. He wanted to travel. He wanted adventure. This was so thoroughly normal that his father had to applaud. But the thought that it might take Baruch away from him made him thoughtful. For how long? Would he still be there when Baruch came back? Before the questions were fairly framed in his mind an answer suggested itself. He would simply follow.

He told his lawyer of his new resolve, and his lawyer looked at him with sympathy and understanding. "You are rich enough to live in luxury anywhere in the world, Mynheer Doctor, without doing another day's work for the rest of your days."

"It is conceivable," Benedict said wryly, "that a very small amount might suffice for that."

For some time now Benedict had quietly been liquidating all his properties and business interests. Their diversity, accumulated over a lifetime, surprised even him: real estate, negotiable notes, leases and subleases on houses, apartments, windmills, barges, and shares in shipping ventures. The process of converting these multifarious assets into liquid assets was tedious and time-consuming, for it all had to be done through third parties and under many names. He could not appear to be panic selling lest the prices go down. Above all, Baruch must not know. Baruch would instantly turn his keen young diagnostic eye on his father and divine why. "He'll know when the time comes," Benedict said.

"I will pray in the synagogue that that time will not come for many years." Benedict's lawyer was as devout as Benedict was not.

"I thank you," Benedict said. "And I shall heartily echo your prayer. I shall do so, hm-m, *in absentia,* however. If Baruch were to catch me going to synagogue he'd think I had taken leave of my senses."

One instruction greatly surprised the lawyer. "I want it all in gold," Benedict said. "Gold and jewels."

Here the lawyer protested. "Paper is safer — letters of credit, sight drafts. They would be instantly honored. We have congregations all over the world."

"I want gold," Benedict said positively. "Gold and jewels."

The lawyer shrugged. "As you say, Mynheer; but it will take longer."

Benedict did not like the news of the world that Baruch had brought home from Leyden. He liked it less and less as Baruch divulged more and more of it.

Baruch missed the busy cosmopolitan atmosphere of the University, with its thousands of students from every nation under the sun and the latest gossip, rumor and legitimate news on everyone's tongue.

France seemed particularly ominous, and France was universally acknowledged as the leader of Europe.

In France the Protestant Huguenots had fallen upon evil days.

"Isaac Newton —" Baruch began.

"Isaac? One of us?"

Baruch chuckled. "No, Father. Newton's a Christian. He says in one of his papers, 'To every action there is always an equal and opposite reaction'; and so it seems to be happening in France."

For many years the industrious Huguenots had worked and lived in France in total freedom. Their schools, hospitals, factories, churches and homes were secure, protected by laws of toleration and equality, the Edict of Nantes of 1598.

But the edict was drawn on broad lines and in general terms. Now the reaction had set in, and an assembly of Catholic ecclesiastics armed with strong powers, were scrutinizing those terms with inquisitorial eyes and reinterpreting them in specifics never dreamed of when the edict was promulgated. Everything not specifically accorded the Huguenots must be interpreted as specifically forbidden them.

Were Huguenot colleges and hospitals mentioned in the edict? Were they mentioned by name? Since they were not they must be closed.

Some of the minutiae would have been ludicrous had they not

constituted so obvious a threat of persecution to come. Did the edict state that a Huguenot woman could be a midwife? Obviously the broad terms of toleration had not dealt with such a detail; and henceforth no Huguenot woman could practice midwifery.

Were the activities of tailors, shoemakers, weavers, cheese merchants, wheelwrights and stone masons specifically mentioned in the edict? Since they were not they were proscribed.

The learned professions fared even worse: doctors, lawyers, educators — since they were not specifically mentioned in the edict they too were proscribed. Nor were bankers specifically mentioned, so no Huguenot could lend money to a friend, write a bill of sale or collect a debt.

"It isn't happening all at once," Baruch said, "but the foundation is being laid, precedents are being set that will deprive them of the very means of existence. Many are leaving France. Where will they go?"

"Where did we go, Baruch, when the same things happened to us? We wandered among the nations. But we took with us the Torah and the Talmud, and we survived."

"I don't think the Huguenots have anything like that."

"Nobody has."

But they both hoped Protestantism would survive.

Across the generations Benedict seemed to catch a whiff of burning smoke, as when Baruch ben Baruch ben Baruch had perished in flames that by now were almost mythical. It was only his pipe, and very distasteful.

There was bad news even from faraway Brazil, a Portuguese possession in the New World. Portugal was engaged in a commercial war that had greed as its origin, greed for the rich East Indian spice trade. Holland also had commercial interests in the trade, and opposed vigorous competition. Portuguese and Dutch vessels fired upon each other in storied East Indian waters, while turbaned infidels looked on in amusement and raised the price of pepper. The Dutch had better ships and heavier guns and usually won. Thereupon Portugal retaliated by expelling all Dutchmen from Brazil, many Jews among them.

As Benedict's days slipped into a routine that consisted almost entirely of conferences with his lawyer, Baruch found that he had taken over virtually all of his father's practice. He made all the calls.

He disliked the narrow confines of Amsterdam; he felt walled in; he looked hungrily at the ships in the harbor, arriving from everywhere in the world, departing for everywhere in the world. He voiced his discontent to his father:

"I am not unappreciative, sir," he said, "but I'd like to acquire experience in some place on my own, some place where I am not known merely as your son. Here everything is practically handed me on a silver platter. I am accounted able simply because you are. I'd like to —"

Benedict smiled, nodded, approved.

"Would you diagnose your feet as wanderlustful, son? Wouldn't you say, without all this politeness and circumlocution, that what you really want is a bit of travel and adventure? Perhaps I have pushed you too hard. Ever since you were a boy I have crammed education into your head. When did you ever have a year off to travel? Most craftsmen do. But you could not. I was greedy for you, son, in a whirlwind of hurry. I could not face interruption of your studies at the University for the journeyman wanderyear that most young men take in every profession. Take now, therefore, the travel that my haste deprived you of."

It was almost too good to be true.

"Would I go with your blessing?"

"I started blessing you the day you were born. Is it likely I'll stop now?" And then, lest he display unwonted sentiment, he added lightly, "Unless I have lost the ability to detect eagerness in a young man's face, you would go anyhow, blessing or no blessing. Where will you go? The world is big. You can go anywhere."

Baruch knew exactly where.

"I went aboard a ship the other day," he confessed. "A sailor stopped me at the quayside, recognizing my gown, and told me his captain was sick — it proved to be nothing but a monumental headache brought on by a night of drinking several bottles of geneva. I gave him a draught of poppy, enough to put him to sleep for thirty hours; and before he drifted off he got a bit light-headed and began to describe the whirling windmills, the bowling green and the beautiful canals of New Amsterdam. I said to myself, 'I could work my passage as a ship's doctor —' "

"By God! You will do no such thing! You are Dr. Benedict van Benedict. No son of mine shall sign on to a ship as an underling, living belowdecks with a scrofulous rabble of gallows birds that are crawling with lice, eating maggoty biscuits, suffering from every known disease —"

Baruch laughed heartily.

"You make it sound like an ideal surrounding to practice my craft."

But his father did not laugh. "There are easier ways to die," he said, still angry.

Baruch had not meant to rouse his father's ire. He was a little ashamed of his levity, which had wounded his father's deep professional pride and loosed such a blast of temper. He was awed by the warmth of his father's blessing, like a benediction, and the profundity of the understanding from which it sprang. And he was practical enough to see certain advantages: it would unquestionably be more pleasant to go as a passenger.

As he converted his assets into gold, Benedict placed it in a small box, about the size of the microscope case, that a man could conveniently carry under his arm. The notion rather tickled his fancy that Baruch, when he came to open it, would find himself a rich young man, rather decidedly rich — and it was all in so small a compass!

First the bottom of the box was covered, then the level rose; bullion and bars took the place of minted coin as more and larger of his properties were converted. Here and there shone a diamond, a ruby or an emerald, like a star but less unreachable and far more negotiable. The jewels he placed in a small chamois pouch, lest they get scratched. Save for the Golden Key to the House of Baruch in Spain, which he had not looked at in years, Benedict realized that he had never seen much gold. Gold had always passed quickly through his hands; he had always invested it in income-producing properties. As for the golden key, actually he had some doubts about its purity. The last time he had looked at it there seemed to be tarnish on its surface. But the box contained pure gold, gold, the safest investment in the world with the world in its present unsettled state.

Then a sort of panic seized him. He had not realized how heavy gold was. So small a box of so great a weight would certainly arouse suspicion. He transferred it all to a sea chest, with rough rope handles, such as travelers put their less valuable belongings in when they traveled by ship and which porters would carry without comment or question. Then he breathed easier.

He breathed easier. Till one day when he bent down to lift the chest. The rope handles seemed to elude his grasp. He lifted it with difficulty and straightened up with an excruciating pain in his chest. The pain traveled like lightning through all his members, radiating from his heart. "No! No! No!" He wept. "Not yet! Not yet!" He became violently sick to his stomach. He could feel the cold sweat bathing his limbs, the blood draining from his face, the feeble pulse. "It isn't *that* heavy. I lifted it only yesterday." But he could not rationalize it away. He knew what had happened. It was the second warning.

He thanked God that Baruch was not in the house. Even the apprentice was out on a call. He was alone, with a desperate fear and a desperate resolve. Savagely he shook his fist at the empty air. "Azrael, Azrael, begone!" he gasped in a strangled voice. "Out! Out! Out of my house! I defy you! Some other time! Out, I say!"

He knew he was far beyond the reach of foxglove. But he had other tricks to cheat the dread angel. He stumbled toward a locked cabinet where he kept drugs so secret, so powerful, so dangerous that neither Baruch nor the apprentice knew he possessed them. They were all deadly poisons.

Instinct guided his hands; fury gave him strength; he found the key and opened the cabinet. Stronger than pain was the glowering sense of a monstrous injustice: he would not be cut off before Baruch was provided for! Azrael must find other employment this night.

In Siam there grew an ugly tree with a crooked trunk. Its reputation was grim. Legend surrounded it. It was said that men died if they so much as slept under it. In Siam suspected criminals were given its seeds to eat. If they were guilty they died in convulsions and unspeakable agony. If they were not guilty they survived. Hence it was called the "ordeal tree."

In Holland it was called the Strychnos Tree, the tree of death.

From an unmarked vial Benedict took one of its seeds, a greenish circular thing covered with gray withered hairs. He crushed it in a mortar and poured brandy over it, and waited for the sediment to settle. There was no time to clarify it. There was no time to measure the dosage. Then he drank half a spoonful, glanced at the clock, washed mortar and pestle and locked the secret cabinet. "I shall know in twenty minutes."

His mouth was full of the bitter taste. He poured a glass of sweet wine and sipped it, his eye on the clock, waiting.

So it was that they found him when Baruch and the apprentice returned perhaps an hour later. Both noticed how well he looked, how good his color was.

By luck, or perhaps it was so ordained, the enormously powerful stimulant had had precisely the right effect. His pulse was strong and steady. Touch, sight, hearing, all his senses seemed heightened. His strength had returned; he had lifted the chest without effort and restored it to its inconspicuous corner. He was reading a book when Baruch looked in at the study, drinking his second goblet of wine. It tasted wonderful, and his mood had never been better.

When Baruch asked him how his evening had been he replied, "Delightful, son; perfectly delightful. I had a visitor, but I sent him away."

Soon, far too soon for Benedict, the day came for Baruch to depart. What does a father say to a son about to go traipsing off to the ends of the world? How to explain that in all likelihood you'll never see him again? How tell a full-grown man with a medical doctorate that to you he is still a beloved little boy whom you would like to tether at home just a bit longer?

Benedict spent a sleepless night and begrudged Baruch the healthy snores that came out of his room. "Doesn't he know how I feel? But I'm not being fair. Of course he doesn't. I have hidden everything from him, even the fact that I propose to follow him as soon as I straighten out his affairs just a bit more." His affairs? Yes, his.

Benedict no longer thought of them as his own. His brush with Azrael's dreaded wing and the wonder-working seed of the Strychnos Tree that had cheated the rascal were too present, too ominous.

The chest of gold still stood in its inconspicuous corner in the study. Books carelessly piled on top of it concealed it more thoroughly than if it were out of sight. No one but his lawyer knew what was in it.

Benedict had planned to send it off with Baruch's other luggage; but during the night as he tossed sleepless on his bed he changed his plan.

"That is the trouble with the really big things of this life," he grumbled. "They only happen once, and you never know how to handle them. Spinoza used to say that you could never step into the same river twice, because the water keeps flowing and therefore it's not the same river. Then he told me that a great philosopher had proved by the same reasoning that you could not step into it even once, and I asked him how it came to be that your feet got wet when you —"

Benedict awoke with broad daylight streaming into the room and Baruch shaking him by the shoulder, laughing.

"What about Spinoza, Father? You were dreaming."

"Oh, it's you, son. Spinoza? I haven't heard from him since he moved to Leyden. Did you see him there?"

"No, nor heard of him."

"Then he's much better, I suppose."

"I suppose so."

Baruch was thinking only of the ship, which sailed with the next tide.

"You'll be going aboard soon, son?"

Baruch said, "I've just time to get my things down to the ship."

Benedict would have liked a leisurely hour to bid him farewell, to give him much fatherly advice that he had evolved in his mind during the last few days: Keep your thoughts to yourself; be friendly, but not vulgar; such friends as you have,

[199]

grapple them to your soul with hoops of steel, but beware of untried friends who will always want something from you and forget you when they get it; do not quarrel, but if you do, win; listen to many, tell few your decision; dress well, but not gaudily, since the commonalty see first the outer man before the inner; neither a borrower nor a lender be — where had he heard such wisdom for a son? Ah, yes, it was in one of those writings by the Englishman, Shakespeare. It stuck in Benedict's mind, however, that the character who voiced the wisdom was a doddering old fool with whom he did not wish to be associated; and in any case, the advice was too broad, too vague, too general to be heeded by a young man.

So he simply said, "I have thought, Baruch, that I might take a little trip myself, when a few unimportant financial matters here at home are somewhat further advanced. I would like to see Dr. Benedict van Benedict set up in practice in New Amsterdam."

Baruch said he hoped his father would not steal all his patients; his father said he promised to leave a few of the simpler cases. Each man kept the conversation light and bantering, for each had his secret concern about the other.

A two-wheeled beer wain arrived at the door, a patient, well-fed horse between the traces. Benedict looked askance at the unprepossessing vehicle. Baruch said, "I physicked the driver's wife. The good man had to pay me in kind: he offered me a barrel of beer. I said I'd prefer transportation to the ship, and the fee was so arranged. Will you hop into my chariot, Doctor?"

Benedict hopped, convinced that advice to such a practical son would have been as unnecessary as unwelcome. As they rumbled over the cobbles to the quayside Benedict said, "When I come to visit you, son, I shall not be surprised if I find you taking your fees in arrowheads. I hear New Amsterdam is full of Red Indians."

"Fuller of Dutchmen, I hear."

"Yes, New Amsterdam must be very much like home."

"At least there aren't any Frenchmen or Englishmen. That's a blessing."

At the quayside the ship was waiting; sailors were in the rigging ready to loose the sails. "Good Lord!" Baruch said. "I nearly missed her."

Benedict said, "I think they'll wait."

His son looked at him suspiciously. "What have you been up to?"

A cheerful voice from the quarterdeck hailed them. "Dr. Benedict? Welcome aboard, Dr. Benedict! Your quarters are all prepared. Come aboard, sir, you and your honorable father. We wait upon your pleasure."

"Honorable Father," Baruch said, "there is skulduggery here. I wanted to be inconspicuous."

"I just wanted to make sure you didn't miss the boat," Benedict said, "so I gave your good captain a small honorarium."

He still had a word or two to say to his son. Willingly he would have spun out the farewell for an hour, but time and tide wait for no man, even a man with an honorarium. He glanced about the cabin. A luncheon table was set for two. He sent away with a goldpiece the apple-cheeked youngster who had been delegated to serve them and whose ears looked too big. "My last goldpiece in the world," he pronounced dolefully. "Henceforth you must look to Dr. Benedict van Benedict. If you serve him well I have no doubt —"

"Aye, aye, Mynheer," said the youngster, grinning. "The Mynheer Doctor shall be well served."

Now was the time, heart-achingly short, to make sure that Baruch did not take all his fees in arrowheads.

"It has occurred to me," Benedict said soberly, "that there is always a period, often so much as a whole year, when a young and unknown doctor at the beginning of his practice in a new town may find himself without a single fee-paying patient." He withdrew from his belt a long fat purse and laid it on the table between them. "This should tide you over that famine period, and you won't have to advertise quack remedies for incurable diseases. I know you wouldn't anyhow."

"No, I wouldn't."

"Still, take it, and then you won't even be tempted. Set yourself up in style in New Amsterdam. Mingle with only two classes, the richest and poorest. Beware of the middle class; they will only defraud you, since they are climbers and have everything to gain, whereas the rich and the poor have nothing to lose."

Baruch wrinkled his brow. "I do not quite follow you, sir. But I love you. I will take your advice, insofar as God gives me the light to do so."

The farewell was growing awkward and heavy with sentiment. Benedict heard the tide bubbling and gurgling against the ship's side, the lines straining against the bitts. The capstan had long since clicked around and gone silent as the anchor was hoisted aboard and secured.

"There is plenty of time," called the cheery voice of the captain. "Tomorrow will do just as well."

"That means there is no time at all, Baruch. I must leave you now for a space, till I follow. The vacation I promise myself will come shortly. There is just one more thing."

He laid on the table the golden key.

"This object is freighted with the history of our House. Some-where in Spain, Seville so the story goes, it fits the lock to the door of the House of Baruch. Generations of Doctors Benedict have treasured it. Many have hoped to return to that house. Treasure it also, my son, for I deem it a good omen."

"You, Father, are the head of the House. You must keep it."

Benedict said, "There is nothing in the history of our House that prohibits its temporary safekeeping in the hands of an heir. No, Baruch, it is you who must keep the key. On a temporary basis, of course, for I shall follow quickly and watch how you make out in the New World."

"Plenty of time," called the voice of the captain.

"Fare with God," Benedict said. "Fare swiftly and wisely. Farewell."

He watched the ship sail.

Jolting home in the beer wagon he said to the driver, "Did my son actually commission this deplorable vehicle?"

"Indeed he did, Mynheer," the driver replied proudly in a rich Flemish dialect, heavy as his beer. "Never was seen in this world such a wonderful doctor as your dear son. Before he physicked my poor wife you should have seen her. O-o-of! Shudders one got. All wrinkles and swellings. But now she is smooth like a doll and beautiful like an angel."

Benedict chuckled. The driver's eloquent testimonial was worth all the discomfort of the beer wagon.

"That must be a great satisfaction," he said and let himself be jolted home.

"Did all go well?" the apprentice asked.

"Quite well indeed," Benedict replied.

To his lawyer next day he said, "I gave Baruch a purse with a year's living in it — but the chest? No, I decided not to give him that. I will take it with me myself when I go, and guard it till I give it to him personally."

"It is not quite full," the lawyer said. "You have not yet sold this house."

Benedict rubbed his chin reflectively. "My apprentice has no other home. He will soon be setting up his own practice. Make him a deed of gift in fee simple to the house. He has earned it."

"Subject to your repossession upon your return, of course."

"Of course. Or Baruch's."

The lawyer nodded and made a note.

Benedict asked, "How long do you think it will be before I can go?"

"Mynheer, you can leave at any time."

"Without loss?"

"I will see to that."

"Then I shall go at once."

The prospect of a long sea voyage had wrought a superbly tonic effect on Benedict. It occurred to him that he had never taken a vacation in his life. "I have prescribed rest and travel for many a patient," he thought wryly, "but I never had the wit to prescribe it for myself." Already, by anticipation, he felt better, younger. Even his pipe tasted good again. But in the main it was total freedom from fear that buoyed up his spirit and lent a healthy color to his cheeks. All his affairs were in order. He slept soundly and wakened refreshed.

Occasionally, out of sheer boredom, he would accompany the apprentice on a call. But not often. The sight of sick people was strangely depressing.

The only worry he had was the lack of news of Baruch, and as time passed he grew anxious. A letter should have arrived by now. He took to haunting the harbor and enquiring of ship captains; but, though some had returned from America, none had a letter from Baruch. One ship had a splintered mast.

"Did you encounter a storm, Captain?"

Benedict was not wearing his doctor's gown.

The captain spat angrily, eyed him suspiciously, and said, "I report to the Company what I encounter, not to curiosity seekers with nothing better to do than ask questions," and strode off in the direction of West India Company Hall.

Benedict shrugged off the incident. "If I had been garbed in the gown of my craft the fellow would have been more respectful."

He had told the apprentice he was going to make a sea voyage to New Amsterdam to visit Baruch, and charged him to pay strict attention to the practice while he was gone, stressing the responsibility that would devolve upon the fledgling physician: to keep daily accounts of his fees and watch that he was promptly paid. "I shall inspect your accounts when I return."

"I will put every guilder aside for you, Dr. Benedict. What would I be without your training, your wisdom, your patronage?"

"I'm afraid you can't very well put it *all* aside," Benedict said. "There will be household expenses, with which you are not familiar; there will be the apothecaries' costs for medicines. Give them half what they ask. Treat the practice as if it were your own. The lawyer will instruct you if you need help in your accounting, as is likely. You are a capable doctor, but I fear I've neglected to teach you the fiscal side of our craft. It is not unimportant."

[205]

"Mynheer Benedict, I will be as stingy as — as — as we're reputed to be."

"But maintain a certain standard — and it might be well to grow a beard. You will look older; your fees will be higher. Not the untrimmed orthodox beard of the lawyer, but a neat distinguished pointed thing à la Richelieu."

"The French Cardinal?"

"He had a very distinguished beard. Most good Dutchmen of any substance are adopting the French styles."

The apprentice smiled at the notion of adopting a Christian Cardinal's beard; but Benedict saw eager acceptance in his fresh, intelligent face.

"I shall expect to see you firmly established when I return," Benedict said gravely.

"Believe me, Dr. Benedict, I will not disappoint you."

Benedict had been so well lately that the apprentice no longer feared for his master's health. Nor indeed did Benedict himself. Some miracle had happened. He firmly expected to return. His pipe proved it. The prospect was infinitely gratifying.

A day came, however, when he sustained a momentary shock. The lawyer appeared with a letter. It was from the Jewish congregation in New Amsterdam. "What — what is this?" Benedict said, pale as a sheet. "Why isn't it from Baruch?"

"It is good news," the lawyer said placidly. "The *Shekinah* of The Holy One hovered over your son. He is safely arrived, in a house of his own not far from one of his patients, the Governor Stuyvesant. The Governor's peg leg is said to be much more comfortable now."

"The Governor? Oh, ho-*ho!* Do I hear what I hear? And I was afraid the boy would take all his fees in arrowheads, or etchings." Benedict rubbed his hands together gleefully, beaming with pride, laughing with relief, his tension relaxed, his fear completely gone.

The lawyer chuckled too. Benedict's joy was infectious. "As for the arrowheads, Mynheer Benedict, he probably has some of those also. They say he does much charity work among the savages."

"He listened, the lad listened! Just as I told him — the very rich, the very poor. Ah, Baruch, Baruch, blessed be the day you were born! This I will see. But is there no letter for me in his own hand?"

"The captain has it, Doctor. I have just come from his ship."

"What captain? What ship?"

"Why, sir, the same captain who transported him safely across the sea. He is expecting another Dr. Benedict as a passenger."

"You've already arranged it? Bless you. Can I sail today?"

The lawyer smiled. "Not quite today, I'm afraid. Captain van Ruysdael will have to water and victual and refit — whatever captains do to their ships in port. It is not in my line; but I dare say it will not take more than a few days.

It was a glorious day with a warm spring sun and acres of flaming tulips just bursting into bloom. Bargemen sang at their towlines on the canals. The myriad windmills of Amsterdam turned their great white sails majestically at their centuries-old task of pumping the sea back into the sea. Dutchmen loved them, and they in turn imparted some of their patience and industry to the Dutch, for without them Holland would sink beneath the waves. Benedict had eyes only for the wind. Sometimes the mills did not turn, in a dead calm. Sometimes the great sails were furled, at the advent of a storm. But today, full set, they turned in a strong steady breeze. A perfect day for a ship to sail.

Benedict departed in an aura of elegance that he himself would not have purposely exhibited for fear of appearing ostentatious; but the lawyer, who knew how often he advised others to maintain a certain style, arranged everything. And Benedict was mightily pleased.

"What a lot of money you squandered," he said, with unconvincing reproach in his voice.

"I took my percentage, Mynheer."

"Well, I suppose there's no harm just this once. But see that you spend less when I come back."

"I will make a note," the lawyer said, smiling broadly.

"Well, make it."

"I forgot my pencil and pad."

"Make it later then."

A commodious coach was at the door. Benedict entered with a quick light step, disdaining the hand of the apprentice, who was a bit too late to help him up. He sank back with a sigh of satisfaction among the luxurious cushions. What a wonderful day, what a wonderful world it was!

Around the coach clustered a crowd of friends, neighbors, patients; many of them owed him money, some he knew would never live to see him return; some were so young he had ushered them into this world. All raised their hats respectfully and bade him farewell in the quiet manner that men assume when they are greatly moved. Jan van Benedict had been so solid a figure of the neighborhood for so many years that no one had ever imagined he might disappear for even a few months' vacation.

Following the coach came a light two-wheeled carriage for the apprentice. But its single horse was curried to a high resplendent shine, and a solemn coachman drove it with an air of dignity that would have satisfied an alderman. With the apprentice sat a husky young porter in a suit so new that it looked as if it had been bought for the occasion, which it had.

At the quayside the ship lay waiting. A cheerful voice from the quarterdeck hailed him. "Dr. van Benedict? Welcome aboard, Dr. van Benedict. Your quarters are all prepared. Come aboard, sir. We wait upon your pleasure."

Benedict had an eerie sensation that he was stepping into the same river twice.

"What have you done?" he asked the lawyer. "I am not wearing my doctor's gown. How does he know I am the passenger?"

"I wanted to make sure Van Ruysdael waited. It was past the tide. The captain was impatient to sail. So I —"

"— gave him a small honorarium, I suppose."

"I took my percentage, Mynheer Doctor."

"You will beggar me."

"Have I done so, so far, Mynheer?"

Benedict laid a hand affectionately on his arm. "No, my friend, you have made me rich." He glanced at the chest, which was now literally a treasure chest.

"I may perhaps have been instrumental in conserving and converting," the lawyer began, "a goodly portion of assets which you were too busy, and indeed somewhat uninstructed in the lengthy legal quiddities required to —"

Benedict chuckled, and let him enjoy his meed of professional pride, and the lawyer became aware that he had lost his audience. His voice trailed off. Oh well, not everybody could be a lawyer, he supposed.

There was need of the husky young porter. It was all he and

the apprentice could do to manhandle the chest into Benedict's cabin. Sailors leaned idly against the rail and seemed delighted at the appearance of a passenger so rich that he brought his own servants to handle his own luggage and calculated their probable gratuities. "Let us help you," a few called out with so obvious an appearance of nonintention that Benedict had to suppress a smile.

There was an orderly flurry of activity as sailors scrambled into the rigging while others manned the lines to warp the ship away from the wharf and into the channel; and beyond the channel lay the open sea, and on the other side — Baruch.

Benedict had just time to extend his hand to bid the apprentice farewell as the ship pulled away. "Remember," he said, "while I am gone you are to look upon the practice as if it were your own."

The apprentice had prepared a little farewell speech, voicing all the appropriate sentiments, but the emotion of parting for the first time from the man who had taught him all he knew was too much for him. He stumbled his words and blurted out something far better: "Dear Master, God bless you and speed your return."

The wind held fair and strong astern. Once out to sea after negotiating the shallows around the Dutch coasts, Captain van Ruysdael visited Benedict daily, to smoke his pipe in the comfortable cabin while Benedict smoked his. To his own surprise Benedict discovered that he was an excellent sailor, without a qualm of seasickness.

"Would you believe it, sir," Van Ruysdael said, "I have known sea captains who actually got seasick? Yes, sir, white as a flounder's belly, and couldn't hold a bit of food on their stomachs. Of course, they feel better after those first few days. Why is this, Doctor?"

"It doesn't seem to have bothered you, Captain."

"Not me!" Van Ruysdael thumped his barrel chest and patted his good round belly. "I am never sick at sea *or* on land. You doctors would starve if everyone was like me."

"I've often wished everyone was," Benedict said. "It will be a happy world when no one is ever sick or in pain."

He had read and reread Baruch's letter. It was filial, short and full of enthusiasm, the letter of a busy man in a strange new world. Baruch never wore his doctor's gown, he said. It would not be the thing for horseback riding. He made all his calls on horseback, with his medicines in his saddlebags, because the roads of New Amsterdam were unpaved and knee-deep in mud whenever it rained. The Indians were friendly to the Dutch but scalped the English and French men because they sold them firewater and the Indians went crazy when they drank it. He looked forward to his father's arrival and hoped he would stay a long time. New Amsterdam bore only a superficial resemblance to Old Amsterdam. His house was comfortable, rented not purchased. There were fascinating new drugs. Many European drugs were in short supply and expensive to buy. All writing paper had to be imported and so, with devotion, he must now close.

Benedict smiled. So many new words! "Firewater"? The word was descriptive enough, and Benedict knew it must be some kind of schnapps; but selling it to the savages and its trigger effect on them seemed to betoken a state of body and mind with which he was entirely unfamiliar. What "scalping" might be he could not imagine, but it did not sound like anything he would like to experience. In Baruch's letter there was also a hint of

[211]

unspoken pride, pride that the son could take the father in hand
and show him things he had never seen before. There were ten
thousand Dutchmen in New Amsterdam, Baruch said, and two
thousand Jews. Nobody could tell Jew from Christian, and
indeed nobody ever asked. In New Amsterdam the traditional
freedom of Holland was magnified.

Almost to the point of assimilation, it seemed to Benedict, and
something stubborn in him wondered if that was a good thing.
He noted that Baruch did not mention the other European
colonies in America. He doubted whether things were so good in
French America, English America and above all in Spanish
America. But that wasn't good either. He would wait and talk to
his son. As the ship bore west he found he could hardly contain
his impatience.

"How long do you suppose it will be before we land, Captain
van Ruysdael?"

"If this wind holds," the captain said proudly, "I shall better
my own record, which is the best in the fleet." He had reason to
be proud. Every day saved meant more guilders in his pocket.

The wind held indeed, but no longer directly astern. It veered
around to the north, stronger than before; and the captain,
cursing the vagaries of the unpredictable, found himself under
shortened sail and driven far to the south. He had wished above
all to give a wide berth to the Portuguese Azores.

At night he ran without lights. Benedict was told without
much ceremony that he must retire at sundown, and that if he
read after dark the lamps in his cabin would be taken away. Van
Ruysdael told him why. "Everywhere there are unfriendly
coasts: Portugal is to the east, Spanish Africa to the southeast;
and to go straight south, making my best speed in this wind,
would run me smack into a hornet's nest of Portuguese islands.

To turn back, of course, is unthinkable. It would take weeks of beating against a headwind — and all because of a threat that will probably not materialize. I'd be laughed out of my command. Hence, no lights after sundown, Dr. van Benedict; and add your prayers to mine that I slip unnoticed past the damned Azores. I may already have avoided them, though I cannot be sure. No sun to give me my latitude." Meanwhile he saw to his cannon, powder and shot.

Captain van Ruysdael's sea sense was sound. He was south of the Azores, but not far south enough.

Since Benedict had retired at sundown he rose at dawn, refreshed after a pleasant dream in which he concocted a marvelous new drug out of the simplest possible ingredients, ingredients he already had. It enabled him to perform a most complicated operation without the slightest discomfort to the patient. But on arising from his slumber he could not remember the formula.

He dressed, looked out of the porthole and saw a high-rising verdant coast, which he knew must be an island because it was far too soon to have reached America.

The land was beautiful in the morning sun. The clouds and fog that had obscured the heavens had blown away. He speculated how gratified the captain must be, for now he could get his bearings and slip past the Azores. He lighted his pipe and settled down comfortably to wait for his breakfast with a good appetite.

Somehow the boy was late with it. In fact, it did not come at all. Hungry, he went on deck.

Something unusual was afoot.

The captain had crowded on sail. Sailors were in the rigging with buckets wetting down the canvas to increase speed. The

ship suddenly changed course and veered sharply around at a
barked order from the captain and bore due south.

"Yonder lies San Miguel," Van Ruysdael said to him.

The island that had been on the starboard side was now
directly astern.

"You had better go below, Doctor."

Two sleek black ships had sighted the Dutchman and put out
from the port of Ponta Delgada.

"They are Portuguese galleys," Van Ruysdael said. "The
splashes you see on either side are caused by oars. Oars pulled
by slaves. They are whipped with a lash if they do not pull in
unison. Such craft go fast. Still, I may outrun them. A stern
chase is a long chase." He cursed the sun. "If last night's fog had
held I'd have slipped past invisible."

Benedict had to admire the man. In imminent peril to his ship
his sturdy Dutch phlegm had not deserted him. He seemed
almost to admire the precision of the oars. He did not get
rattled. Directing his crew in a series of rapid-fire orders, un-
intelligible to Benedict, he still had the courtesy to explain a bad
situation that he knew must be novel to a landsman.

He did not confide certain technical problems that caused him
concern. He was badly armed at the bow, even worse at the
stern. There were only light guns in those places. His strength
was in the massive weight of the broadsides he could deliver
from heavy cannon on either side of his ship. Even now they
were sticking their angry iron muzzles out of the open ports. A
landsman would not have understood, and besides, there was no
time.

"I'd like to stay on deck if I may," Benedict said.

"As you please, sir. But stay out of the way, and don't get

killed. If they get within range they'll start firing, and then I might need a doctor."

Benedict had no fear that he would be killed. Was he not a doctor? With a history of two heart attacks? Who could know better than such a man the manner of his own passing?

The sun had not quite reached its zenith, the time when Van Ruysdael would have taken his sight. But today he need not, for he knew where he was.

Benedict's second pipe had just gone out when the Portuguese ships drew within range. He saw a puff of smoke, heard the report, then heard the whistle of the ball as it passed harmlessly over the masts. But the next shot tore a great hole in a sail, carried it away, and further slowed the ship in its effort to escape.

Again Van Ruysdael was at his side.

"You had better go below, Doctor. I do not advise you to come up on deck again, but if you do, wear your gown. They won't fire on a doctor. Besides —" And there was a new grimness in his voice. " — we're going to need a doctor. So will they, I promise you. Gowned, you will be the safest man on the ship, and the most indispensable."

Benedict did as the captain advised. His knowledge of war was cloistered, academic. But this real and present horror, hundreds of men created in the image of God, flying at each other's throats, straining to get close enough to murder each other — the picture appalled him, he who had devoted all his years to saving lives.

He was not afraid for himself; it was not to be a cannonball that would snuff out his days. Some dark night, unannounced, Azrael would steal into his room like a thief, and this time he would be unable to cheat him. Calmly he donned his doctor's garb, stuffed his pipe, lighted it, puffed it with the consolation of perfect diagnosis and went on deck.

They were very close now. Van Ruysdael had swung his ship around and brought his port cannon to bear on the nearest enemy. Suddenly there was a roar like a thousand simultaneous thunderclaps, and the ship slid perceptibly sidewise over the water, leaving a smoothed green surface behind, answering the tremendous recoil of the broadside. A cloud of evil-smelling smoke smote Benedict's lungs. Screams went up from the Portuguese. Bodies flew skyward into the air. Timbers splintered, and from belowdecks a dismal wail went up from the slaves chained to their oars. The Portuguese ship took on a strong list and, disabled, wallowed out of control downwind. Van Ruysdael knew she was doomed and turned his attention to the other.

Yells of fury mingled with moans of the dying. The captain swung around and presented his starboard battery to the enemy, and again the thunderous noise and the acrid enveloping smoke of the Dutch broadside. This time the Portuguese answered. Cannonballs crashed into the starboard side of the Dutch ship, and there, too, men died.

One Portuguese ball smashed into a gun just opposite the place where Benedict was standing. Another ripped into his cabin, destroying much of the floor. The ball burst open the chest of gold; and then, as the deck gave way beneath it, it slipped slowly into the sea.

At the sight of the gun crew lying at his feet, bloody, dismembered, with organs he knew so well and had physicked so often spilling out of their shattered bodies, a sort of madness seized Benedict. He hated the perpetrators of so monstrous an insult to all he held sacred.

The young gunner of the piece was attempting to rise to his

feet. His right arm had been shot off, and the arteries were pumping blood in spurts to mingle with the blood of the dead on the deck behind him.

Benedict ripped off a portion of his gown and with it applied a tourniquet to the stump. "You'll be all right, lad," he said. "Come to me tomorrow and I'll dress this properly."

"But my match! My match! It went with the arm! I can't fire back! The gun's still loaded!"

Very calmly, with vengeance in his heart and a perfectly steady hand, Benedict tapped the glowing embers of his pipe into the touchhole of the gun. It went off with a deafening roar and a jet of fire and smoke. The heavy ball smashed squarely through the open port of the gun that had wrought the havoc he had witnessed, duplicating its death and destruction. Benedict was glad.

A sharpshooter in the roundtop of the Portuguese ship saw the shot and saw the black-robed gunner who shot it. He took careful aim and fired. The bullet penetrated Benedict's unprotected breast and lodged in his heart.

"Something grazed my chest," Benedict thought idly as he lay supine on the deck. "Must have knocked me down. Lucky it didn't hit me square."

He would get up in a moment. It was unpleasant lying among the corpses. Tomorrow he would physic his wound, which certainly could not be serious because he felt no pain. Right now he was very tired. He felt slightly guilty at not helping others, so much worse off than he. But he was getting drowsy, too. A word of Isaiah slipped into his mind. He thought, "I will hide myself for a moment, one little moment until the indignation be overpast."

It was thus that Van Ruysdael found him, among the other

dead around the gun, after sinking one and driving off the second of the Portuguese ships.

In New Amsterdam when he saw Dr. Benedict van Benedict he said, "There were many casualties, but we won. Naturally it was necessary to bury him at sea with the others." He related the manner of Benedict's death.

Baruch, stricken to the depths of his soul, said, "Did he suffer pain at the end? He hated pain."

"None at all, Doctor; and let me assure you, I know. Death was instantaneous."

"Blessed be God for that," Baruch said.

"We found this in his cabin, or what remained of it after taking a direct hit." He gave Baruch a few gold pieces. Baruch took them. "And this." It was a diamond.

"Keep the stone, Captain van Ruysdael, and remember my father whenever you look at it. I have no use for diamonds."

"I shall remember your father as the best man and the best gunner I ever knew."

BOOK III

No two good men could have differed more widely in character. Yet no two good men could have been more magnetically drawn to each other than Dr. Benedict van Benedict and his neighbor, Peter Stuyvesant, Governor of New Amsterdam.

The Governor, who was now well into his seventy-first year, was testy, cantankerous, quarrelsome, perverse, cross-grained, opportunistic, old-fashioned and full of prejudices that were as clashing and unmixable as the colors of his tulips which nevertheless flowered luxuriantly side by side in the gardens of his estate in Holland, gardens on which he had not set eyes during the eighteen years of his rule in the colony but which he still remembered and longed for. "One day I shall see them again."

Dictatorial, often in pain in the stump of his leg, he disliked Englishmen, Frenchmen, Spaniards, Lutherans, Huguenots, Quakers, Catholics and, though he never admitted it in the presence of his doctor, if the truth be known, he did not care much for Jews either. Above all he detested the Portuguese. It was a Portuguese bullet that had cost him his leg years before, when he had led a daring attack against a Portuguese island in the West Indies.

And of course he disliked change. Once New Amsterdam had been entirely Dutch. "But now!" he would sputter, as if the polyglot speech of the city were a personal affront. "A melting pot! That's what New Amsterdam has become. Dozens of languages, Dr. Benedict. Dozens! That is the horrible babble that insults my ears when I walk among the people."

And the Indians. Three times he had led punitive expeditions against unfriendly tribes. "Savages! Stupid, blood-thirsty savages. *Heer God!* Do you know, Dr. Benedict, these ignorant primitives never even invented the *wheel?*"

"Since you speak of God, Mynheer Governor, do you know that God did not invent the wheel either? The wheel is unquestionably ingenious, of infinite use and efficiency. And yet there exists not a single wheel in the human body. How much more convenient it would be if instead of feet we were constructed with wheels at the bottom of our legs. The possibilities for progress would be endless. All streets would automatically be paved, for example. Everything with wheels, including ourselves, would travel faster, with less effort, less wear —"

"Wheels? Instead of feet? My dear doctor!"

"Why not? But it was not so ordained by the Almighty. Therefore, instead of wheels, which neither God nor the savages deemed necessary to invent, we are cursed with a primitive duality of awkward sticks on which we plod our painful way through this life as best we can instead of rolling smoothly on wheels.

"Nor, Mynheer, is there a wheel in the human heart, where we could certainly use one. Imagine it, sir, its smooth and simple efficiency; whirling continually, windmill fashion, circulating the blood like a fan instead of the complicated stop-and-go pump that He gave us. A great improvement."

The Governor chuckled. Benedict's enthusiasms could always lighten his mood. "Maybe that's why I like you, Doctor. You're so confoundedly rebellious, always trying to improve things. Now you're suggesting improvements to God Almighty. Ah well, I used to be like that too."

"You still are, Mynheer Governor. New Amsterdam is far better because of your rule."

"But old, Doctor, old."

"My father was old. But he died young in heart, fighting for freedom, firing a cannon against a Portuguese pirate ship."

Sometimes Benedict would relive that day, seven years ago now, when Captain van Ruysdael brought him news of his father's death. Seven years. How quickly the earth spun! He remembered the few gold coins, the useless diamond, the letter from the apprentice that had followed with a substantial remittance of guilders and a handful of beautifully mounted spectacles sent by Spinoza. He remembered the apprentice's enthusiastic appraisal of the Van Benedict clientele, "which I shall always consider," the apprentice wrote, "yours." Then there were shorter and fewer letters between them, then finally none at all.

Holland seemed far away. Seven years was a long time in the life of a rising young doctor. Benedict had all but forgotten the Old Amsterdam, so firmly was he now rooted in the New. No doubt the apprentice had forgotten him also. He had long since decided, "So it is, so let it remain." The death of his father had severed the silver cord that had shackled him to the city of his birth. Here was a newer city, built on the pattern of the old, as babies are built on the pattern of their parents, but blessed with the certainty of growth and development, bursting with the exhilarating freedom of youth. Here a man rose or fell by virtue of what he had in him, free from all the confining restrictions of the older culture. Freedom existed in New Amsterdam so widely that certain misguided men mistook it for license; and for some of these lawless men Dr. Benedict signed death certificates when they were hanged for murder, for others decrees of perpetual banishment after certifying them as unfit.

The banished would disappear into the forests to the west, to be promptly scalped by the Iroquois or sold into slavery to anyone, red or white, who would buy them. In New Amsterdam there were no slaves except a few Negroes imported by the Portuguese a generation before, and they were fewer every year by reason of the climate: too cold in winter, too damp in summer, or they died of homesickness for Africa and a plethora of New World diseases. "It is odd," Dr. Benedict would muse, "that the white men and black succumb so quickly to syphilis. The red men seem immune." Syphilis was also called the "French Disease," but the French blamed it on the English, the English on the Italians and the Italians, citing the last days of Columbus, blamed it, full circle, on the Red Indians. Whatever race was responsible, the malady was sweeping over Europe like a plague, and no doctor had a cure. There was considerable pain before madness and death put an end to their agony. "Since they are doomed," Benedict would wish, "would God there were a way to alleviate their suffering." The House of Baruch had been dedicated to the conquest of pain for as long as he could remember the history of his House.

The Governor had accused him of trying to improve things. "Accused" was the word, since improvement meant change, and the Governor wanted nothing changed; indeed, if he could have stopped the clock, nay, set it back twenty or thirty years, he would have done so. It was in this, more than anything else, that Governor Stuyvesant and Dr. Benedict van Benedict differed. What troubled the Governor troubled Benedict not at all. He rejoiced in the melting pot of New Amsterdam, he enjoyed the babel of tongues and had learned to make himself understood, if not to speak fluently, in most of the languages generally heard.

A fierce Red Indian was even now teaching him Iroquois. It was the most difficult case and the most difficult tongue he had ever encountered, for the patient was the Indian's five-year-old child and the child was in pain. When he moaned his father would slap his face. "He must learn to bear pain like a man."

"If you slap him again," Benedict said, "I will call down a curse from a great spirit, Hippocrates, who dwells beyond the moon, and the boy's leg will remain permanently paralyzed, nay, it will grow shorter and wither no bigger than the bone."

Benedict's deepest root in the New World was Esther, his wife, and little Baruch, their son, now just the age of the Indian's. Esther had been born in Massachusetts during a short and never-to-be-duplicated period when Massachusetts tolerated useful Jews. But the Massachusetts theocracy soon grew self-sufficient and greedy and began to expel Jews; Louis XIV ascended the throne of France and began a reign of dazzlingly successful bigotry that seemed destined never to end; everywhere tolerance flew out of the window, everywhere but in New Amsterdam. Thither Esther and her parents had immigrated, and there her parents died and were buried on their farm in Haarlem, far north of the bustling city. There it was, in that remote and beautiful pastoral wilderness, that Dr. Benedict van Benedict had first met her. He was on a search for Indian herbs and she was struggling, in her innocence, with a single not-too-bright servant, to breed cattle who inexplicably showed no interest in each other.

As delicately as he could Benedict said, "Mistress Esther, I must, er, tell you, the bulls are no longer bulls. They have been, hm-m, altered."

"Altered, Mynheer Doctor?"

"Bulls they are no longer. They will provide the most tender of beefsteaks, but, alas, no progeny. In short, they are oxen now, patient useful beasts but with a past forgotten and a future forlorn. If I were you I would sell them to draw beer wagons."

Within the year the oxen were sold. Within another Esther and Dr. Benedict van Benedict, inscribed by the elders of the synagogue under his true name, Baruch ben Baruch, went under the canopy; and the next year little Baruch blessed their home, a home no longer rented now but owned in fee simple, thanks to the doctor's growing practice.

The Governor himself took time to attend. Governor Stuyvesant's time was at a premium. New Amsterdam needed all his resourcefulness and all the mature fruits of his long experience as ruler of the new and still raw colony. "The English are getting damned threatening these days," he growled. "Greedy, insolent, worse than the Portuguese, if that's possible. They're stirring up the savages against us. They're a lot more sure of themselves now that they've dropped their decent republican government and restored their damned monarchy. So the savages get bribes, firewater, firearms, promises of Dutch plunder . . ." Then a twinge in his leg compressed his lips and he grunted, "Do you know, Mynheer Doctor, whenever I get angry my stump bothers me more?"

It was advancing age, choleric constitution and sluggish circulation, Benedict knew. There was no cure. Drugs that would speed up the circulation would raise the blood pressure and put a strain on the heart. But drugs that would slow down the circulation would also slow down the heart, give him a dropsy and his foot would swell; worst of all, his spirits would droop. His mood would become depressed and he would probably sit all day feeling sorry for himself. In such a syndrome of self-defeating probabilities there was only one medical desideratum: Calm the man. But how? How can you tell a man to be calm when he is so structured as to be exactly the opposite? How can you tell a man with a brilliant mind to make his mind dull? How can you prescribe against vivid farseeing imagination? Yet there was a way to calm the man.

"Moderation is not for you, Mynheer Governor. Your body functions so fast that it burns up stimulants that would make other men frenetic. Stimulants like coffee, tobacco, brandy."

"That is true," said the Governor, highly pleased; and in his rebelliousness straightway determined to cut down on his intake of coffee, tobacco and schnapps.

"Much sleep?" Benedict waved it contemptuously away. "Much sleep is also of no value for a man like you."

"True, Doctor. I require very little sleep."

Privately the Governor determined that thenceforth he would try a good long nap in the afternoon. He did so. The effect was exactly what Benedict had hoped for. Stuyvesant, though his naps were short, wakened refreshed, full of energy, less irritable and the pain in his stump dramatically subsided.

Esther said to her husband, "You told him to do all the wrong things and he did all the right ones. Now he adores you."

"It was the only way to manage him, dear."

"Is that how you manage me?"

He looked at her so earnestly, kissed her so fondly that she said, "If you do, I don't care. I adore you too."

"You are not Governor Stuyvesant, darling; and your legs — well, I don't think I'd like you in a wooden leg, no matter how beautifully decorated with solid silver bands."

Esther grew pensive and looked a little sad. "I hope it doesn't hurt him anymore," she said softly. She was speaking not of the Governor but of the little Indian boy with the painful, paralyzed leg. "Dear God, suppose Baruch were similarly afflicted!"

"I have only seen the disease once or twice before," Benedict said. "It seems not to be contagious when the fever goes away and paralysis sets in. I have offered the father and his squaw — the Iroquois squaws must always be consulted — to physic the child."

"I will help," Esther said.

"No, dear; you'd be constantly exposed and I can't be absolutely sure it's not contagious. The mother must nurse the boy back to health, not you. I'll have to give them shelter; they're far from home, the other Indians are afraid to let them into the longhouse, partly out of fear, partly because they feel disgraced by a cripple. But I won't have them here with you and Baruch. I'll put them over the stables where it's warm and clean and airy."

They would be comfortable, he knew. And Esther and Baruch would be safe.

Among the misfits who found the freedom of New Amsterdam irresistible was a young English sailor who, with a back still smarting from a few light blows of the cat for stealing a bottle of his captain's favorite port, committed the far more serious crime of deserting the ship when it anchored momentarily in a Long Island inlet before proceeding on its voyage.

Fearful that search would be made for him, a totally unwarranted assumption, the youth hid by day and emerged only at night, eating seed corn that the Indians were planting and even, when hunger drove him, gnawing on fresh-caught fish that were destined for fertilizer, one fish to each hill of corn. He congratulated himself that he had eluded his pursuers. He would have been irked to know that his captain had considered his desertion good riddance. That the Indians saw him stealing the corn and raiding the fish supply and did nothing to stop him would have deflated his sense of supreme self-importance. There was plenty of corn, plenty of fish, and so deep was the Iroquois hatred of the English that they were pleased and amused to see dissension and desertion in the ranks of their enemies. His scalp was in no danger.

From the western shore of Long Island he beheld in the sunset the windmills of New Amsterdam. With a log to uphold him he paddled across the short stretch of water and arrived late at night at the door of Dr. Benedict van Benedict, the only house where a light was burning.

Soaking wet and scared as a rabbit the fugitive presented a deplorable spectacle. "They'll hang me if they catch me," he said.

Benedict knew the British custom. The deserter was speaking the literal truth.

"They're not going to catch you, lad," he said. The early spring night was cold; the boy's teeth were chattering; a week of malnutrition showed in his face. "How are you called, young man?" And he hastened to add, lest he be taken for an informer

[229]

seeking reward for reporting a fugitive, "My name is Benedict, Dr. Benedict van Benedict. You look as if you could use something in the way of a restorative."

"Port is my favorite," the fugitive said grandly.

Benedict frowned, but put it down to the nocturnal chill and probably a bit of youthful braggadocio.

"I think a bowl of good hot soup would be better. I'll have it prepared. I asked you your name."

"My name is Charles," he said.

"So is your King's, if I am not mistaken."

"Yes, it is, Dr. van Benedict," the deserter said, not quite implying that he was of royal blood. "But certainly," Benedict thought, smiling inwardly, "he'd be willing to have me think so. He's a sly one. But I'm damned if I'll let them hang him."

He sent him aloft to the fragrant haymow above the stables, then routed the cook from her slumbers and shortly Charles was wrapped in a thick warm blanket and eagerly spooning up a hot bowl of bacon-bean-corn soup.

"I don't like his looks," said the cook when she returned.

"Would you like to see him hanged? They would, you know."

No, she wouldn't like that either, she said, good woman that she was, and waddled off to her room. Gentry and British deserters! Indians and the Governor! Why couldn't Dr. Benedict be like other Dutchmen? He didn't even act Dutch. Him with a brilliant clientele, starting with Governor Stuyvesant, who had to pay like a prince — she had listened at the door. Well, she supposed the Governor could afford princely fees. But this solicitude for the underdog, this preoccupation with cast-offs and the hunted — oh well, there was no accounting for Jews, even Jews who ate bacon and lobsters, which she cooked to perfection and of which Benedict was very fond. Long since she would have left the Benedict household (she was not *that* old and fat, she assured herself) save for the fact that no one else had ever been able to soften the pain of the gout in her foot.

"You know, Mistress O'Rourke," he had said when she first came to cook for him, "you ought not to tipple before breakfast."

"I do *not* tipple," she had said belligerently. "I only use a little wine for my stomach's sake and my often infirmities. It's in Holy Writ, it is."

"What isn't?" he said. "Now take this, Mistress O'Rourke. It is a little drink of meadow saffron, a sort of tea, concocted of a beautiful flower almost like a shamrock."

It always did her gout good; she could not remember the shamrocks of Ireland; she had been too young when her parents, fleeing the Antichrist, Cromwell, had found welcome in the all-sheltering colony of New Amsterdam. Meadow saffron sounded like something acceptable to her pantheon of saints. She would light a good Dutch candle — Dr. Benedict would never miss it — for the repose of the souls of her parents, who had died of smallpox contracted from the Indians. She had never liked Indians since.

Un-Dutch he might be, this Doctor Benedict; but meanwhile he paid her well, physicked her painful foot, never scolded her as black Protestants would have done when she hobbled off every Sunday morning to Mass in the little chapel just off the Bowling Green. She stayed on, and when Charles came, she accepted him as she accepted everything else in the happy but baffling Benedict household.

Charles lived comfortably above the stables all during the spring and hot summer, and now that the season was verging on autumn he almost felt that he owned the place. He had a genuine way with horses. They whinnied with pleasure when he approached. He curried them sleek and shining, proud of his handiwork.

"They like me, Mynheer Doctor," he would say in Dutch, which was improving by contact.

"Because you like them," Benedict would say in English, which, by contact, had also improved.

Benedict wondered how this deserter, now proudly styling himself "the groom of Mynheer Doctor Benedict van Benedict," would react to the intrusion of a family of Red Indians. Charles reacted unexpectedly well, almost too well, Benedict thought. It was not ordinarily in the nature of the British to share quarters with savages. With horses, yes; with dogs, yes; with any other dumb brutes that were unambitiously animal and hence no threat to British complacency. But not with Indians. In many respects Indians were disturbingly human.

Yet Charles was cordiality itself. Benedict searched to ascribe a motive; he found none and reproached himself. "The good free air of the New World must have remade the lad." But he could not help adding a cautious, "perhaps."

"The poor boy!" Charles cried convincingly when he first saw the crippled child.

"But not beyond help, I hope," Benedict said.

By a coincidence which may have jogged Benedict's memory of the obscure disease, the father's name was Tonawanda.

"Tonawanda means 'running water'," Benedict explained. "Water is the treatment I shall essay, with your help if you will."

"I shall be honored, Mynheer Doctor."

"Hot as the boy can stand."

He gave him a blanket. "Soak it, keep it wet and hot. Wrap

the leg. As soon as it cools repeat the treatment. Between applications the parents will massage the leg."

"Mynheer, you will make me a renowned doctor like yourself," Charles said, smiling at the Indians, who he thought were still out of earshot. They smelled vile and were crawling with lice.

"I'll try to get them to bathe," Benedict said under his breath.

Charles said venomously, "All Indians stink," and as they approached greeted them with a flashing smile. "Welcome, my friends."

They had heard him, but their impassive features did not alter.

The early weeks of their installation above the stables started with something of a problem for the cook. At dawn the day after their arrival she stormed into the doctor's bedroom without knocking. He was deeply asleep after a full night of calls.

"Yes, Annie?" Esther said, raising her head from the pillow.

"I have been raped!" bellowed the O'Rourke.

"Incredible!" murmured Benedict, still half in a dream. "Who would be desperate enough to do such a thing?"

"Raped?" Esther said.

"Raped, ravished, set upon. The red heathens in the barn have ravished my best stew pot too. The curse of Cromwell upon them!"

"The stew pot too!" Benedict said, now fully awake, laughing in spite of himself. "That is what I call a double improbability."

Esther, Massachusetts born and more familiar with the archaisms still current in Puritan New England as well as the rural districts of Ireland, explained, "Annie is using the words in their old meaning, dear. 'Rape' and 'ravish' simply mean 'stolen' in her idiom."

"Ah," Benedict said, "I am greatly relieved. Reason is restored to the universe. I was afraid human nature had changed. Now, Annie, if you'll just get my dressing gown I shall listen to your account of this ravishment and do what I can to amend it."

The cook took up her tale of woe.

She hadn't heard a sound, she said, not a sound, and she was a light sleeper, too, especially since the doctor was so careless about locking his doors and the saints only knew who might not break in and steal; but somehow in the night somebody had sneaked into her kitchen and stolen a bowl of corn meal and a couple of smoked fish, and how she was going to cook a decent Christian breakfast this Friday morning she couldn't imagine.

Her tone seemed to accuse the doctor.

He considered the tragedy gravely.

"Well, Annie, in that case I'm afraid we'll just have to make do with ham and eggs this morning for breakfast."

By a manful exertion of willpower she succeeded in overlooking the enormity of such a breakfast on such a day.

But there was more. The thief had also stolen one of the doctor's cigars and (though she did not mention this item) a full inch had lowered in the level of her hidden bottle of wine which she kept for her often infirmities.

But she had caught the culprit, she said.

With catlike grace, quiet as a teeny-weeny mouse, unobserved — the poetry of the Irish was flowing full flood in Annie as she recounted her exploit — she had crept from her kitchen and caught the Indian in the act.

Esther, stifling her laughter in her pillow, wanted to say, "Redhanded, no doubt," but listened in silence.

"There he sat, would you believe it, Doctor, smoking your cigar just outside the barn, and there was my pot with the fish and mealies in it, bubbling and stewing away without so much as a by your leave, and his skinny red squaw stirring it with my best long-handled wooden spoon."

"Where was the Indian boy, Annie? Not out there in the cold, I hope."

"No, Doctor, he and Charles were still asleep in the loft."

Benedict was thankful for that and listened with mounting amusement as Annie continued.

Well, she wasn't going to let any dirty smelly heathen savage steal from her dear Dr. Benedict, that she wasn't, with him so kind and generous, but careless about some things, she hated to say it but he was, so she walked right up to the Indians and said, "Give me my pot," just like that, though where she got the courage to face those murderous redskins she wouldn't care to say, not to Dr. Benedict, but the courage didn't come from a human source, she could say that much, it came from a saint, that's where it came from, and if you asked *her* it was Saint Patrick himself, bless his dear Irish — phew — soul — phew —

She had to pause for breath in her pious monologue and Benedict said hurriedly, before she could start again, "Mightn't the Archangel Michael have had a bit to do with it too, Annie?"

"Would that be *Saint* Michael, now?"

Benedict did not quibble over the title. After all "saint" merely meant "holy."

"Saint Michael is very much honored by us," he said. "In fact, he is the guardian angel of Israel."

"No-o-o!" In wonderment. Then, "Oh, go 'long with you. You're making fun of me."

Still, she was shaken, and she concluded her Indian tale.

"What I wanted was my pot," she said, "and what I got was a blow on the bum with my own wooden spoon." She rubbed the smitten area and looked as if she were going to cry. "So I came in to tell you about it, Doctor."

Benedict replaced the pot with a bigger one and the spoon with an even longer-handled one to Annie's complete satisfaction. Privately he was pleased that the Indians had stolen so little. "They didn't steal for profit, Annie; they took only enough to sustain them for one day. They're practically ostracized, you know. No other Indians will go near them, at least till the boy is cured. As for the cigar, you know as well as I do that a smoking Indian is a peaceful Indian. I advise you to forget the incident and let Tonawanda have a cigar every day and whatever food he needs. You wouldn't want them in the house, would you? Well, neither would I. They're my guests, in a way. And isn't it Christian charity to feed the hungry and shelter the homeless?"

Well, since he put it that way she had to agree that it was; and she certainly didn't want her spotless kitchen cluttered up with smelly savages.

There were no further incidents after that first skirmish. Quiet was restored to the Benedict establishment, and Annie came to watch as eagerly as the doctor for signs of improvement in the boy's condition. He was a pretty child with great brown wondering eyes, wondering why he had been taken from the longhouse, why he never saw any of his playmates anymore, why his leg did not walk right even when he gave it definite orders with his mind, and why it hurt. He was clean as a white child now, cleaner than many, since no boy in New Amsterdam was soaked so constantly in steaming wet blankets, and several shades lighter than his parents. He was too young to have their savage aversion to water. This water soothed his pain. He liked water.

To take some of the monotony of the treatment away from Charles and give him more time for the horses, Benedict put a big wooden tub in the yard when summer came and there the boy would soak in hot water for hours.

Colonies of well-nourished lice remained happily undisturbed on the parents, however, and posed a problem: whenever they came to massage his leg some few of the insects migrated to the boy, where, finding nothing else to bite on the surface of his clean copper skin, they bit him, causing discomfort and insomnia.

To order Tonawanda and his squaw to bathe was an unthinkable impossibility. Tribal habits are not so easily uprooted. But perhaps there was a way.

"The treatment is succeeding," he said to the squaw. "Already the leg muscle is fleshing out. Soon he'll be running and shooting his arrows at birds in the forest like the other boys."

She had tended him with Indian patience and the self-denial of comfort displayed by mothers everywhere, devotion that knew no racial boundaries. Her burning eyes betrayed the intense hope she felt in her heart. Tonawanda also had helped, though he tended to put the boy too soon on his feet and his face assumed a wooden sullenness when Benedict warned, "Not yet. Not yet." In Tonawanda the hurt pride and the stigma of ostracism urged him to hurry the treatment so that he and his family could go home. There, since the cause of their disgrace would no longer exist, they would be reinstated in the longhouse as if nothing had happened. Their allotted place in the communal dwelling would be cleared for them. Such few primitive possessions as they had left behind or had been appropriated by others would find again their usual place. There would be no comment or thanks. It would be as if they never had left. And if you never leave there is no cause to welcome you back.

To get them to bathe Benedict adopted a stratagem appropriate to the level of their understanding. One evening in the deepening twilight, as the full splendor of a copper moon rose over the peaceful pastures of the Bouwerie where the Governor's fat cattle were grazing, he said to Esther, "Please look in the closet and see if you can find my old physician's gown."

She was startled. "Why, dear?"

"Am I not a medicine man? Tonight I will make big medicine against almost cosmic resistance. I've got to get those Indians to take a bath."

She saw he was really serious. "I'm afraid it smells awfully of camphor," she said.

Benedict occasionally complied with the requests of ship captains, who, departing on long voyages, asked for camphor as an antaphrodisiac to safeguard the morals of their crews. He used it principally to keep moths out of seldom-worn clothing.

"The odor will only enhance my big medicine. I predict that by tomorrow our Indians will smell sweet as a rose." He dropped a bar of scented soap into the black sleeve of his gown.

In the gathering darkness the Indians saw a ghostly black figure silently approaching them. From it emanated a mysterious penetrating odor. His long gown accentuated his tallness. Fear of the unknown gripped them. Tonawanda made a motion as if to get up and run, but the squaw held him down with an imperative grasp. "Stay still," she whispered. "Maybe it will pass by."

Benedict drew close and said gravely in his familiar voice, "My friends, I have a message for you."

He addressed the squaw first, as head of the family, protocol in the matriarchal society of the Iroquois.

Their faces lost their fear, so relieved were they to discover that he was not a malevolent spirit but human and a friend.

Tonawanda found his voice and said, "What is the message, Dr. Benedict?"

Slowly raising his arm and pointing beyond the moon, Benedict said, "Tonight I enquired of the great spirit Hippocrates, who can make people sick and make people well, and I thanked him for all he has already done, through me, to bring back the strength to your son's leg; and I sought his further help in speeding the cure that is already so far advanced. His breath came to me in a cloud of sweet-smelling smoke, and I heard his voice."

They listened, rapt. They could smell the sweet breath of Hippocrates, who dwelt beyond the moon.

"I heard his voice, and the voice said, 'Tell my people to bathe themselves and their garments, even as their son is bathed.' Then the voice of the spirit ceased. I have spoken my message."

The Indians gazed at the tub thoughtfully for some time after Benedict left them.

In the house Esther said, "Do you think they will actually do it?"

He chuckled. "You never know about Indians. We'll find out in the morning. Anyhow, I left them the soap."

Next morning when Annie took them the food for their breakfast she was confronted by a miracle. She greeted the doctor with something like awe in her voice. "What did you do to them, Doctor? They don't smell anymore. And divil a bug to be seen. How did you do it? Even their clothes, what there is of them, are clean now."

Benedict said with mock solemnity, "I quoted them a profound religious text that everyone ought to follow. Haven't you ever read, 'Be clean and change your garments' "?

She looked doubtful.

"It's in Holy Writ, it is," he said, so nearly mimicking her brogue that Esther raised a warning eyebrow. Annie was too good a cook to be laughed out of her job.

"Is it really?"

He nodded. "It's in Genesis, Annie."

Annie was glad it was in the good Christian Bible and not some heathen Jewish book.

CHAPTER 2

As the year approached its end and the days grew shorter Dr. van Benedict noticed an appreciable falling off in the collection of his fees. He had as many patients as ever but fewer of them could pay. New Amsterdam had come upon hard times.

Prices soared. Food could be had in plenty if one wished to subsist on the local abundance of Indian corn, turkeys, pumpkins, squash and fish; but the Dutch taste for coffee, chocolate and schnapps could not be satisfied without copious imports from Europe. And imports from Europe had virtually halted. Both British and French ships looked upon Dutch vessels as legitimate prizes as the last quarter of the year 1663 approached.

The cause of this undeclared war was a harmless little aquatic animal living in freshwater rivers and lakes of the New World. Its fur was of exquisite softness, warm, easily worked into garments and richly lustrous. It possessed a further quality that made it commercially valuable. It could be felted. It made the best hats in the world, and hats, especially for men, were getting bigger every year as the French fashion of wig wearing broadened the brim and heightened the crown. Some haberdashers actually predicted that the time was not far distant, if the trend continued, when the brims would grow so broad they would have to be cocked up in front, lest they fall into the wearer's eyes; perhaps cocked up all round in a three-cornered shape. Others averred that fashions were quite unpredictable and no such thing as a cocked hat would ever exist. Meanwhile, the beaver, the innocent source of the beautiful fur, flourished in the clear lakes and streams as they always had.

In less troubled times the Indians had loaded their canoes with the pelts and paddled peacefully by twos and threes over the waterways from the hunting grounds to the Hudson River where, up and down the valley, the Dutch would buy them, trading in return cloth, beads, hatchets, iron pots and pans, looking glasses, sugar and some few fowling pieces to make turkey hunting easier. In all his years as Governor, Peter Stuyvesant had forbidden muskets and punished severely any Dutchman who sold the Indians rum. He had seen what firewater did to them. The French and the English were neither so scrupulous nor so wise. From New England and New France the Indians could buy anything they wanted, particularly the firearms and rum that made them so dangerous to the Dutch.

The fur-bearing beaver thus lived in a region that one day would be a battleground and already was unsafe. Frenchmen and Englishmen robbed the Iroquois canoes before they could get to New Amsterdam. Hostile Algonquins, hereditary enemies of the Iroquois, ambushed and stole from them, slaughtering them with European muskets.

The Iroquois mood grew vengeful and hardened. Under their copper skin, behind their impassive features, despite their skill at agriculture and near-to-representative tribal government, lurked the untamed Stone Age savage, who had not invented the wheel.

To protect themselves they no longer arrived in little groups of two or three canoes to trade their beaver pelts. They instituted a convoy system, scores of canoes at a time, and begged the Dutch, who still would not let them have firearms, for protection.

Minted coin grew scarce in New Amsterdam. Counterfeit coins made their appearance. The Governor threatened public hanging for anyone in the colony caught clipping coins or striking counterfeit ones, but they continued to multiply. The silver rusted. The gold tarnished. Real silver and gold sold at panic-inflated prices. It was suspected that the British and French were responsible for smuggling this secret and most effective weapon into New Amsterdam to weaken further the already hard-pressed Dutch economy.

Horse stealing became common. Horses were the only means of transport in rugged terrain like the Catskill mountains, and there the rough-and-ready frontiersmen took the law into their own hands and strung the horse thieves up to the nearest tree. Grimly the Governor winked at the practice. There were prime beaver in the Catskills. But horses continued to disappear, even from within the city limits of New Amsterdam.

Lately Benedict had taken to warning his stable boy when he finished his calls, "Keep a sharp eye on the horses, Charles."

"That I will, Mynheer Doctor," Charles would reply.

Benedict had always kept two horses of his own, and Esther had brought him two from her farm in Haarlem when he married her. One was too old to be of any use, but she was attached to it and he kept the worthless beast as a pet because she loved it. The other was a trim little mare that Baruch was just learning to ride. The saddle was much too big for him and his legs did not reach the stirrups even when Charles shortened the straps to the highest hole. Nevertheless, it seemed to Benedict and Esther that the young man had an excellent seat, and one day, they fondly assured each other, young Dr. Baruch would be making his calls on horseback too. Or perhaps the streets of New Amsterdam would be paved by the time he grew up and then he would ride in a fine carriage.

So it surprised them one day when Benedict returned from his calls and Esther from visiting a neighbor to see Baruch riding barefooted, bareback except for a blanket, with a rope for a bridle, not even in the horse's mouth but looped around its neck.

"Tonawanda's been teaching me how to ride Indian fashion," Baruch piped gaily in greeting.

Tonawanda stood nearby in the courtyard with something very close to a white man's smile wreathing his stern features. Beside him stood his squaw. Their son was jumping up and down, crying in Iroquois, "Now it's my turn. It's my turn now!"

After the first shock Benedict and Esther both laughed and clapped their hands. "Good boy, Baruch!"

Charles appeared from the barn, sidled up to Benedict and said in a whisper that seemed meant to carry, and did, "I could not stop this savage performance, Mynheer Doctor." The nascent smile on Tonawanda's lips died stillborn.

"Why should you stop it?"

And to Baruch, "Give your friend his turn now, Baruch."

Baruch slid off. It was not far down but it was farther than his feet could easily reach. Esther sprang forward to help him, but Tonawanda was already there. He did not actually touch the lad, but he was ready. Benedict saw his strong copper hands

[244]

poised to plant themselves just under the armpits and furnish support if Baruch should slip. Baruch did not. Clutching the mare's mane he lowered his feet solidly to the cobblestones and ran over to his father and mother, his face flushed with excitement and pleasure.

The Indian boy stood on the overturned tub, the tub he no longer needed, and vaulted up onto the mare's back.

"While this equestrian lesson continues," Benedict said with relief, "let us go inside and see what Annie has managed to find for our supper. I could use a good hot soothing cup of chocolate for my nerves."

He sighed. He knew there was no chocolate. There had been none since the blockade.

"It will be mealies and chicken again, I'm afraid," Esther said. Sometimes she regretted selling her farm. But the price had been good and Haarlem was too distant for efficient absentee ownership.

As they entered the door Esther caught a whiff of something delectable roasting in the kitchen. "It certainly doesn't smell like chicken," she said.

Annie appeared with a frightened face and set a pot of steaming chocolate on the table.

"Where did you steal this ambrosial brew, Annie?" Benedict said.

"It wasn't me that stole it, Dr. Benedict. I found it in the kitchen. There was a great big piece of prime beef, too, all ready to roast, freshly slaughtered it looked like."

"Maybe one of my patients —"

Annie shook her head. "Beef they might have, if they'd part with it, I wouldn't know, but not chocolate. No, sir. And not this."

[245]

With the stern air of a judge who has examined all the evidence, determined the guilty party and is about to pronounce sentence, she placed on the table an earthenware bottle of imported Holland geneva. It was unopened.

"It's that thieving heathen Tonawanda, that's who it is. The saints only know where he stole it from and who's been hoarding it, and who maybe they stole it from theirselves. That redskin gives me the creeps. He never seems to move, just sits there and smokes, and then all of a sudden something disappears from my kitchen or something pops up that wasn't there before or something's been moved, like a ghost did it. It's uncanny, that's what it is."

"Never look a gift horse in the mouth, Annie."

"And that's another thing. The horse. Teaching young Master Baruch to ride horseback like a heathen savage, it's unchristian, it is."

"No harm came of the riding lesson, Annie. But you're absolutely right. Everything about the riding lesson was unchristian. Unless the horse was baptized there wasn't a single Christian in the courtyard. Except Charles, of course. I forgot about Charles."

"That one!" Annie grunted. "He's worse than the Indians. He's Church of England. And he wasn't in the courtyard. He was up in the loft where he always is, the lazybones."

"Was he?" Benedict asked Baruch.

"I didn't see him when Tonawanda was teaching me to ride, Father."

"Has Tonawanda given you lessons in Indian riding before?" And sensing in Baruch's face the fear of being chided, he added, "You rode so well I thought he might have given you other lessons."

"He gave me a couple before."

Benedict said to Annie, "No harm's been done, Annie. If Tonawanda is the thief he cannot return the beef to its original owner, which was a steer, and the steer is no longer in this world."

He watched Annie's good honest face overspread with confusion as her slow mind struggled with this bit of *pilpul,* a trick of dialectic used by teachers of the Talmud to sharpen the wits of their students, who were taught to analyze statements critically for the purpose of uncovering contradictions, fallacies and ultimately where the truth lay. The results were often as fallacious and ludicrous as this one. It was far beyond anything poor Annie could grasp.

"As for the bottle of schnapps," Benedict continued, "Tonawanda must return that. Unopened."

Annie looked pensive. "Then I'd better keep it in my kitchen, don't you think?"

"I do indeed," Benedict said. "Unopened."

Annie sighed and disappeared into the kitchen with the bottle.

Baruch said, "Father, was the steer really the owner of the beef?"

"No, son. Cattle cannot own anything. God made the beasts to serve man. It was the human owner of the steer who was the real owner of the beef. That was the point of my little joke with Annie, who didn't quite catch the fact that I was making an illogical statement. When you reason, Baruch, reason logically. For example: if I say, 'All Indians are red men, therefore all red men are Indians'; is that true or false?"

Baruch thought a moment.

"It's false," he said.

"Why is it false?"

"Isn't it?"

"Yes it is. But why?"

"Because men get red when they get sunburned even if they're not Indians."

Benedict beamed his approval.

Just then there was a tremendous clattering of hooves in front of the house, a neighing of many horses and an imperative pounding on the door as if someone were trying to smash it in with a club.

"Dr. van Benedict! Dr. van Benedict! Confound you, man, open up!"

Benedict said mildly, as the pounding continued, "There is only one voice that loud in all of New Amsterdam. If he would only lift the latch he'd find that the door is not locked. I'd better open it before he breaks his wooden leg."

In stomped Governor Stuyvesant, his face red with fury.

"Observe, Baruch, that anger too can make men red," Esther said, and whisked the boy off to the comparative quiet of the kitchen.

CHAPTER 3

THE Governor had scarcely seated himself at the table when he began to scowl and glower at the doctor. He said in an angry voice that carried through the house, "Are you rich, Van Benedict? You people usually are."

Benedict shook his head. Stuyvesant's accusatory manner set his teeth on edge. But he controlled his anger. Three thousand years of history confronted him in the man across the boards of his own table in his own house. It might have been Pharaoh of Egypt, it might have been Torquemada of Spain, it might have been any ruler of any nation. Good men at heart, he firmly believed, men made like himself in the image of God, tolerant friendly, intelligent when all went well — but in times of trouble when pressed too hard a sickness came upon them and the Jew was the easiest to blame, the likeliest scapegoat. Benedict knew sickness of the body as a doctor, as a Jew he knew sickness of the soul. "Scapegoat," he thought to himself. "The compulsion to blame someone else. Everyone has it. We have it too. In fact, we invented the scapegoat. When Israel sinned,

Aaron laid his hands on the head of a goat; all the sins of Israel went into the goat; when they chased it into the wilderness and let it escape and everybody felt better. But at least we blamed a dumb goat, not a living human being."

"Well, are you, Van Benedict?"

"Am I rich? No, Stuyvesant, I am not."

The Governor started as if a scorpion had stung him. It had been years since anyone had dared address him as anything but Your Excellency or Mynheer Governor.

Benedict saw his dart had struck home and pursued his advantage.

"Since you have deprived me of my title of Doctor, sir, permit me to deprive you of your title of Governor," but he said it without rancor.

"I note also that you call me 'you people,' as if I were some undesirable alien instead of a born Dutchman. If you consider me un-Dutch because I am a Jew at least do me the courtesy of calling me Baruch ben Baruch instead of Van Benedict."

"I meant no offense," the Governor said, limp and deflated. "You have always been my friend. I am greatly overwrought. The Colony is in dire need."

Benedict could afford to accept the half apology.

"I know. Nothing reaches us from home." Unconsciously he stressed the word "home"; it was his home as well as the Governor's. Holland and New Amsterdam constituted the greatest love of the Governor's life. Holland and New Amsterdam possessed a tradition of freedom unparalleled in the world. Stuyvesant's devotion to that tradition was as deep as Benedict's own. The Governor would beggar himself, nay, die, for it. He had often faced death for the freedom that was Holland.

He was about to face death again.

Benedict said, "Our congregation here has contributed heavily to our cause. And I think you know the extent of my own contribution. You must have seen the rolls."

The Governor nodded. He had. He knew to a guilder the exact amount.

"Short of starving my family I could contribute no more," Benedict said. "And now, my good friend, I beg you to put aside your suspicion of the Jew's hidden wealth. It doesn't exist. There is no logic in it. What would I do, Mynheer Governor, where would I go if New Amsterdam were strangled by the British? By the French? They are not noted for their love of Dutchmen."

The Governor nodded again. These were his sentiments too. "What we need most," he said, the administrator in him taking grip on his thoughts, "is gold, gold, Mynheer Doctor, and silver. When you are in dire need only the precious metals can help."

"Love of country helps, also."

"That is something we Dutch can take for granted, except for the few foreign spies among us that I haven't caught yet. We could buy off the French with silver and gold. The British are a different breed: stubborn, scheming, more dangerous. They're the ones who are flooding us with counterfeit coin, and very well done, too. The French ones you can detect; the first rain washes off the plating; but not the British, till they tarnish, which takes several weeks. Powder and shot we need also. Fortunately we've a pretty good supply of that, but no more can get through the blockade. What I need most, this very night, is horses. How many horses have you to lend to the cause, Dr. van Benedict?"

"Four, Mynheer Governor. They are yours, and not as a loan, as a gift, every one of them. I do not even ask why you need them."

"You do not need to. I can tell you in a breath."

An Iroquois runner had arrived with news of a sixty-canoe convoy richly laden with beaver pelts now halted under the protecting guns of Fort Orange in the upper reaches of the Hudson, but unable to proceed downriver to New Amsterdam. Hordes of Algonquins, French *coureurs de bois,* and British frontiersmen, degenerate white men, half outlaws, half civilized from years in the woods, living like savages themselves, had pinned down the convoy.

"Sometimes I wish I had armed the Iroquois," the Governor growled, grinding his teeth, his color rising again. "And yet, had I done so, they'd long since have gone the way of the Algonquins."

But if the convoy could beat off the enemy, then, once out in the broadening waters as the river flowed south, the rich cargo of pelts could proceed safely to New Amsterdam. "Once secure behind the Wall," the Governor said, "I'll have no difficulty disposing of them."

"How?" Benedict could not help asking.

"Why, Doctor, it's simplicity itself. Privateers, both French and British. I get offers every day. And they're well supplied with good solid coin to buy. The line between a duly commissioned privateer with letters of marque from King Louis or King Charles and an out-and-out pirate is thin and easily crossed."

That was why he needed horses, to supply swift mounts for the gathering body of well-armed men who this very night would ride to the rescue of the sixty-canoe convoy. "And we will, oh-ho! It will be a pleasure!"

His enthusiasm was contagious. What an amazing old man he was. At the age of seventy-one, with a wooden leg, to lead a small army of fighters into a wilderness to beat off a vicious band of Red Indians!

"Let me show you my horses!" Benedict cried. "Two are swift and tireless. One could carry a man, if he weren't too heavy. The other — well, let me show you."

As they walked through the courtyard toward the stables the Governor remarked, "I hope they're still there, Dr. van Benedict."

Benedict chuckled. "Don't worry. I've got a stable boy who practically sleeps on top of them. Charles? Charles! Come down at once."

There was no answer.

They entered the stables. There in their stalls were Benedict's two horses, and there was Esther's sleepy old pet placidly munching his hay with yellow worn-down teeth; he cast a rheumy eye on the doctor, snorted contentedly in a sort of equine sigh and went on with his meal. But the little mare was gone.

Suddenly Tonawanda was at their side. He appeared so silently that the Governor started. His two Iroquois feathers identified him as an ally, but just to make sure the Governor said to him in his own language, "I did not notice you at first, young man," and listened intently for the reply.

Tonawanda said, "I wasn't here at first." No Algonquin could have spoken Iroquois like that. Stuyvesant was satisfied.

"This is Tonawanda, Mynheer Governor. I had the opportunity of treating his son. Where is Charles, Tonawanda? Why isn't he watching the horses?"

"I am watching."

"Where is the little filly?"

"Charles took her for a ride. He will be back."

Benedict grunted in disgust. "I told that youngster to watch."

"He will be back," Tonawanda said.

[253]

"It's a beautiful moonlight evening," the Governor said laughing, "and if I were a young stable boy I just might sneak off for a little ride too. On a filly." He winked broadly.

Well, you old rascal, thought Benedict. It was a side of the multigifted septuagenarian he hadn't suspected.

Actually Governor Stuyvesant's mood was soaring. The prospect of danger always rejuvenated him. His fierce temper relished action. He was delighted with Benedict's horses.

"But I'm afraid I can't use you," he said, patting the soft muzzle of Esther's pet. "You're a bit elderly and weak in the legs. If they were made of wood, now, like mine —" He laughed at his own joke on himself. Then, more seriously, "You know, Dr. van Benedict, I'd sell the silver bands off this thing if I had to. Every scrap helps."

Benedict was thoughtful.

"We all feel that way, sir."

"And I'm afraid I can't wait for your moonstruck young man to come back with the filly. Use her for your calls."

Stuyvesant stomped around to the front of the house. Many more men had gathered, all armed. Tonawanda delivered Benedict's horses to them. With incredible speed the Indian had saddled and bridled them.

Stuyvesant leapt into his saddle with the agility of a man forty years his junior and stuck his peg leg into a round leather cup that served him for a stirrup.

"Keep an eye on your old horse, Mynheer Doctor. They'll steal anything these days. I lost a bottle of schnapps and a cannister of chocolate just last night. And somebody butchered a steer of mine. I didn't mind the steer, except that the thief cut the meat from the living animal and left the poor beast to bleed. Had to shoot him. What I really regret is the schnapps. Good-bye, Mynheer Dr. van Benedict, and many, many thanks."

He took his place at the head of the troop, shouted a thunderous order, and the little army moved forward.

Benedict retraced his steps slowly to the house.

"Tonawanda," he said, "I'd like a word with you."

The Indian followed him silent as a shadow. They went into the doctor's study.

"Will you smoke a cigar, Tonawanda?"

"No."

"Please sit down."

Annie appeared.

From the flush on her face Benedict suspected that the bottle of schnapps was no longer sealed.

"Oh Dr. Benedict, Dr. Benedict, that Charles, the spalpeen, he was skulking round the kitchen door like he wanted a cruller or something and Lord knows all he had to do was ask and I'd have given him one, and then when he heard the Governor he sneaked round under the window without a cruller or anything and just listened and listened, though heaven knows the Governor's voice is loud enough to wake the dead, and pretty soon he went into the barn and off he was on the little mare and he's not back yet, and I own I don't like him but I never thought he was a horse thief, though as the Governor says, they'll steal anything these days —" She clapped her hand to her mouth and her flush deepened guiltily.

Benedict sighed. So Annie had been listening too. Well, the Governor's voice did carry.

"There's no harm done, Annie — I hope."

"And Doctor —"

"Yes, Annie?"

"Oh Doctor, since I got so nervous tonight with all those men on horses and guns and noise and all, and the rubbish he talked about you being a Jew at first, and I hope Baruch didn't hear —"

"It's all right if he did. He'll hear it again, Annie, and learn not to let it upset him and how to cope with it."

"— and you so kind, almost like a father confessor, so I have to confess that, all nervous like I was, I took just a teeny-weeny nip of the bottle. There. I've said it."

"Is there any left?"

"Oh yes, lots — I think. I was awfully nervous though."

He looked uncertainly at Tonawanda. Hospitality was hospitality and one did not drink alone. On the other hand, an Indian was an Indian.

"No," said Tonawanda, reading his thoughts.

"TONAWANDA," said Benedict sternly, "did you steal Governor Stuyvesant's chocolate, did you steal his geneva and steal a cut of roasting meat from one of his steers?"

"Steal, Mynheer Doctor?" There was honest lack of comprehension in the Indian's voice. "What does 'steal' mean?"

Benedict reflected that he knew no word for "steal" in the Iroquois language. He had had to say it in Dutch.

"Did you take the chocolate, the schnapps and the meat without telling him?"

"Yes. Did I do wrong?"

Sometimes it was very difficult to talk to Indians. When you seemed to reproach them they lapsed into monosyllables, as if they feared censure for some wrongdoing which they did not know was wrong. Then it was that their features took on the wooden impassivity that made white men assume they were stupid or had no feelings.

True it was that they could endure hunger, thirst, pain, fatigue, even torture without demonstrating the least outward sign of discomfort. Such was their training. Benedict knew that in certain initiation ceremonies, when Indian boys entered into manhood, skewers would be passed through the muscles under their armpits, cords would be looped through the holes and thrown over the branch of a tree, and the initiate would be lifted by his own flesh till his feet left the ground, to hang for some time to teach him to bear pain without complaining, while all the tribe looked on. One whimper and the initiate was disgraced. The longer he hung the higher his status. Such was the source of the Indian's refusal to show emotion, and his monosyllabic speech when confronted with reproach that he did not understand.

At other times Indians were talkative, even garrulous. At their dances, feasts and celebrations their faces lit up with vivid expressions of pleasure, their voices rose in paeans of song and their bodies danced tirelessly in uninhibited joyfulness. But a single word would change their mood. So it was, Benedict remembered, with children — one moment all bubbly and exuberant, and the next, at a frown from their parents, withdrawn, sullen, taciturn, confused, rebellious against they knew not what.

"No, Tonawanda, you did not do wrong."

Tonawanda smiled his almost-white-man's smile. Benedict had removed the reproach. "You had expressed a desire for chocolate, Mynheer Doctor. Fat Annie likes schnapps, and has been good to me and my squaw and my boy. So I 'stole' as you call it. As for the meat, meat belongs to everybody, like fish in the rivers, like corn in the fields even when you plant it yourself. When white men plant a field do they not leave a portion ungarnered for hungry people who have no field of their own?"

Peah, thought Benedict. He had not thought of the Hebrew

term in years: the Portion of the Poor, the unharvested corner of the field, the ungarnered sheaf, the not-to-be-gleaned, left by the planter for the stranger. Here was a Red Indian teaching him Torah.

"I'm afraid we don't always, Tonawanda; but we should."

"I'll return it all if you do so, Mynheer Doctor," Tonawanda said, a fear of the reproach lurking behind his eyes.

Benedict laughed heartily, and Tonawanda seemed to join in, in a silent Indian sort of way. "I'm afraid it's all gone by now, my friend," Benedict said.

"Then I'll steal somebody else's and return it to the Govenor's house. There's plenty more if you know where to steal it."

Here, perhaps, was how the notion of "Indian Giver" originated: give a thing, take a thing back. But it was not a moment to enter into an elaborate explanation of European concepts of private property.

"Tonawanda, where is your squaw?"

"She is back in the longhouse with our son. Everything is now as it was. Our son's leg is strong and sound again, thanks to Hippocrates and you. You are not like our medicine men, Dr. van Benedict. You have stronger magic. Strong magic comes from here." He touched his breast. "This I have learned from a white man. I have learned much, living with a white man. I have even learned what it means to steal. I will never forget your kindness, nor will any of the Iroquois." He added with neither modesty nor vainglory but simply as a matter of fact, "I was chief of the council till my son became sick. Now that he is well I am chief again. No, Doctor, my tribe will never forget you, nor the Dutch."

Benedict, having sipped his schnapps, was smoking. The blue

smoke hovered like a fragrance in the room. He offered Tonawanda a cigar. Tonawanda's eyes shot fire.

"No!" he rasped in his throat; then, recollecting himself, "No,
thank you very much, Dr. van Benedict."

Never had Benedict beheld a more peaceful Indian than
Tonawanda at this moment, yet the Indian would not smoke the
tobacco of peace, which Benedict knew he loved.

"Charles isn't back with the filly yet," Benedict said. "I have
many calls tomorrow, and I can't make them all on foot."

"Charles will be back, Mynheer Doctor."

"You too, Tonawanda, are not like our chiefs, not like Governor Stuyvesant, for example. You are not like us at all. Maybe at
one time men were all alike; maybe we've changed and grown
apart with the passing of time."

Tonawanda said, "What used to be no longer is. Men change.
Whole tribes change. You, for instance, Dr. van Benedict, are
Dutch, and the Dutch are not like the English and the English
are not like the French; and you are not even like most Dutchmen, probably because you are also a Jew — you make me think
of the great Hiawatha."

Hiawatha was a name Benedict had never heard, but he
assumed that Hiawatha, whoever he was, must be an Indian.
Tonawanda expatiated dearly on the history of his tribe, the
Iroquois.

Hiawatha was once an alien, a Huron; he came to live among
the Iroquois and the Iroquois adopted him as one of their own,
with full voice in the Iroquois council and full Iroquois citizen-
ship. For the Iroquois of those days had no chiefs or dictators,
unlike the Algonquins, but elected representatives from their
midst, and each representative had an equal voice in the council.
Men of genius rapidly rose; in the council their wisdom shaped

policy; on the decisions of the council the Iroquois made treaties of friendship and trade, made war and concluded peace.

So it is in Holland, thought Benedict. So it is in all representative governments, all, alas, too few. How few Europeans had any notion of the extraordinary polity of the New World savages.

Hiawatha had a dream, Tonawanda related. He rose in the council, the Iroquois shared his dream. It was a dream of universal peace and equality, where every man could dwell secure in the longhouse. Children were cherished, squaws voted on a par with warriors, everyone smoked the tobacco of peace, the tomahawk was buried in the earth. No one "stole" since no one coveted. The fowl of the air, the fish of the rivers belonged to no one because they belonged to everyone. If a man planted a harvest the harvest was his, but he never harvested the entire crop lest someone whose field was less fruitful lack corn.

Hiawatha's dream was embodied in an oath; the oath, in the absence of writing, was passed down from generation to generation by word of mouth. Tonawanda knew it. This is how it ran: I, Hiawatha, now uproot the tallest pine tree; into the hole thereby dug cast I the tomahawk. Into the depths of the earth I bury the hatchet and all weapons of war and the war paint and war drums and all implements of strife. Deep down in the underground rivers that flow otherwhither away, I bury from sight all that sets man against man in hatred, and I plant the tree again. Thus is the Great Peace established.

"There was peace, there was abundance of corn and game throughout the broad territory of the Five Iroquois Nations," Tonawanda said, sad legends of things now lost remembered in eyes that seemed fixed on a distant past. "Among all the red men we, the Iroquois, were known as Those-Who-Do-Not-Go-on-the-Warpath. But Hiawatha died, and with him died his dream."

[261]

Then came the white man, Tonawanda said bitterly, you people with your cannon and muskets and horses and firewater. Everything changed.

("Things must have changed drastically," Benedict thought, "for the reputation of the Iroquois is now the most warlike and brutal of all the Indian tribes of the New World.")

"We dug up the tomahawk," Tonawanda said. "It is always ready now. True, we attached a peace pipe to its top side, and we smoke it whenever we give our word to keep friends with those we trust, and we do not break our word. We trust the Dutch, Mynheer Doctor van Benedict." Again he almost smiled.

"But we trust no one else. Especially Frenchmen and Englishmen and those who serve them. Them we cut up, or roast, and take their hair."

In this queer mixture of lofty ideals and horrible savagery Benedict could not help saying, "I hope when you kill them you do so without causing pain."

Tonawanda was noncommittal.

Next morning at breakfast Annie served the Benedict family hot chocolate and imported Holland rusk. The rusk was sweet and fresh as if just delivered from a ship. It was doubtful if even the Governor had anything so tasty in his pantry. Annie was pale as a ghost and her hand shook as she poured the chocolate, but she did not appear to have been tippling, and indeed Benedict suspected the bottle of geneva was probably no longer in this world.

"The mare's back in the stall and she's got a bloody mane," Annie said.

Benedict rose from his chair in alarm. "Is Charles with her?"

"I — I can't tell for sure." Annie fled. Not to the kitchen but to the doctor's study, where she shut and bolted the door.

"Sit down, dear," Esther said; but Benedict hurriedly walked toward the stable the shortest way, through the kitchen.

In the kitchen was Tonawanda, quietly arranging cannisters of chocolate, bottles of imported geneva, rare Holland wines and boxes of Dutch cigars, which Benedict preferred over the local tobacco. Tonawanda was contentedly smoking one himself as he worked.

"I wished to give you something before I said good-bye," he said.

"Tonawanda, I am grateful, but I do not want you to continue this stealing for me."

"Mynheer Doctor, I didn't steal it. I bought it from the master of a privateer ship in the harbor, just like a white man."

"Where did you get the money?"

"I stole it from the master of the ship."

"I see," said the doctor. Never had the gap seemed so wide between his moral sense and the Indian's.

"I must look at the mare," he said. "Annie tells me she's hurt, her mane is all bloody."

"It's not the mare's blood," Tonawanda said placidly. He followed the doctor out to the stables, almost strutting with pride. It was clear that he expected praise.

The mare's mane was bloody indeed, and the hair was not all her own. A human scalp was tied to it with a long white tendon that Benedict recognized as freshly excised from a human leg.

Benedict's voice rose in a scream of fury. "What is this horror, Tonawanda!"

Tonawanda said, "It's Charles."

"I KILLED him without inflicting the slightest pain," Tona-wanda said, "because I knew you would want me to kill him in that manner, quickly. It is customary among my people, however, to kill traitors slowly, explaining to them as we kill them the reasons for causing them discomfort. We begin at the fingers and toes and work in. They retain consciousness and just before the end we roast them and take their hair. In this way justice is done, since it is wrong to execute a spy without telling him wherein he has been at fault."

"I wouldn't have killed him at all," Benedict said miserably.

"Then you would have been at fault, Mynheer Doctor van Benedict. Do not white men execute spies?"

Poor Charles, thought Benedict. I saved him from a hanging. But if he was fated for death thank God he died painlessly. I have civilized this primitive at least to the point where he did not torture the boy. Spy?

Tonawanda was still speaking.

Tonawanda had discovered, Benedict could not guess how,

that Charles was a deserter from the British Navy, that he had grown weary of the menial chores assigned to a stable boy, and he had envisaged one scheme after another that might enable him to return to his ship, any British ship, with something of value, some secret intelligence that would blot out the crime of desertion and reinstate him in King Charles's service. "He said to me," Tonawanda said, " 'Now I shall be an admiral.' "

This secret intelligence Charles had acquired when he heard Governor Stuyvesant disclosing the details of the plan to protect the Indian convoy.

"Under a wharf in the canal on Canal Street," Tonawanda said, "Charles told the master of a British privateer. I heard them speak. The master of the British privateer said, 'We shall sail up the Hudson and capture them all, and the pelts, and you will be with us and you will be a great man.' So I killed Charles."

"And the master of the British privateer?"

"I killed him, too. He would have intercepted the canoes. There is a new master now. The Iroquois convoy is safe."

Sadly Benedict shook his head. Tonawanda caught his thoughts.

"I have traded many good lives for the loss of two worthless lives, Mynheer Doctor. Their words were wind. But the lives of my people and the lives of the Dutch are not worthless."

Benedict said, "I am glad the convoy is safe. I am sorry you killed Charles. I will wash off the blood and say a prayer over his scalp."

"I will do that, Mynheer Doctor; I will do it now before I depart, since you wish it. I thought you would be content with the way I had managed." Was there moisture in the Indian's eyes? Was there the veil of misunderstanding?

"I do not judge you, Tonawanda."

[265]

There was a soft plashing noise in the courtyard from the old tub. When Benedict looked out again both tub and Tonawanda had disappeared. The little mare was curried to a high shine and munching her hay, clean, bloodless, scalpless and glad to be home. Benedict wondered, "Shall I ever see him again?" He rather thought not.

An exhausted Iroquois runner now brought hard and heavy tidings to the beleaguered colonists of New Amsterdam. The convoy on which they had pinned their hopes had been destroyed.

The doughty Governor had arrived too late. The protection he sought to bestow found nothing to protect. He arrived with his troops to witness a scene of perfect quiet, an empty wilderness. The river shone blue, fish leapt in the sparkling waters, a pleasant breeze murmured softly through the forest. Only a few vultures gorged with carrion wheeling lazily overhead, only a few scavenger dogs with muzzles still bloody from feeding upon dead bodies, bore witness that yesterday there had been a disaster.

The hapless Iroquois had been ambushed, riddled by grape-shot from hidden British cannon, shattered by slugs from French muskets. Their frail birch-bark canoes were shot through, overturned and sunk, while the precious beaver pelts floated into the hands of their enemies. Those of the Iroquois

who survived were taken prisoner, to be mercilessly put to death
by slow ingenious tortures that even the French could not look
upon. *Mais parbleu,* what did one expect? *Les sauvages sont
sauvages,* are they not? Meanwhile one could quaff a glass of
better vintage than the firewater that one gave to one's savage
allies, that had such a violent effect upon them, and try not to
hear the burning children's screams or smell the roasting flesh of
their warrior fathers. And one must be sure one got one's share
of the pelts, since the English had a nasty skill at snatching
everything that floated, the result, no doubt, of their excellent
naval training. And what was this rumor one heard? King
Charles had given his brother, the Duke of York, all of New
Amsterdam? Which he did not own and had no right to give?
One would see about *that.* It was not in the interest of the
French for New Amsterdam to be transmogrified into New York.
One would make representations to one's King, Louis XIV. His
Most Christian Majesty would know how to put a stop to such
British arrogance, even if it meant sending an army to extermi-
nate the Algonquin allies.*

Governor Stuyvesant returned to his farm in the Bouwerie in
a sober and somber mood. His mission had failed. He was sorely
beset on all sides. His empire was shrinking, shrinking like the
empire of the Romans when the barbarians surrounded them
and compressed them tighter and tighter into an ever-constrict-
ing space. He found the harbor empty. The pirates and privateers had disappeared. The blockade tightened.

From Fort Orange he floated down on rafts a few ancient
brass cannon and melted them into bullion to make pennies. A
few disreputable Spanish ship captains accepted them, but

* He did, and decimated them; but too late to alter the course of history.

offered no silver or gold in exchange. "You are fighting a lost cause, Señor Gobernador."

"If you will not give me silver and gold, have you powder and shot?"

"Si, Señor. A little."

He took it, but the powder would not burn and the shot was not iron but common stone, disguised.

"Get out of my harbor!"

"Adios, Señor Gobernador."

Even the Spanish now deserted the harbor of New Amsterdam. Its broad waters, formerly so crowded with shipping, now stood empty, empty as they had been before the white man came. Some Iroquois took it for a sign that the white man's rule was at an end, he would soon go back to wherever he came from, him and his horses and big canoes with white wings that conjured the winds and forced them to do his paddling. Wiser Iroquois said no, this is a period of change; and the white men will soon go to war with each other; we have given our word, we will keep our word to be faithful to the Dutch.

On a chilly autumn night a young servant from the Governor's farm knocked on Benedict's door and said, "Mynheer Doctor, my master is in pain and desires me to ask you to physic him."

"Where does he hurt, lad?" A doctor must know what medicines to provide.

"It's his leg, Mynheer Doctor. But he puts his hand on his belly also as if it hurts; but this I saw for myself; all he complains about is his leg."

Elevating the youngster, who was an engaging lad, to the status of a consultant, Benedict asked, "Do you think it's serious?"

The boy replied, "He's been wretchedly moody ever since he came back from the lost convoy, Mynheer Doctor."

Benedict hoisted him up onto his horse — his horses were now back in the stables — and with the doctor ahead, the boy in the croup, they galloped to the Bouwerie, where they were met by an aged servant with a lantern.

"It must be grand to be a doctor," the Governor's boy said, holding on tight to Benedict's waist. "How fast you ride!"

"That's because people get sick fast."

"I'm going to be a doctor too."

"Now you just do that, young man. Where is the Governor?" he asked the ancient servitor.

"In here, Mynheer Doctor."

Governor Stuyvesant sat with the stump of his leg propped up on a chair in front of him. Tonight he looked his years. His face sagged and his voice had lost its fire.

"The stump throbs, Dr. van Benedict. I can hardly walk. Every time I put my weight on it it feels like fire. Can you give me something to stop the pain, even temporarily? I've got a lot of walking to do."

Benedict examined the stump, which was swollen, chafed and inflamed.

"From the looks of this you've been walking too much already, Mynheer Governor. Best to stay off it a few days."

Stuyvesant sighed wearily. "I know I should. But I know I won't."

Since his return from the abortive expedition to Fort Orange he had walked tirelessly inspecting the defenses on the Wall, stood long hours at the State House trying to devise with the council some means of raising revenue, paced the deserted wharves looking for ships from Holland, which never came.

"For all the good I can do now I might as well sit here and wait till the British come."

He too had heard the rumors that King Charles had given New Amsterdam to the Duke of York. "But I expect the French heard it first. Anyhow, it may not be true. British agents often plant false rumors to confuse an enemy they hope to weaken. But I'm damned if I'll just sit."

Other things troubled the Governor also. The faithful Iroquois were seldom seen in New Amsterdam of late.

"They will not desert us," Benedict said with utter conviction.

"I know," Stuyvesant said. "But they're on the warpath now in their own private dispute."

The Iroquois had massed in a terrible war of revenge against the Algonquins. There were sickening atrocities on both sides in the depths of the forests. Such information as seeped out of the wilderness to the white man seemed to indicate that the advantage lay with the Iroquois, who, in their fury, were retaliating with even more savagery than the Algonquins.

"Just fix me up so I can walk again," the Governor said.

Benedict swabbed the stump with alcohol, applied a healing unguent and wrapped it in soft cotton bandages.

"Apply this every day, Mynheer Governor. Above all keep it clean."

Stuyvesant already felt more comfortable. He nodded. "I will."

Though the Governor had not complained about his stomach Benedict recognized symptoms of extreme nervous tension and depression. He poured him a dram from his chest. The Governor drank it without question. It was a powerful stimulant combined with the pain-killing poppy. It would lift his despondent mood and alleviate the pain in his stump. "I shall leave you a bottle of this with instructions for the dosage, which is small. Do not take more than I write on the label, or you will feel like dancing."

Stuyvesant grinned. "You tempt me to drink it all."

"You would break the skin and the stump would become morbid, and then you might never walk at all. You would behave incautiously."

"No, that I cannot afford. Not in these times."

Benedict looked around the room for the Governor's wooden leg. It was carelessly tossed in a corner. He went over and got it, thinking he would be wise to place a pad of cotton wool in the leather cup that fitted the stump to ease the chafing when Stuyvesant put his weight on it again.

The thick rod of hickory which formed the lower portion of the artificial limb was much darkened by exposure. Three lighter rings where the wood had not darkened caught the doctor's eye. The silver bands were gone. Benedict looked at the Governor in amazement.

Stuyvesant nodded. "They weren't much, but they were sterling," he said. "I had to set an example."

Pleading with the burghers in the State House to donate their last silver tureens and family plate he had donated all of his own, even down to the silver bands on his leg.

"All the gold in New Amsterdam is long since contributed," he said, "except the women's wedding rings, of course, and I can't ask for those or they'd probably join the Algonquins. Then we *would* have a war on our hands, wouldn't we!" He smiled grimly.

Benedict's admiration for the brave old fighter mounted almost to awe.

"In the end I may lose the colony, Doctor. But I'm going to try my damndest not to. Now let's put on the leg, shall we?"

[272]

He grunted, but he could stand.

"It will be better tomorrow, Mynheer Governor. Do not overdo the walking at first."

But he knew he would.

He rode home thoughtfully. He wished he could have been of more help.

Perhaps he could.

I N a smoky smithy beyond the protection of the Wall where land was cheap there lived and labored a blacksmith. He was wizened and short of stature and so dark of complexion that people said he never washed the soot of the forge from his face. Despite his diminutive size he had hulking, muscular shoulders and arms so powerful that fractious horses soon learned the futility of protesting when he wrenched their legs into position to shoe them.

The Dutch knew him as Joseph Smid. It was an easy name to remember since it so perfectly described his craft. It was a name that the elders of the synagogue had suggested when the man disembarked from a Turkish ship, seeking asylum. The Turks no longer wanted Jews in Yemen, especially Jews skilled in a competitive trade.

They asked him his name. He had no history, no learning, no genealogy; he could write no language, though he could calculate on the abacus and write down the amount of his bills in recognizable Arabic numerals. He spoke a debased Arabic-

Turkish dialect and a few ancient Hebrew words that seemed to have survived among the Jews of the Yemen throughout its long centuries of conquest and domination by a succession of foreign despots. He said he thought his name was Joshua Tubalcain. At least he had been so called by his father. The name possessed acceptable credentials if one remembered the very obscure mention of it in the Torah, and the scholars of the synagogue did, but it had not been used for a long time in Europe — just such a name as still might linger in the desolate deserts of Yemen.

Did he have a craft? Could he make a living in the New World?

"Horses, metals, iron," he said.

Blacksmiths were needed in New Amsterdam. The congregation loaned him the purchase price of a smithy just north of Wall Street and registered him as Joshua Tubalcain in the rolls of the synagogue.

"But no one will patronize your shop with a name like that," they said. "We too are largely newcomers to the colony, but mostly we are Europeans and we know nothing of the Yemen. It sounds foreign. Do you know the meaning of the name Tubalcain"?

He shook his head. "It's just my name," he said.

"It means Hammer Blow of the Smith," they told him. He nodded his head. What else should it mean? Wasn't he a smith?

"I hammer good; I hammer hard; I hammer —" He could not find a word. He touched his breast, he touched his forehead in a curious Eastern gesture. They understood: Tubalcain hammered skillfully, with confidence of craftsmanship in his head, with respect for his craft in his heart.

"To attract customers and not appear foreign," they advised

[275]

him, "you had better call yourself Joseph Smid, which means the same thing."

Joseph Smid soon paid back the congregation's loan. He was the most sought-after blacksmith in New Amsterdam. Not everyone had shod Arab stallions. Smid prospered and learned enough Dutch to drive the hardest bargains in the New World. But since he also did the best work no one objected; after a little haggling all paid, till lately, of course, when no one had money. Then he took payment in kind.

Benedict had often taken his horses to Smid to be shod. Noting the intricate ironwork of his tools, he had asked, "Who made these, Mynheer Smid?" and of the grills that he had constructed around the horse stalls, "and these?"

In answer to each query Smid had pointed to himself and said, "Me," as if to ask, "Who else?" unaware of their artistry.

To Joseph Smid, Dr. van Benedict took the Golden Key to the House of Baruch.

"Is this real gold, Mynheer Smid?"

Smid scarcely needed a glance at it.

"It is gold," he said.

But to Benedict it looked tarnished and he wanted to be sure.

"It is gold," said the blacksmith.

"How can you be certain?"

From a shelf Smid took down a dirty green bottle of some sort of workingman's acid that Benedict did not recognize; perhaps it was a flux that the artisan used in his metalwork. Smid rubbed the key with a swab that he wet with the liquid.

Like the sun emerging from mist in the dawn the pure gold of the key blazed forth in glory.

"Gold?" said Smid, smiling.

"Gold," said Benedict, convinced. "Thank God."

"*Omayn*," murmured the blacksmith, as if to himself.

"Melt it down," Benedict said, "if you know how, and watch that you do not lose a single precious drop."

Smid worked the bellows and blew the coals on the forge up to a hissing fire. Skillfully he raked the coals into a small volcano with a fire-spitting concavity in the center. Into the white-hot flames of the cone he inserted a ceramic crucible. Grasping the key with a small pair of tongs, delicate as the doctor's own surgical instruments, he poised it over the crucible, which now blazed so brightly that it hurt to look at it.

Raising a pair of singularly understanding eyes to Benedict's, he said, "This key is very ancient, very holy. There is still time. Am I to continue?"

Benedict said, "Yes. But hold! What is your fee?" He knew Smid's reputation for outrageous charges.

"There is no fee."

Benedict startled.

"Many good men have come to me to melt down their metal. I know why. It is for a great good. I never charge. In Yemen I was nothing. Here I breathe free and I am respected. There is no fee."

He dropped the key into the crucible. It began to glow dull red, then white. Slowly the metal sweated and ran; it melted, settling downward, beginning with Solomon's seal, sinking to the serpents which signified the physician's art, and finally, into the pool of shining gold, sank and dissolved the ancient hieroglyphic symbol that had represented since time out of mind the tremendous concept that life is eternal, life is good, life is hope, and deserving of dignity.

Benedict contributed the gold to the common cause.

"The key was pure gold, Esther. I donated it to the Governor's fund. Do you know, I never was sure."

"It was the right thing to do," she said.

"I have seen base metal disguised as gold." He was thinking of the counterfeit British coins. "But I never before saw gold disguised as base metal. I wonder how it happened." He shrugged; he supposed he never would know.

"It didn't fit any lock we care about." Esther smiled. "And besides, as Annie tells you, you never lock doors."

"I don't have to lock my door here in New Amsterdam, Esther, and we're certainly not going to Spain where the key is supposed to have come from."

"When I am a doctor I am going to Spain," Baruch said.

Benedict opened his mouth to speak; but Esther knew he would utter a warning that Baruch would not understand — yet. She quickly said, "Of course you will, Baruch."

"There are lots of sick people in Spain," Benedict said.

"And Holland and England and Germany and France — and —" He was running out of foreign nations. "And Fort Orange, if Tonawanda's there."

"Yes, son, you will travel," Benedict said. "All young doctors ought to travel before they settle down. There are sick people everywhere."

"And I'll cure them, like you cured Tonawanda's boy and made him walk."

"But first you have to go to medical school and learn how to cure them, son. You will have to work hard."

"It won't be work. It will be fun."

Benedict wrinkled his brow thoughtfully. The lad was right. "Yes it is, Baruch. It is fun to be a doctor, if you have the aptitude, and it's in your blood to have. It is fun to work at something you believe in, and that's where a man always works his best. But there is much, much to learn; a doctor must never stop learning; and there is much that doctors do not know, cures that doctors still must discover." He thought of the tragic unknowables. Would they ever be known?

Why was it that the Indian boy had responded to treatment when other innocent little children were hopelessly paralyzed, disabled for life if they lived? Why did cancers appear in the body for no reason and doom patients to lingering sickness so painful that they would pray for their inevitable death to come quickly and put an end to their agony? Whence sprang the plague of small pox that was decimating the Indians, and the great pox that was epidemic in Europe? So many mysteries for which there was no remedy, so much, so much to discover. And over all the failures of the healing art hung the dreaded specter of pain that caused patients often to postpone the simplest surgical operations until it was too late.

Pain must be conquered.

Probably it would take a long time, probably he would not live to see it, but the conquest of pain was a shining goal. He would never cease trying to achieve it.

"Governor Stuyvesant said an interesting thing to me yesterday," he mused. "He said, 'I may lose the colony, Doctor. But I'm going to try my damnedest not to.'"

"It was a brave sentiment for the Governor to think of," Esther said.

Benedict raised his eyebrows. "Oh, he wasn't the first to think of it, my dear. We did. Centuries before our good Annie's Holy Writ was written by our separated brethren, an ancient rabbi, Tarphon, taught the selfsame courageous sentiment: *It is not incumbent upon thee to complete the work, but neither art thou free to desist from it altogether.*"

[279]